IGNITE
A MM Mercenary Romance

Abigail Glenn

Portal World Publishing

Contents

TRIGGER WARNINGS

This book is heavy. I would say in some ways, heavier than anything I've ever written. While there are plenty of sweet moments, nuggets of comedy, and a HEA, it does touch on very sensitive, difficult topics.

This story was not approached with a light heart. I did my best to handle these topics as delicately as possible. Everyone processes trauma differently. Everyone has their own unique journey with mental health. There are pieces to these characters that are a mix of truths, and yet I had to give them a bit of rein to tell their own stories.

With that said, please tread carefully if any of the below topics may put you in a bad headspace:

Mental health struggles, self-harm, suicidal thoughts/behaviors, violence, mentions of child trafficking (good guys fight against it), and trauma as a result of previous child sexual assault (not detailed on page).

PLAYLIST

I went a bit unhinged with this one...
Check out the playlist on Spotify.

Weak & Powerless - A Perfect Circle

High Water - Sleep Token

Take Shape (feat. Billy Corgan) - Code Orange

Forward! - Anaal Nathrakh

Stranded - Gojira

Walt Disney Wormdog - Grim Salvo

Custer - Slipknot

Send the Pain Below - Chevelle

Right In Two - Tool

Outside - breakk.away

Two Tens (feat. Anderson .Paak) - Cordae

The Summoning - Sleep Token

Die On The Cross Of The Martyr - Unprocessed, Tim Henson, Scott LePage

Heavier - Rain City Drive

Legend Has It - Run the Jewels

Seasons of Flies - Bind the Sacrifice

Do Your Job - Irving Force

The Grudge - Tool

Dr0nched In Sw0t - KAMAARA, Grim Salvo

PROLOGUE

EZRA

TWELVE YEARS OLD

There's too much blood.

It drips from my trembling hands as I stumble toward the stairs of my concrete prison—a small, windowless basement in a creaky suburban house.

Fourteen stairs to climb. Fourteen stairs, and I will have escaped hell.

Come on, Ezra.

The choking, gurgling sounds from the man I just stabbed twists my stomach into sickening knots.

No. Not a man.

Evil given flesh and bone. He deserved death. I shouldn't feel a lick of remorse over giving it to him. He kept me in the dark so long I'd nearly succumbed to a lifelong sentence of torture.

As my heart slams against my ribcage, I keep my head tilted up, eyes focused on that rectangle of golden sunlight painting the first floor of the house. Nothing else matters. Nothing else except reaching the top of those stairs.

Nine more to go. The demons won't follow me. They'll stay buried with the corpse I'm leaving behind.

Eight. I'll survive this. Everything will be better when I make it to the top.

I stumble up the next few steps on weak legs, and the little scrap of confidence I've worked so hard to coax out of the chasm where I've shoved everything away shrivels.

By the time I reach the landing, tears I swore I wouldn't cry leak from my eyes, trailing hot and endless down my face. God only knows how long they've been collecting inside of me.

I drag myself into that pillar of warm sunlight and break down, quaking so hard with sobs I'm certain I'm going to fall apart.

Is this shame normal? This disgust over what I'd done? I'd grabbed that screwdriver so fast, jabbing it into the soft flesh of my captor almost on instinct. It was like some raw, primal beast had overcome me as soon as I saw him drop it on the floor. Once warm blood spurted over my small hand, that beast fled, leaving me utterly lost in its wake.

Eyes blurry and fingers slick, I crawl to the front door and battle with the locks. My pulse continues to throb under my clammy, dirt-streaked skin.

What if this isn't real? What if I'm dreaming again?

Another sob escapes the depths of my tattered soul. Oh, God. Don't let me wake up. I don't want to wake up. Don't give me hope just to take it away.

Flicking the last lock on the door, I stumble out onto the porch and suck in my first breath of clean, humid air. Is it summer? I'm really not sure.

My shaking legs fail me, dropping me onto the concrete hard enough to rattle my bones.

Gritting my teeth against the jolt of pain, I pull my body down the front steps, leaving bloody handprints along the way.

I sprawl out on the grass. The soft tickle of it against my skin feels absurd. I'd long forgotten the burn of the sun, too. I'd let it bake me right here if not for the panic swimming through my veins, jolting my brain with alerts to keep moving.

Not safe. Not safe. Never safe.

That man is dead. I stabbed him. I watched him bleed.

Why am I still so scared?

I can't get my breathing under control. The weight of all these un-leashed emotions is crushing my lungs. I might die right here, bleeding out from internal wounds.

That panic jolts me upright, snapping me back into survival mode. I scan the tiny property that I had once foolishly believed would become my first true home. A quaint two-story, robin's egg blue house. A leaning chain-link fence. A cracked driveway spilling out into a street flooded with traffic.

I don't know what I'm looking for, only that I need to keep moving. I need to wash my tainted skin clean before anyone sees what I've done.

My gaze locks on a glistening body of water peeking through lush trees across the congested street. I break into a pathetic run toward it. Cars blare their horns at me, barely swerving in time to avoid taking me out. I'm skin and bones. The impact would kill me in an instant.

I spent so long wishing for death, but now that I've had a taste of freedom, I want nothing more than to *live*.

I *choose* to live.

As soon as I breach the line of trees bordering the river, I leap into the cold, murky water. I sink all the way down to the rocky bottom and hold myself there until my lungs ache.

Still, that sick feeling in the pit of my stomach won't leave. I want to claw my skin off. I want to scream until my throat goes hoarse. I want to incinerate his touch embedded into muscle and bone. Into the very center of my being.

That man is dead. But deep down, I know he has forever broken me.

CHAPTER ONE

EZRA

ELEVEN YEARS LATER

S tanding in the middle of a pockmarked, blacktop street, I stare at a rundown warehouse and sift through my latest thefts, trying to figure out where I fucked up.

It shouldn't come as a surprise that I'd get myself into trouble. Fate had my name on a list from day one. I cheated it once, and now it wanted payment in blood. Not just mine, either.

Dragging fingers through my chin-length blonde waves, I spin my lip ring around with the tip of my tongue. Fuck my self-preservation instincts today. I don't have much to show for my short time on this earth, anyway. Just a backpack stuffed with ratty clothes, a shitload of trauma, and a long-time friendship with an old homeless man I call Jakey, who might not even realize if I never make it back to our side of the city.

Jakey.

Visions of my reed-thin friend, battered and bruised, flash through my brain, his favorite tattered Carhartt jacket I stole for him freckled with blood, and a fucking piece of paper stapled to his chest with a map of this location sketched on it.

To say I wish I had the strength to mess these people up for hurting my Jakey is an understatement, but even after all these years of freedom, I can't seem to steal enough food to keep more than lean muscle on my bones.

As I stride to the chained gate, my eyes trail the razor wire fence surrounding the massive warehouse. Might cost me a few new scars to clear it if shit goes south, but it's doable.

Four men clad in black with balaclava masks spill out of a graffitied security booth, rifles cradled in their arms. I dig my black-painted fingernails into the soft flesh of my palms as my heart dips in my chest.

I really fucked things up this time, didn't I?

Stealing began as a means to ease the gnawing ache in my stomach. With no true skills or education, I had zero hope of finding a job when I escaped that basement. Humans aren't designed to handle my amount of baggage, but I've done my best to cope on my own.

I'd expected the police to pick me up and convict me of murder. No one ever came. And I had no desire to ever return to a foster home. They'd all proven just how little my life actually meant, especially when the CPS visits stopped altogether.

That should have been my first red flag to run.

Eventually, I stumbled upon kind, quirky Jakey in a scrapyard. Catching sight of me lurking among the trash as he warmed his hands around a barrel fire, he invited me over. Told me wild, fantastical stories to settle my nerves. Promised me he would never hurt me.

Jakey restored my faith in humanity. He *wanted* to care for me like the parent I'd never had, but I quickly realized how much he needed me to take charge.

I can't say that was the start of my troubles, but the pressure to make sure I always had cash on hand definitely pushed me toward the edge of a cliff.

One I now actively choose to leap off.

The adrenaline rush of stealing made me feel alive. Invincible. Even when I sometimes got bloody. My injuries were never enough to stop me from having another go, like some fucked up thrill ride I couldn't quit.

So, when the offer came to take on bigger thefts—mostly swiping confidential business files for a random guy that haunts the docks—I hadn't put much thought into where those jobs would lead me. I was desperate for the money to get me and Jakey on the other side of the river. *Permanently.*

Chest leaden with guilt, I approach the warehouse gate. The closest gunman drags it open enough for my thin body to slip through. Guns immediately point at me and shouting commences in another language, deep and throaty. I don't understand a single word of it, but I lift my hands in submission.

"Um... I think I've been summoned," I say, battling the urge to fidget when one wrong twitch of a muscle could have me turned into swiss cheese.

I'm motioned toward the warehouse, three of the gunmen closing in around me, and my pulse shifts into a higher gear. *Nothing but a rat in a cage.*

The thought makes me sick.

I'm not afraid of pain. These guys can torture me all they want. I've endured far worse. It's the fear of being confined in that boarded up warehouse that has fresh adrenaline shooting through my veins.

I can't wither away in the dark again. Mentally, I don't think I'd survive it.

Running my fingers over the rows of safety pins fastened to my tight black pants, I shove down memories before panic can take root. *Definitely not the time to lose my shit.*

I glimpse another figure dressed in black walking the perimeter. It triggers me to scan the decrepit lot once more for an escape route. My attention snags on the vision of sleek high rises staggered across a glassy, cloudless sky on the other side of the murky river.

East Bank. A mythical land of big business and affluence where people worry more about sales deals and balancing checkbooks than where their next meal is coming from or who is going to shank them in their sleep.

Moving there was me and Jakey's grand plan. A dream that may never come true, but it still inspired the mind while laid out on wafer-thin shelter beds in the middle of the night.

The leading gunman smacks a palm on the warehouse door hard enough to rattle it. When the door screeches open, revealing a musty, dim interior, my combat boots find themselves nailed to the ground.

Pain lances through my lower back as one of the gunmen slams his gun into my kidney. Normally, it would be enough to focus me, but the idea of strolling into the dark space has cold prickles spider-walking down my spine.

My brain replays the soundtrack of my life. *Not safe. Not safe. Never safe.*

"No trouble from you," the gunman utters in a thick accent.

I throw him my best glare, though it's hard to intimidate anyone with my soft, youthful features. His icy eyes reflect nothing but a desire to inflict harm, and I drop my gaze, catching the hint of a neck tattoo peeking out from his mask—a series of numbers and letters.

He tugs his mask back over the ink.

"Cheat your way through preschool?" I taunt. "Or just a big fan of alphabet soup?"

A wad of spit hits my cheek, and anger surges through me. I weigh the consequences of throwing a fist at his face. But now all three gunmen are shouting at me in their indistinguishable language, so I figure I better get my legs to cooperate.

"Heathens," I mutter under my breath, wiping the glob of tobacco spit on the sleeve of my tattered jean jacket as I step inside the warehouse. All of me, clothes included, will need a wash later.

I'm escorted through towering rows of wooden crates and smaller rooms overflowing with corroded machinery and yellowing paperwork. This place hasn't been touched in decades, which only nudges me further toward meltdown territory.

The gunmen shove me into a boxy, cluttered room with an extensive wall display of guns. Forcing down the terror eager to hook razor claws into me, I focus on the man behind a metal desk.

I assume he's in charge. He's not very intimidating in size, and I get the feeling that he tries to make up for that fact with piercings and tattoos. He also doesn't appear much older than mid-thirties. His dark hair and stubble are free of gray. The only signs of aging are the crows feet at the corners of his lifeless eyes.

How does one rise to the top of so many armed criminals so young? Is there a box on the job application to check that reads: *I've killed at least five whole humans?*

"Cozy in here," I mutter, fighting the building energy in my body urging me to move. To run. To freak the fuck out.

I need to keep my wits about me if I plan to make it out of this shit-pile situation. If I die, then Jakey won't have anyone to look out for him. And if I live, but somehow piss these people off, Jakey might become a victim of their aggression again.

The leader swivels in his chair to face me. I take in the name Gabriel stitched on his mechanic's shirt. Something tells me he doesn't actually fix cars for a living, and I doubt that's his real name, unless he's got an inflated ego, but it's something to report back to the police, I suppose. Not that I can rely on them to get involved in anything on this side of the river.

"This is him? The notorious street thief?" Gabriel asks, his gaze sweeping over my lean frame and ragged clothes in clear disappointment. I mean, I'm not petite, but I'm not a six-foot hulked out viking like the masked gunmen surrounding me.

"No bowing needed, thanks," I reply. Something solid hits me in the back of the head. "Ah, fuck! Not my skull, please." I rub fingers over the pounding warm spot, certain I can feel the bruise developing already.

"I hear you've been doing some jobs for an acquaintance of mine at the docks. Says you never fail to deliver," Gabriel comments.

Shit. I should have known better than to assume I'd found a quick way to earn some cash. The bleach blonde man at the docks was shady as fuck, but I'd convinced myself he wasn't any worse than anyone else that roamed the streets in West Bank.

"Give me a few weeks, and I'll probably fuck something up." I shrug, trying to make light of the situation.

Gold and silver teeth gleam from Gabriel's wide smile. "Cocky. You'll need to be for the job you're about to do for me." He props his boots up on the corner of the desk. "You ever heard of Sinro Enterprises, kid?"

I bite back the urge to correct him on my age. Still, my words come out sassy. "Hard to miss their name posted on the tallest building in the city."

Gabriel smirks. "Funny kid. I like him. Maybe we keep him." No one chimes in, and Gabriel shrugs. "Do you know what Sinro Enterprises does?"

I fiddle with my lip ring, flipping it back and forth. "Stuff with numbers. Pose for handshakes in the news. Who cares?"

Gabriel's humor dissolves, and I swear black doom clouds coalesce behind him. "I care. I get paid a lot of money to do certain jobs in this city, and their CEO keeps *fucking* interfering."

I clamp my jaw together to hold back another smart-ass comment that he's the one hiding out in a creepy tetanus shack in the literal worst part of the city. Don't think it'll help my cause.

Though, I do have to wonder what a large company like Sinro Enterprises could want with crusty warehouse criminals.

"He raided my operation down by the docks. Killed dozens of my men. Stole important information from me."

Jesus, were the docks the local hangout for all scumbags in this city?

I try my best to force sympathy. "I'm sorry?"

Gabriel doesn't buy it. He leans back to pull one of his revolvers off the wall and examines it in his hands. "Yeah? You're going to be real sorry if you don't retrieve what he took from me."

Swallowing, I jab a thumb at Alphabet Soup. "Why don't you ask these guys to help you out?"

A boot strikes at me, and I go down to my knees hard, my hands snapping to the edge of the metal desk to keep from bashing my face against it.

"My men are good at killing, but they are not stealthy like little Ezra." Gabriel emphasizes the letters in my name, and I hold back a shudder. The fact that they know my name means they've put some time into me. Made an investment. I'm not getting off the hook anytime soon. One job will surely turn into two. Next thing I know, I'll be on their payroll, and not by choice.

A captive all over again.

I push up to my feet, a prickle of unease in my chest. "So you want me to break into Sinro and steal from them?"

Gabriel tosses a cell phone across the desk at me, lit up with a picture I can't quite make out. "No. I want you to slip in undetected and retrieve what belongs to me."

I lean over the desk, but this earns me a smack, this time to my temple, hard enough to have my head snapping to the side.

"Ah, fuck! Can I look at the thing your boss wants me to snatch?"

The urge to poke Alphabet Soup in the eyeball nearly has me acting a fool.

Gabriel nods at his men, and I'm allowed to examine the picture of a large hard drive. I file the serial number away in my memory, pushing down questions over what could be stored on it. From the sheer volume of firepower these criminals own, I think I have a good idea.

"What if I don't want to accept the job?" I say, meeting Gabriel's steely gaze.

My stomach dips as he loads a bullet into the cylinder of his gun. "Then I kill you, and your crazy old man, too."

I frown. "Guess that's settled, then."

"Not so easy, little Ezra," Gabriel warns. "Any of Sinro's employees catch you, and you'll be wishing I was the one to put a bullet in you."

"Ah. Death all around. Just how I like it," I mutter.

Why couldn't I have excelled at painting street art or bagging groceries or something fricken normal?

I know the fucking answer. But I also know there's no fixing me.

"Five days, Ezra. Then I start carving up your homeless friend. See how brittle his old bones really are."

CHAPTER TWO

CAIN

Sprawled on a winter-chilled rooftop, I settle into practiced breaths as I peer through the scope of my MK18 rested on the ledge of a pawnshop.

Heady adrenaline floods my veins—a welcomed thrill after too many stressful weeks holed up in the office.

I get high off the hunt. The fear I summon in others when they catch the barely audible snip of my silencers or the crack of my rifle from somewhere in the night when I don't care to be stealthy. Possibly the screams of the unlucky souls I chose to carve up with my knife instead.

But this target was clever. More than I gave him credit for. He'd managed to slip through our strike at the docks in West Bank last night.

While my teams delivered the hard drive we'd snatched from Gabriel's operation to my head of IT, I'd taken off after this fucker, only to lose him when he'd dipped into the lobby of a convention center hosting some medical professional event.

Honestly, I was beginning to question who the fuck I was. Four years in the Special Forces, and more than a decade into running a highly successful security consulting business, and I can't even take out one target.

Did I lose sleep over the failed kill? Fucking hours of it. White-hot rage was still coursing through my veins when I rose out of bed before sunrise to a call from my staff with updates on my target's whereabouts.

Too much time in the clown suit sitting behind a desk and not out in the field, Rev, my VP of HR, had teased me as soon as I'd stormed into the office this morning. I'd nearly slammed my empty coffee thermos into his face. Wouldn't be the first time I'd broken his nose.

I spot my target now, a tall man with bleached hair and neck tattoos, exiting the subway. Head on a constant swivel, he drifts into a swarm of people on the sidewalk.

He knows I'm watching.

Had I more time in between meetings with clients and planning out complex security jobs, I'd take my time torturing this one. But after tailing him for hours, hopping countless subway lines, I was over it. I'd anticipated his route and posted up, and as soon as I had a clean shot, I was going to send this guy to hell with a few more holes in his body.

Adjusting the angle of my rifle to counteract the bitter wind, I keep my finger hovered over the trigger. The slightest error could cost the wrong person their life. The whole reason I started up Sinro Enterprises with my inheritance was to protect innocent people.

After being exposed to the wickedness of this world during my service, I couldn't imagine returning to a civilian life where I wasn't still fighting evil. I would have served longer, but two bullet holes in my shoulder and a fuck ton of PTSD had me shipped home instead.

Before I can line up my target's head in the scope of my rifle, he darts into a crumbling public library building, phone clutched to his ear.

I unleash a growl. He must have eyes looking out for him. These motherfuckers keep multiplying faster than I can hire mercenaries to wipe them out.

Hefting my rifle off the ledge, I swiftly collapse the stock to fit in my briefcase. Then I grab my Glock and tuck it into the shoulder holster beneath my bomber jacket.

With my briefcase locked up for later retrieval, I drop down the ladder at the back of the pawnshop and sprint toward the library.

Cardio was not on my agenda today. Not when I'd spent hours punishing my muscles in the gym last night. Nor did I expect to have to cancel two meetings this morning. This shitstain is cutting into important business.

I burst through the entrance of the library. Immediately, I'm tossed a concerned look by a shapely woman behind the long counter. I give her a curt nod, as if that would reassure her I mean no harm—one glance at my looming size and cold, sharp features and everyone thinks I mean harm.

I prowl through rows of bookshelves, one hand beneath my jacket, resting on my gun. Dusty shelves soon part for low computer tables. My eyes scan over the heads of people typing away, coming to rest on a pretty face that tilts my world on its axis for a few slow breaths.

He tips his head up at me in curiosity, and it's like a higher being sank a fishing hook in my cheek, lurching me to a halt to have me questioning my entire purpose. I think the answers to the universe might be hidden in the beautiful depths of his hazel eyes. My fingers twitch with the urge to sink into his chin-length, dirty-blonde waves and pull him closer. And that gold ring speared through his sinful, plush bottom lip...

His beauty is an unwanted shock to my system, forcing my battered heart to pound hard against my ribcage.

Fuck. Whatever. This. Is.

I hit reset on my brain, hurrying to find my target before he decides to open fire in a public library.

I catch him sneaking through a back hallway toward an exit. Glock poised for the kill, I rush after him and kick open the heavy emergency door to the alley. Three bullets immediately tear through it. At least he's using a suppressor, but the punch of the bullets on metal is enough to stir up concern inside the library.

I let the door slam shut with a curse. Yeah, I'm definitely using my knife today.

Sneaking back down the hall to submerge myself in bookshelves, I tap a button on my earpiece to call my head of IT.

"What do you need now?" Alaric asks in irritation.

To some in my company, Alaric is a legend. A mythical creature capable of working magic on computers and security systems. To me, he's my lanky younger brother who prefers to lurk in the lower levels of our high-rise, excited by the blue glow of computer screens and the whir of high-powered fans.

"I need surveillance on my target," I demand. "Back street of the public library on Cincinnati and 7th. He must have friends."

"Geez, Cain," Alaric mumbles. "That guy's not dead yet? Are you really that rusty?"

I grit my teeth as rapid clicking ensues from his mechanical keyboard. "Alright, I'm tapped into cameras. You know we have a team that specializes in tracking targets, right? I only see one guy. Northwest corner of the building. Quick access from a side door about forty feet behind you. Why didn't you send Rev on this one?"

"Check surrounding buildings. I'm not about to walk into a trap."

Palming the hilt of my knife tucked into my jacket, I half-tune out Alaric, rattling off confirmations that the area is clear as I backtrack through the library to the second exit point. I tap my earpiece to hang up the call, not wanting Alaric to ruin the buzz from my kill.

Silent as death, I slip out the side door. A fresh wave of adrenaline surges through my veins as I creep toward my target still facing the door he shot up.

With no witnesses or other enemies in sight, I wrap an arm around his neck. I jerk him back hard and thrust my blade into his kidney. His gun clatters to the street, but I'm not done. I stab him again, closer to his spine, my pressure on his windpipe strong enough to keep him from producing more than a pained wheeze.

Warm blood sweeps over my gloved hand, slithering down my bare wrist. My face twists in disgust at the idea of this guy's fucking fluids on me.

Shoving my target forward, I tear my blade across his throat. His body crumples, and the anger I've been harboring since last night finally wanes. It should make me feel better, but this fury is the only thing that makes me feel alive most days.

Flicking blood from my knife, I tuck it back in my jacket. Only then do I become aware of eyes on me.

I whirl on the figure standing at the mouth of the alley, Glock aimed at his skull. My hands drop slightly when I see the pretty guy from inside the library. He's not holding a weapon. He's just staring at me with wide eyes.

God dammit.

Is he an accomplice? He did lock eyes on me in the library for a questionable amount of time. Why the fuck else would he hang around to watch me stab a guy?

I wait for him to make a move, my finger refusing to put that final incremental pressure on the trigger.

No longer hidden behind a computer monitor, I can properly take him in. Dressed in worn punk rock clothes, he looks young. Maybe twenty, if I had to guess. He's average in height, but lean. Safety pins line the rips in his tight black jeans. He's speared quite a few of them through his ears, too. I can't help but grimace. Is that what the youth are into these days?

The fact that I'm hesitating is further proof I should have sent Rev on this job.

"Hey," I call out to the guy, not really sure what I plan to do with him, or why I'm even talking to him.

He turns and bolts for the busy street, and I let out a string of curses, lowering my gun. I debate giving chase. First, I need to dispose of a body.

Local police don't stand a chance at shutting me down. But the public might raise flags if they discovered just how many people my company skillfully drops in this city.

I toss the dead guy and his gun into a dumpster and call Henry, head of my clean-up crew, as police sirens wail in the distance.

"Hey, boss. I was just wondering when I'd hear from you. How many you got for me?" Henry asks.

Irritation flickers in my chest. "Just one. Side street of Cincinnati. First green dumpster."

"Consider him gone." Henry drops the line.

Striding out onto the busy main street, I sweep the crowds for my runner. Henry turns into view in a garbage truck. Even from this distance, I can see his villainous grin behind the windshield.

Henry enjoys clean up work. Personally, I think it's fucked up. Then again, all of us at Sinro Enterprises are a bit fucked to be doing what we do and still operating a normal business by day. Monsters parading around in the skin of humans, pretending to feel a whole spectrum of emotions when some of us just... don't.

My phone vibrates, and I groan when I see Rev's text pop up across the screen. *Heard you got another runner, hotshot.*

Fucking Alaric. Did he have eyes on the guy the entire time and didn't care to inform me? Granted, I know Alaric's been hyper-focused on figuring out what's on that hard drive, among all the other shit we throw at him.

Rolling my eyes, I slide open the text and fire back a message to Rev. *Get on the hunt. I have a 1PM meeting I can't miss.*

With a heavy sigh, I send off one more message I know I'm going to regret. *Runner is young, Rev. Assess before you shoot.*

Several messages buzz in response as I shove my phone in my jacket pocket. Rev's never going to let me live this down.

After retrieving my briefcase from the pawn shop roof, I stride into a hotel lobby to change back into the three-piece suit I'd stowed away in a bathroom stall.

I give in to the craving for a massive craft coffee from the hotel lobby before crossing the river bridge to find my black Benz parked in a public garage.

Pulling into traffic, I weave toward the glistening steel and glass monstrosity I've transformed from one of my grandfather's hotels into Sinro Enterprises, determined to make my next meeting. But once I'm there, seated around the large oak table with three burly men eager to protect their assets, I can't get a leash around my wandering mind.

I can't stop thinking about the guy in the alley.

If he was running with criminals, why did he look so shocked by my actions? Was it his first time on a job? Or was he just in the wrong place at the wrong time, and I'd handed his fate over to Rev, potentially the most bloodthirsty of my hired mercenaries?

Fuck. It didn't matter. Pretty boy was as good as dead.

CHAPTER THREE

EZRA

There are people in this world that draw your awareness without explanation. You notice them, even if you don't understand why. Could be physical attraction. Could be something deeper—a recognition of someone's soul.

I'd felt that man's presence in the library even before his towering, broad frame stepped into view, his dark locks mussed over his forehead. Under straight, full slashes for brows, his deep brown eyes held nothing but glacial, bitter fury when they'd met mine.

He radiated absolute confidence, and my pulse took notice.

Shortly after he'd run off, I'd heard what I'd thought were suppressed gunshots. Instinct had me racing out the front doors, worried I'd find the man laid out in the alley. Wouldn't be the first time I'd stumbled upon a dead body. Probably wouldn't be the last.

What I hadn't expected was to catch the man burying a knife in the shithead from the docks. You know, the one that gave my name to Gabriel.

Shock froze me in place while my brain struggled to process what the fuck was happening. Distorted bits of memory threatened to take me under like a tidal wave.

My hands, stained in blood.

My captor's grip on my wrists going slack as the life drained from his body.

Stunned, near-black eyes searing into me, twinged with fear but promising punishment for my disobedience.

You don't want to be a sinner, do you? You want to be good like me?

"Hey." The man in the alley spoke in a deep voice, breaking me free of my demons long enough to run.

Submerging myself in the crowded streets, I push out a few long breaths to calm my ragged nerves. I've done well to keep the past buried, but something had shifted under the stress of the trouble I'd stirred up recently.

I just needed to keep moving. Keep running so nothing could catch up to me. I needed to make sure Jakey was okay after I spent hours at the public library researching Sinro Enterprises.

Bursting into the Hartman Shelter, I rush through the yellowing cafeteria tables and rub my palms together to get warm blood flowing.

My eyes skim over people huddled in small groups, dressed in mismatched, ragged winter clothes. One of the regulars, a nice woman named Gloria, waves at me from her table.

"Hi, Ezra," she calls out. She's working on stacks of paper snowflakes. One wall of the shelter is already covered with her excellent designs.

I put on my best smile, despite the panic stirring in my chest. "Hey, Gloria. Think we need more decorations. Not quite festive enough."

She beams at me, and I'm hit with a wave of guilt at the thought that I might have lured bad people here. I'm a popular guy now, in the worst way possible.

It's definitely not the first time I've messed up. I've been threatened, roughed up, stabbed, shot at, and even bitten by dogs over the years. But the shit I'd waded into this time was on another level.

Would the murderer hunt me down? Was it fucked up that I find myself attracted to him when I know he likes to play hide the knife in the human body?

I mean, I've murdered someone, too. Probably with the same level of unhinged aggression. I'm not sure I would have recognized the boy white-knuckling that screwdriver. He's not me. He exists completely outside of me, like I've shedded a second skin.

I *should* swing by the police station and report what I witnessed, but I've mostly avoided interaction with law enforcement. Normally they just turn "crazies" like me away. They might offer to escort me back to the bus stop or the nearest shelter. One time, they bought me fast food for lunch.

What a treat.

Right now, I just needed to forget the murderer and focus on Gabriel's job. Wipe me and Jake's names from the lists of criminals and search for greener pastures where we would be safe, though I knew the likelihood of that was slim.

I spot Jakey nestled in a corner by the kitchens, our two backpacks—everything we own—tucked under one arm as he knits another pair of rainbow-colored gloves. A breath of relief rushes through my parted lips. *Right where I left him.*

Jakey enjoys knitting when he's in a good mood, which is most of the time. Other times, he's battling monsters in his head—hallucinations from a past filled with too many drugs.

His head tips up, his floppy knitted hat nearly falling off his silvery locks of hair. He's wearing fingerless gloves, his stained brown jacket, sweatpants, and sneakers with holes in the toes, showing off dirty socks that I swear were white two weeks ago.

I frown. *Need to get Jakey some new clothes soon.*

"My precious Ezra is home." He smiles, and it crinkles the black and blue bruises around his eyes. He's got a cut along his ear, too, right above the starburst piercing I gave him because he said he wanted to look cool like me. Who was I to deny him his happiness?

When I'd first arrived at this shelter, people warned me to keep my distance. Old Jakey was senile. Jakey saw fairies. Jakey had scratched people. Bit them, too.

But Jakey had recognized me for what I was—shattered on the inside. No better than a feral animal clawing my way through life, failing to pick up on normal human behaviors.

He'd asked for my name, and when I told him I didn't have one anymore, he gave me one.

Ezra.

I liked it instantly. It was pretty. It was the first gift I'd ever received. More importantly, it had belonged to Jakey's son, long gone from this world, so I knew it held special meaning.

I had meaning for once.

Plopping down on my butt right in front of him, I rest my hands on his bony shins. I'm not one for touching, but it's how Jakey knows it's me and not a monster or a changeling or someone out to beat him down for food or money.

"Damn. I'm worn out, Jakey. I think I need a nap." I crack my neck and curl my body over his legs like a child in need of affection. "How was your day?"

"It was wonderful, Ezra." He pats a gloved hand on my hair. "I finished a scarf for you. Now I don't have to worry about you being so cold when you go out on adventures."

Fighting back a sting of tears, I rise up to accept the rainbow scarf he holds out for me and snuggle my face into the warm, soft fabric. Sparks of joy light up Jakey's good eye. The left one has an ever-growing milky sheen. I've been keeping watch on it. Not that there's much I can do for him.

"It's perfect, Jakey." I sniffle. "I love it so much."

Beaming, he gets back to knitting his mittens, his gnarled fingers working at impressive speed.

"Have you eaten today?" I ask, glancing at the kitchens where I spot a worker with a hair net stirring a large, steaming pot of something that smells a bit spicy and rich. Maybe chili.

"Not sure," Jakey admits, like food isn't essential to survival. Usually, the workers were better about making sure he ate.

I give his shins a light tap. "I'm gonna clean myself up and get us some food. Then I gotta go out again, okay?"

"Course. You're such a hardworking boy. I'm so proud of you. My Ezra!" Jakey shouts my name, and the closest table of people shake their heads at him. Senile Jakey, at it again.

My chest tightens. Shit. I really love this old dude. I'd do anything to keep him safe.

Which means I'll have to find a way inside of Sinro Enterprises, even if my research proved just how truly fucked I am. The company specializes in security consulting, training, intelligence, and combat operations. They were professionals, for god's sake.

After I retrieve a bowl of chili and cornbread for Jakey, I sprawl out on the floor, using the scarf he made me as a pillow, knowing when I wake up I'll have to deal with this clusterfuck of a situation I've gotten us into.

CHAPTER FOUR

EZRA

This was a suicide mission.

I spend half a day circling the steel and glass wonder of Sinro Enterprises before I come to the disheartening conclusion that there is no way I'm sneaking in anywhere but through the front doors. Heavy gates block off the parking garage entrances, and all the side doors are tucked behind stone walls, locked down with biometric security.

Sometimes you had to walk directly into the fire, and if you put out the right energy, nobody blinked twice in your direction.

Buttoned up in a hunter green dress shirt and black slacks I'd swiped from a tux shop, I stride into the expansive, granite lobby. I permit myself a few seconds to appreciate the grandeur, watching a dual set of glass elevators rise and fall in the center of the proud building.

I'm sure I look daft, head tilted up and jaw hanging open, but the reality of where I'm standing, in one of the wealthiest buildings in East Bank, hits me square in the chest.

My gaze drops to the line of metal detectors and half a dozen men and women with tactical vests sporting weapons. Impatient employees crowd around them to swipe their badges and haul ass to work.

God, I hope my lack of a solid plan works out.

"Sir, can I help you?" the receptionist, an older Black woman, calls out.

Shit. Mistake number one, Ezra. Lingering too long.

"Um, yeah. I have a meeting with Cain Vincent." Uncertainty bleeds into my tone. Does anyone actually request the CEO of a company?

The receptionist looks me over. Should I have stolen a full-on suit instead? I know my hair needs to be cut, but with criminals breathing down my neck, I'm feeling a little rushed for time.

She pops her gum. "Name?"

I peek over at her partner's computer screen and spit out the first name I see listed there. "Brian Richards."

This is so stupid. So incredibly stupid.

But really, all I need to do is get past their line of security and locate some sort of data room. Architectural plans online showed another set of elevators along the west end of the building. I'd also memorized stairwells and emergency exits.

And if the drive wasn't stored with their data? Well, I'd just have to get creative...

The receptionist spins her chair to reach for her phone, and I break away from her desk. My hand dips into my pocket to grab the badge I'd stolen from an employee on the way in. A bump against his shoulder, and I'd snatched it right out of his pocket.

Sweat beads along the back of my neck as I scan the badge on a pad at the beginning of the security line. It blinks green, and I hurry through one of the metal detectors under the scrutiny of two armed guards. No need to remove anything on my body. Might be stupid for me not to carry weapons, but I'm better trained with my hands and feet than with a gun or a knife.

I give the guards a nod of respect, trying to keep my movements fluid like I belong here, though my heart is slamming against my ribs. Any fricken second and the receptionist is gonna call me out.

The guards wave me forward, and I break into a fast walk toward the back elevators.

"Meetings," I mumble when a few employees glance my way. "Meetings all damn day."

My badge scans green on the pad by the elevator doors, and I dart inside. *Hey, maybe this hair-brained strategy is gonna work out.*

As I'm looking over too many buttons, a hand snaps between the closing elevator doors. My blood pressure skyrockets, expecting more guns pointed at my head any second.

A suited man with tamed black curls and a cruel expression steps on, followed by a woman with a tall frame and pin-straight, platinum blonde hair. I scoot to make room for them, shoving down the urge to reach out and touch the woman's magical hair.

My impulses sometimes, I swear.

"What floor?" the man asks, turning his gaze to me. My eyes dip to his hand hovering over the buttons, inked with tiny, intricate bone tattoos.

Why do these business people look like they could rip me apart?

"Oh, uh... Sorry, I'm a bit nervous. Here for an interview. The receptionist told me where I'm supposed to go, but I may have forgotten..."

My cheeks burn red-hot. Was it too much? I'm not great with pretend games.

"Ah." The guy turns away. "You'll want thirteen then. Gwen will get you straightened out."

He presses the button for me, and we fall into a strange silence. I tap my fingers anxiously on my thighs. Is there a code against talking in elevators? I fight the urge to loosen the tie constricting my neck. I spent nearly an hour figuring out how to tie it. No way I'm messing it up.

I have no interest in meeting Gwen on the thirteenth floor, assured Sinro Enterprises isn't going to store the drive in an easily accessible place, but I need to blend in.

Tattoo guy steps off on floor twelve. Platinum lady, who looks like she might be an angel of death, is headed for eighteen. Which means I'm forced to exit when the doors open once more.

I give her a shy smile and step off, quickly clipping the stolen employee badge on my shirt pocket backwards so no one can accuse me of wearing the wrong face and name.

There's another pad to scan my badge beside a set of glass doors. A woman behind a desk has eager eyes on me already.

Sweet Jesus, please let me have the right access for this floor.

I hold my breath until the light on the security pad flickers green. Then I push through the glass doors.

The woman rises from her chair with a polite, "Good morning."

Her name tag lists her as the office manager. She's got a round face, freckles, and a wild frizz of light hair.

My attention drifts from her almost instantly, my mouth parting in awe as I take in the thirteenth floor. Honestly, this place is kind of fucking cool. The modern space has an open layout, with the exception of a couple closed up offices. Walls of windows offer panoramic views of the city and its lush parks. Business professionals sit in fancy cubicles, typing away with complex software pulled up on their dual monitors and answering calls in hushed voices.

Directly to the right of Gwen's desk, I glimpse a breakroom down a short hallway, adjacent to more closed off rooms and a door to the stairwell.

Bingo.

My heart skips as I put on my most innocent smile. "Um, hi. I'm here for an interview with... IT?"

"Oh, did Alaric finally decide to hire help? Let me just phone him real quick."

Before Gwen can dial a number, I cut in. "Do you mind if I get a drink of water?"

"Of course, dear. Help yourself. There's tea and coffee, if you prefer." She waves me past her desk, and I slip into the breakroom, just for a couple of seconds, knowing my time is running thin before someone reports a lying sack of shit in their presence.

I fill a cup of water and snatch a donut from a box on the counter as I drift closer to the stairwell door. There's a meeting taking place directly across from the breakroom entrance. Glass windows reveal a full table of suited men and women tuned into a presentation given by a startlingly attractive man. He's all dark tones and sharp edges against beautiful, creamy, pale skin.

Blood drains from my body when the man turns toward me. His frigid gaze meets mine as I'm mid-bite into my sprinkled donut. *What are the fucking odds?*

I guess Sinro employs murderers because the one I witnessed stabbing one of my enemies outside the library is staring me down. *Maybe he won't recognize me.*

But when his nostrils flare and his hands clench into fists, I know I'm completely fucked. Tossing my cup of water, I dart for the stairwell.

Still chewing through the last bite of delicious, sugary donut, I throw myself into the gap between stair railings and fall two flights before I catch myself on another railing.

I hiss at the tug on my shoulders, hoping I didn't damage anything. This stress on my body had better be worth something.

I race for the lower levels of the building, the most logical place in my mind to store data. It's cooler underground, and no one could ask to venture there without seeming suspicious. No easy entry points or exits from the plans I studied.

God, I should have stolen an energy drink this morning. I feel like I'm running on fumes, even with my little nap at the shelter.

As soon as I burst through the door marked lower level one, I hear the glorious sound of buzzing computer fans. Rows of server towers blink from behind a glass wall, sealed in a temperature controlled room.

Now I just needed to find the drive with a matching serial number. No pressure. Just a hulking, sexy killer, probably on the way to snap my neck any second. Possibly armed guards right behind him.

Holy hell, I've never dealt with a situation like this before. I should have taken more than a day to scope this place out. Cockiness mixed with desperation is a dangerous combination.

I scan my badge on the security pad. It blinks red. Heart thundering and pulse pounding beneath my sweaty skin, I slam my combat boot against the glass door to shatter it.

Careful not to wipe out on the broken glass, I rush between the first aisle of server towers. Along the back wall, I scrounge through built-in desk drawers loaded with computer parts. I try every drawer, finding a row of them locked.

Frantically, I search for something to pick the main lock. I locate a toolkit for computer repair in a cabinet, and I get a tiny screwdriver to fit it right before the stairwell door slams open.

The murderer appears, cool and collected, despite the inferno burning in his dark eyes. Why the fuck did I think this was a good idea?

Because Jakey's safety is on the line, that's why.

Frozen in place, my brain scrambles for a plan. The only ways off this floor are the elevators and the one stairwell, both blocked by the murderer. There must be other rooms down here where I could possibly lose him, right?

His gaze moves from my hand on the locked drawer to my eyes. "Don't even fucking think about it," he warns in a deep voice.

With a flick of my wrist, the lock clicks. I rip the first drawer open, grab a handful of hard drives inside, and bolt down the towers of flashing electronics.

Shit. This is where I'm going to die. Why hasn't he shot me already? Was he going to use a knife on me? I'd rather take a bullet than be stabbed again.

I spot an unmarked metal door ahead. It swings open before I reach it, a small man with cropped, light-brown hair and bright caramel eyes, holding a steaming cup of coffee. His eyes go wide as I barrel toward him.

"Uh, Cain?" the guy calls out.

"Move, Alaric!" Murderer shouts.

Alaric disappears behind the door, and I'm slammed against the metal surface by the murderer apparently named Cain. As in Cain Vincent. The fricken CEO.

An arm locks around my neck, another slamming into my hip to drop me to the ground.

I don't even have time to cry out before my vision goes black.

CHAPTER FIVE

EZRA

My head is shrouded in fog when I finally peel my eyes open to a small, gray room flooded with sunlight.

Cain stands in front of me, his powerful form leaned against a closed door, arms folded to draw his navy suit jacket tight over the cut of his powerful arms.

Instinct has my body lurching to flee, but I've been zip-tied to a chair in the center of what looks like an office. *Fuck zip-ties.* Why are they so handy in so many situations?

I crane my neck, seeking something to cut me free. An empty desk is the only other piece of furniture in the room, tucked in the corner of two walls of windows overlooking East Bank.

Movement in the glass windows on either side of the door where Cain's posted up snag my attention. Business people swap internal memos and converse like it's a common occurrence to hold someone prisoner here. Thick silver letters hung on one of the walls tell me I'm still at Sinro Enterprises, which gives me hope that I'm not about to be murdered just yet. Surely they don't want the carpet stained with blood.

Eventually, my gaze returns to Cain. How long has he been watching me? Shouldn't the CEO of a billion dollar company have more important things to do than babysit a low-life thief? Doesn't he have people or whatever?

When he doesn't speak, I can't help but break the tense silence. "Did you have to choke me out?"

"Better than shooting you, no?" His smooth baritone wraps around me, and I fail to hold back a shiver, my body reacting in a most unusual way. His eyes narrow. "Though that option is still on the table."

The flash of madness in his hard gaze tells me this guy has killed tons of people. Those deaths are practically carved into every lethal edge of his body.

Cain begins to pace around my chair in slow, predatory strides. "Who are you?"

And the interrogation begins.

My pulse quickens. Maybe I could tip my chair over and use the pointy legs to shatter a window. Seems reckless, though. We're pretty fucking high up, and I've never had the desire to become a human pancake.

Cain reappears in front of me, brown eyes searing into me like hellfire. I wriggle in the chair as my heart skips a beat.

"What's first? A finger or a tooth?" I taunt.

Despite my attitude, panic looms at the edges of my mind. I hear Cain's low voice demanding answers, but his words are nothing more than a fading rumble in my ears as I start to mentally spiral out.

I grit my teeth. *Not the time, Ezra.*

A firm, calloused hand slides around my throat, choking me back to reality. Strangely enough, warm blood rushes low in my body. I shift in the chair again.

Woah. Do I... do I like this? Since when have I ever not cringed away from a human's touch that wasn't Jakey's?

Again, he demands, "Who are you?"

His fingers constrict tighter around my neck. Without thinking, I tip my head back to expose more of it for him. Fuck. The pain he's giving me only seems to be confusing my body, strangling the panic seeking weakness in my brain. I don't think I want him to stop.

"Batman," I wheeze. "Wait, shit. Redo. I'm your worst nightmare. Does that sound more threatening?"

He digs his fingers into the soft spots just under my jaw, and I whimper. Not because I'm afraid, like he assumes, but because I want more of this. Which is a wild thought. I blame my inability to think straight on my stiffening dick. Why is it doing that?

"You don't know who I am, do you?" he says.

"Sure I do. You're the guy that's going to fuck me up, right?"

He shoves at my neck, tipping the chair backwards. I brace for impact with the floor, lifting my head enough to avoid hitting it. The force is still enough to draw a grunt from my chest.

"I don't think you understand your situation," he says slowly, coming to squat beside me. His head cocks, and a lock of dark hair falls over his forehead. He shoves it back into place, the only sign of his irritation with such an emotionless mask over his face.

"Obviously not," I reply sarcastically.

"How did you get into my building?"

My heart hammers in my chest under his scrutiny. Lying has never got me anywhere in life, so I stick with honesty. "By being invisible."

His mouth turns down, confusion kneading his brows together. "You a spy?"

I run the tip of my tongue along my lip ring. His eyes dip there, watching the movement. I don't miss the way his pupils dilate before he tears them back up to glare at me.

Faster than I can blink, he flicks out a small pocketknife and swipes it across my cheekbone. White-hot pain blooms there, but what he doesn't know is that the pain only serves to ground me when I'm all wound up.

I grin at him as warm blood drips into my ear. "What kind of business is this? Do you often cut up clients? Offer consulting on how to dish out torture? Or do you order bone tattoo man to rip people apart like pulled pork?"

Cain leans in closer, and I glimpse the little flecks of gold in his red-brown eyes and the faint scar on his chin. His teeth are a bit sharp. And his scent... I draw the hint of eucalyptus deep into my lungs, trapping it there.

My throat tightens as my hard dick jerks in my slacks. I've never had a reaction like this to anyone, and it throws me for a loop. I test my restraints again, desperate to move. Pace. Run.

"You're not a client," he replies in a cold tone. "You're a thief. A bad one, at that."

He flicks his knife closed, splattering droplets of my blood on his polished leather shoes. He doesn't seem to care.

"I snuck in here, didn't I? Would have snatched that drive, too, if you hadn't recognized me," I say, beginning to enjoy this little exchange more than I should.

I can see the effect my sass is having on him, making him bristle with rage. Slowly, I'm breaking through his polished exterior. I think I'd like to see him lose his cool. Which is just further proof that I've lost my mind.

Cain snarls. I brace for another cut, almost welcoming it. He lurches my chair upright. Seconds later, my hands and feet are cut free. He yanks me to a stand, practically carrying me by my neck over to the desk, where he pins me down.

His weight pressing against my hips makes it impossible for me to move. And impossible for me to ignore the hot desire coursing through my body when he glares down at me, his chest rising and falling with aggravated breaths.

Oh, fuck. I definitely like this.

"Is this your first time interrogating someone? Seems like you don't know what to do with me," I say, unable to resist further teasing him.

His knife makes another appearance. I should be frightened. I know that. But somehow I'm more turned on than anything else. When he kisses the tip of his blade against my chin, I can't help my hips from pushing against him, rubbing my aching length against his muscled thigh.

Cain rips his body away.

"Too late," I whisper, voice sounding husky in my ears. "I felt that."

The evidence of his arousal strains against his slacks, far too thick and long to hide. His pupils are blown wide now, nearly hiding the warm brown irises. The fact that he's turned on by our exchange, too, has my entire body thrumming with excitement.

Funny, he came in here to intimidate me, but I think the roles may have reversed.

"Do that again, and I won't hesitate to kill you," he threatens, as if I'm to blame for his body's reaction. Shit, he's really painfully attractive, though. What was I supposed to do? The knife tease isn't helping cool me off, either.

I palm my dick through my soft pants. "Can't help it. Upsetting you is pretty fun."

Cain struggles to regain his rigid composure as tension sizzles between us. I'm laid out, fighting a boner from hell, and he's acting like he wants to carve me up for it, but he's too scared to put his hands on me again.

The door knob turns, and Cain moves out of its path as it swings open.

"You've got a call on line three," a male voice sings.

The man who appears in the doorway has striking blue eyes and a shag of silver hair. The rest of him is all grayed out, too. Silver earrings. Charcoal suit. The outline of silvery white-ink tattoos barely visible on his pale hands. They almost look like scars.

"Is this the little thief who broke in?" he asks.

Cain tucks away his knife. "Told you not to disturb me when I'm in a meeting."

"Is this a meeting?" Silver guy questions. "I think I'm going to need your definition of meeting. Last week, it was wet work in the interrogation room. Today it's torturing intruders in the empty corner office that *should* be mine. Next week it's going to be sex swings in the break room. Again, your definition is so broad."

Shit, wet work? Yeah, I'd say these guys are bad news, and I somehow avoided getting dragged into whatever torture chamber they're hiding in this building. Doesn't mean they won't still take me there. Maybe this is just the initial "give me hope" portion of their fuckery.

Cain growls. "Wouldn't have to waste my time here if you'd done as I'd asked and tracked the guy down, Rev."

Rev's face lights up with pure joy. "This is the runaway witness? Why, he's on the wrong side of town!"

Cain brushes past him. "Finish this up. I want a summary report on my desk by the end of the day."

Rev sighs. "Always stuck with the grunt work. You owe me."

The door clicks shut, and Rev turns those startling iceberg eyes on me. "Exceptionally sunny day outside, isn't it?"

"Torturing me isn't going to work," I tell him, though my pulse is pounding under my skin.

"No?" He approaches slowly, hands reaching out to pat over my body. I grit my teeth through the process, and when he draws back with the stolen employee badge, he flashes me a wicked grin. "There's Seth's badge. You telling me you snuck in here and you didn't bring a single weapon? Should we be offended?"

"I don't get caught."

He raises a brow. "Like... ever?"

"Ever." I nod, and the movement causes more blood to drip into my ear.

He looks amused. "And how often do you go about breaking and entering?"

I rub fingers over the marks the zip ties left behind, my brain working every angle to get me out of here. I can't leave without the hard drive. That was the whole purpose of this trip. The only way to assure Jakey doesn't become a target again.

"Couple times a week." I shrug. "West Bank is a bit easier to navigate for me. This isn't really my scene."

Rev cocks a brow. "I see. And what would motivate you to foolishly break into our company?"

Witnessing Cain's efficient way of disposing of criminals has me wondering if I shouldn't disclose information about Gabriel. Maybe Sinro could get me and Jakey out of this mess. Cain might not be so easily convinced of my innocence, but Rev seems entertained enough by what I have to say.

"I had no choice. Either I steal the hard drive or my friend gets fucked up again by some bad guy and his gunmen."

Rev clicks his tongue. "And I didn't even have to get my hands dirty. Got a name for me, kid?"

I nod. "Head of the rodeo had on a shirt stitched with the name Gabriel. He seemed like a typical drug lord, but he had a ton of weapons."

Rev considers this information, running his thumb under the curve of his bottom lip. "Sounds like we may have a common enemy. Why don't we see if we can help each other out?"

Heart skipping, I roll up to a seated position on the desk to better examine him. Blood rolls down my cheek to the corner of my mouth, and I flick my tongue out to swipe it away before it dribbles onto my shirt. I *had* planned on returning the stolen clothes, but I don't think the shop owner will appreciate the new stains.

"Cain's the bad cop, isn't he?" I say.

Rev flashes a grin. "Caught on to us already. We'll have to shake things up. Though Cain really sucks at faking sympathy." His head drifts to the interior window, and I watch Cain march out of an office, phone in hand, body coiled up with near-palpable fury.

"So, any idea on where this fuckhead's holed up?" Rev inquires, drawing my attention back to him.

Was he honestly this trusting? Or was this part of the mind games he'd mentioned? I couldn't get a good read on him. He smiled a lot, but that humor never touched his pale eyes. He probably got away with fooling most people, but I've become hyper-critical of others out of necessity. I pay attention to details.

I spit blood onto the carpet and draw my feet up on the desk until I'm curled in a ball, which only makes his smile grow. "So look, I'm all about spilling the beans on this dude, but I need reassurance that you're not going to kill me or toss me out just to get off'd by this guy."

"A negotiator. Have you considered a corporate job before?"

I fiddle with one of my safety pin earrings. "Suppose I wouldn't turn it away for the right pay."

Rev's head tips back with a musical laugh. "Oh, Cain's going to have a field day with my summary report on you, kid. You're something else."

"Summary report?"

"Yeah, he trusts me to pick you apart. Figure out if you're gonna be a liability to the company."

My brows hitch up. "Do I look like a liability?"

Rev's grin is wicked. "Oh, you're a liability. Just not in the way Cain thinks. What's your name, pretty boy?"

"Ezra," I reply. "Just Ezra."

"How about this? I go grab my laptop and we pin down where you met this crime lord. Then I'll talk to Cain about some sort of protection for you and your friend."

"I'd prefer that in reverse order," I mumble.

But Rev's already striding for the door, leaving me to mull over if I've made a colossal mistake.

He returns with a laptop, two cans of Mountain Dew, and a box of tacos. Again, I have to wonder if he's fucking with me. Earning my trust just to chop me up into pieces or something.

However, I'm not going to turn away food. Crunching away at our tacos, we dig up old satellite images of the abandoned warehouse. Rev leans back in his chair. "I'm not good at sugar coating shit. You're in deep, Ezra. We've been tracking this guy for months. He's rapidly moving up rank on our priority list."

He clicks through records of Gabriel on his computer. Arrest reports for every kind of crime you can think of involving cars, drugs, and guns.

A sliver of fear burrows into my chest. Did I just permanently etch my name onto Gabriel's shitlist by giving up his location? What if Sinro isn't equipped to handle this situation?

"How is he not still in jail?" I ask, frowning.

Rev taps his fingers on the desk in perfect rhythm. "Good chance he's got the right connections. Might be why police don't try to fuck with his operations."

The door to the office opens, and Cain appears. His features twist with barely restrained anger. Rich brown eyes coast over me, then Rev, then the food wrappers from our little gathering.

"You," Cain says with force, a finger pointed at Rev. "My office. Now."

Rev closes his laptop and drags it off the desk. Before striding out the door with his boss, he gives me a wink. "Don't worry, Ezra. I'll handle the big bad bossman."

CHAPTER SIX

CAIN

I storm into my office, ignoring the curious glances from my staff over their cubicle walls.

Closed off from straining ears, I whirl on Rev. "What the fuck are you doing? I asked for a report, not for you to make friends with the guy and buy him goddamn tacos!"

Lack of sleep and chasing around criminals has me in a mood today, though some would argue I'm always in a mood.

Add in the fact that my dick decided to wake up at the worst fucking time possible. Why did the little thief have to have to be so fucking pretty? Who the fuck has a right to look like that?

Failing to restrain his grin, Rev takes my fury in stride. He's known me long enough to not be afraid. Sure, I'd slugged him a couple of times. He'd swung on me, too. But we'd never raise a weapon against each other. He's the one guy I can't shake, no matter how dark I go.

Rev's an anomaly. He'd waltzed into Sinro Enterprises shortly after I'd started it up. Told me he didn't need an interview, just a few minutes to prove his skill with pistols at the gun range. I hired him after two perfect shots. It didn't take long after that to discover the heartless killer beneath his mask of light-hearted amusement.

Rev leans back against the slate gray wall of my office and slips his hands into his pockets. "The guy took a job under duress, Cain."

I slam a fist down on my desk, uprooting a can of pens and my stapler. "I don't give a fuck!"

Rev just blinks back at me. "Why didn't you shoot him, then?"

"What?" I ask incredulously.

"If you think he's such a threat, why tie him up in the office and not in the lower levels where we normally do this work?"

I blow out a hot breath. That's the million-dollar question of the day, isn't it?

"I...needed to be certain he wasn't working with our enemies."

"Name the last time you've dragged someone back here to question their alliances. You're quick to pull the trigger, Cain."

"Yeah, because those other people were all confirmed criminals!"

"And we both know this guy's innocent."

I tug at the longer pieces of my hair while pacing behind my desk. "Fuck you."

Radiating a calm I wish I possessed, Rev continues, "He has no clue what's on the drive or how to access it, but he did help locate one of Gabriel's warehouses."

I scoff. "Gabriel threatened a fucking kid into stealing the drive back? He can't be serious. He's gotta have another team moving in on us."

Rev tilts his head, his silver chain earrings swinging with the movement. "I don't know. He said he's never been caught. And his name is Ezra, by the way."

"I don't care," I snap back.

"Sure, boss." Rev gives a quiet laugh. "Ezra's apparently quite the con artist. Clever, too. We should consider hiring him, if not for his potential, then for the fact that Gabriel would slaughter him the moment he steps out of this building empty-handed."

I drop into my chair. Stressful days and nights of shitty sleep weigh heavy on my bones. I had a tough sell with a new client this afternoon. Not to mention, criminal operations seem to keep popping up left and right. If it wasn't for my business, this city would be overrun with corruption.

"He sneaks in, and you want to offer him a job." I shake my head. "You've gone soft, Rev."

"I just recognize talent. You hired me as HR, after all."

Rev was good at reading people. He studied them like they were all experiments. I knew the real reason he did it. Made it easier to mimic emotion so he could better fit in with society.

While Henry enjoyed picking apart bodies, Rev liked to play with them when they were still squirming and crying, and he did it without an ounce of remorse or regret. He slept soundly at night. Enjoyed working long hours, too.

I run my hands up and down my face.

"Just go talk to him. Maybe without dicing him up," Rev says, opening my office door. "We don't need Henry unsettling the floor with his strange cleaning methods."

When he's gone, I ease back in my chair and spin it side-to-side. What the hell do I do now? The little thief strolled through my front doors like he was out for a leisurely walk.

But if Rev is convinced he was being manipulated, I had to give value to that. I don't have much of a moral compass anymore. However, I don't condone the slaughtering of innocent civilians.

How was it I now felt responsible for this guy? Because, yeah, Gabriel would tear him apart if he left here without the drive.

I could keep him locked up until we dealt with Gabriel. That seemed like the best solution.

Deep in my thoughts, I lose track of time behind my desk. The flicker of half the office lights shutting off signals the departure of the cleaning crew. I glance out at the dark skies. The streets are already flooded with traffic, lit up like a circuit board.

Releasing a heavy breath, I check my email and review the notes Rev sent me from his conversation with Ezra, ever the star employee. After today's shenanigans, he sure as fuck isn't getting that corner office.

Apparently, our little thief doesn't have a last name. I snort. A lie. His first name was probably a cover-up, too.

After some failed searches for Ezra in our system records and on Google, I pick up my desk phone and hit the number for Alaric. He doesn't try to mask his frustration when he answers my call.

"You know I can't finish anything if you keep dumping tasks on my desk."

I permit my brother's attitude because he's our most skilled person at cracking systems and talking code, but I'd hoped in time he'd pick up proper social skills working here.

"You earned this task. The guy that snuck by your supposedly hawkish eyes twice? I want you to dig into him."

"He didn't sneak past me," Alaric mutters. I remain silent until Alaric gives me the response I'm looking for. "Okay, whatever. Not like I had plans or anything."

"I know you don't, so quit acting like you're put out by my request."

"Maybe one day I will be," he counters. "You know, when I find somebody."

I chuckle, envisioning his pout. "People like us, who obsess over work, don't find significant others."

Almost too quietly to hear, I catch him saying, "You did once."

That wipes the smirk from my face.

"Give me a bit. I'm in the middle of hacking into a security system for Salem. Then I need another bag of Cheetos."

Alaric hangs up on me, leaving me remembering why I rarely call him. His ability to drop social bombs doesn't mix well with my inability to channel anything but a prickly nature ninety percent of the time.

Pushing up from my chair, I grab my thermos to refill it with coffee, knowing I'm going to be pulling late hours tonight.

As soon as I step out of my office, I can't help my gaze from drifting to the glass windows of the corner office.

Irritation burns in my chest. The thief—*Ezra*—is laid out on the desk in his blood-stained button-up shirt and slacks. He has one leg propped up, and his arms are draped wide, hanging over the edges.

I suppose his quirkiness is why Rev likes him. They both seem to enjoy pushing buttons to get reactions, almost as if life is just one big game to them.

Maybe he's smart like Rev. A master of manipulating emotions.

I hold back a growl of frustration. Regardless of what Alaric digs up, I know I won't be satisfied with my decision on what to do with Ezra until I have another discussion with him.

I set my thermos in the break room before cutting back to the corner office. Turning the lock, I step into the room and close the door behind me.

"Okay, little thief." I force a deep breath to keep my head level. "Either you're cunning enough to fool a diagnosed psychopath with an IQ off the charts, or you're actually in a tight spot with a notorious crime lord."

Ezra's head lulls to the side, blood now crusted on his cheek. I'm thrown off by the dark shadows forming under his eyes. If he's been running around with Gabriel, he probably hasn't had much rest lately.

His gaze sweeps over my body, and I'm enraged by the skip of my pathetic, weak heart. I fiddle with my cufflinks, not wanting him to catch on to how he affects me. Whenever Rev senses discomfort, he leans into it with honed claws.

"Is that supposed to be a question?" Ezra asks in a bored tone.

So much for maintaining my cool. His lazy posture and lack of fear shove me to the edge of reason. Crossing the room, I wrap my hand around his delicate neck and shove him down hard on the desk.

"Enough with the jokes. Which is it, Ezra?" I push through clenched teeth.

He swallows, and I feel his pulse quicken against my fingers, a beautiful little flutter under sun-kissed skin.

A strange warmth floods through me when his pupils expand. It only makes me clutch him tighter.

"You like this position, don't you?" he murmurs, thick eyelashes fluttering.

I squeeze hard enough to bring a flush of red to his skin. His soft, warm hand encircles my wrist, but he doesn't attempt to fight me. Overwhelmed by a surge of guilt, I draw back from him.

"I would like to think I'm smart, but I'm really not," he replies softly. "Got myself into serious trouble."

I shake my head, frustrated by my lack of control over my emotions right now. "I have someone looking into you. I'll find out what you're all about, Ezra. And if there's anything questionable, anything at all, your life is forfeit."

He turns his gaze back up at the ceiling, and his body sags. "Okay."

"Okay? That's it?" I huff, ripping my tie loose. Why couldn't I leave this guy alone?

I watch his tongue slip over his full bottom lip, flicking his lip ring back and forth. It shouldn't captivate me. Shouldn't make my mouth water or my cock throb hard enough to have my hands twitching with the need to grip it.

"Cut me up all you want. Just... please don't restrain me again. I don't like that."

My brain short-circuits. "What?"

"I mean, I get that I'm at your mercy. Just thought I'd ask nicely."

A jab of concern hits me, and I shut it the fuck down. Seal it away with every other troubling thing ricocheting in my chest. Today's been a whirlwind. I shouldn't have come in here thinking I'd gain anything of value.

But I couldn't stay away.

Ezra leans up on his elbows, his tousled, decadent locks and mesmerizing eyes alerting my body to just how much I like the way he looks. I'm both enraged by his careless behavior and slightly impressed. I can't stop my eyes from circuiting his features.

"Cain." His voice is so soft, so vulnerable, my hands curl into fists. "Can I ask you for a favor?"

I force a low laugh, though I can't help but watch him spin that lip ring around and around. What would it feel like against my mouth? Running over the shaft of my cock?

Fuck. No.

"You're being held captive, and you're asking me for a favor? You know I could kill you, right?" My words hold no edge, my tone dipping into something deep and raspy.

"No doubt." Sadness bleeds into his expression. "I have a friend in West Bank at the Hartman Shelter. If I'm missing for too long, I worry what might happen to Jakey."

It takes me a few breaths to process what he just shared with me. He's concerned about someone in a homeless shelter? What is this Jakey to him? A family member? A friend? What would Ezra be doing in a shelter?

All these questions only serve to further erode my sanity.

"Jakey?" I scoff. "What kind of name is that?"

Timid hazel eyes meet mine. Where was the sassy boy from earlier? The one who seemed to take pleasure in driving me crazy?

"It's the nickname I gave him when he found me."

My chest tightens. Suddenly, the office feels too small. Too warm. Why is the fucking heat cranked so high on this floor today?

"Jakey," I repeat, the name tasting sour on my tongue. "He a thief, too? Someone close to you?"

Why didn't Rev include more in the summary report?

I hold back a growl. Because I would have criticized him for diving into personal details. That shit doesn't matter.

Ezra blinks at me like he can see the gears whirling in my head. "He's just a harmless old man without a job or a place to live. I take care of him. Make sure no one takes advantage of him. Gabriel's guys messed him up and threatened to kill him. That's how I wound up in this mess."

This guy must be an expert manipulator. My insides feel slithery. I can't seem to get a wrangle around my emotions or regain control of the logical part of my brain.

Why the hell would he risk his life for some old guy on the streets?

I shift my gaze to the black and blue bruise peeking out from the hair along his temple. A shocking burst of anger makes me want to peel Gabriel's flesh from bone for putting hands on him.

Next, I take in the scabbed cut along his cheek. Yeah, I feel wrong for doing that now, but in the grand scheme of harm I've inflicted on others, this is definitely mild.

I yank my fingers through my dark hair. Normally, I'm better at keeping my composure, but this day is fucking with me.

Before I can give away any more signs that Ezra is effectively clawing his way under my skin, I turn and shut the office door.

Lock it.

Storm away.

I can't keep him in an office much longer, but I'll wait for Alaric to report back on his findings to decide where to move him.

In the meantime, I text Rev to check on Ezra's friend.

CHAPTER SEVEN

EZRA

A corner office in a high-rise building isn't the worst place I've been forced to sleep. Actually, it might be the safest. Which is saying a lot, considering Cain, or Rev, could barge in here any minute and decide to play operation with my organs.

I lie down on the floor beneath the desk. The windows are chilled from the winter air, but the room itself is warm, and the carpet is soft beneath me. Plus, there's a ton of the city to take in from this height, all symmetrical lines and architectural beauty challenging gravity.

My stomach growls in protest, but I'm used to ignoring that particular signal. Curled up, I let my thoughts turn to Jakey, hoping he's safe. Gabriel wouldn't be expecting me back this soon, right?

I should have made Rev promise that Jakey would be protected. Instead, I'd been too caught up in helping him research Gabriel while shoving tacos in my mouth.

Unrest stirs up in my bones, and I sink my fingers deep into the fibers of the carpet. I really don't want to lose my friend. My life has never mattered, but Jakey... he's something special. He carries such an envious light. Mine was extinguished long ago by the people who were obligated to care for me.

I suppose Jakey's been messed up by people, too, what with his previous tendency to dip into bad substances. At least he can't remember most of those troubling memories. I still go to war against mine every time I drift off to sleep or get too overcome with unexplainable energy.

Over the years, I've gotten better at winning that fight. I'm good at convincing myself that I'm just experiencing nightmares.

But when I lose...those are the nights I wake up in a cold sweat with my heart racing, convinced I never got out of that basement.

My throat tightens, and I sense that all-consuming panic slithering toward me. I squeeze my eyes shut, willing it to go away. Sometimes it feels like a living entity. Acknowledging its existence gives it more power over me.

I lurch up to my feet and pace the room. The streets allow me an outlet for this excessive need to move. Trapped in here, I fear what my mind is going to do to me.

Scrounging through the desk, I find nothing but some old newspapers, trash bags, and more loose paper clips. I scoop them up and begin winding them together into some sort of lock pick.

Then I sit in front of the interior window until I confirm that Cain has left for the day, a shiny metal briefcase in his hand. I lift a hand to mock-wave at him, but he doesn't look my way.

It's not hard to see how tightly wound Cain Vincent is. Aggression bubbles just beneath his surface, barely contained. I wonder what could have filled him with such rage.

More overhead lights shut off. I make my move, working the paperclips into the lock on the door. Freed from my corporate prison, I do a quick walk around the office floor, scoping for cameras. Two by the glass doors to the elevator, which really limits my options. No doubt the hard drive has been moved from the lower levels by now.

Still, the chaos unfurling inside of me needs a fucking distraction. Dropping into a chair in one of the cubicles with a puppy calendar hung on the wall, I rifle through drawers. I let out a low whistle and prop my legs up on the desk as I scan through documents.

Sinro Enterprises has some interesting paper trails. High-dollar purchases for military-grade weapons, armored vehicles, passports, and plane tickets. I'm beginning to think they lean more toward taking people out rather than protecting the average politician or celebrity.

Do they work for the government? Special Forces hidden under the guise of a consulting business? Considering Cain's skill and his unique staff, it's a valid possibility.

I can't leave it a great big mystery. Hands on an invisible string, I keep tugging and tugging, seeking answers to curb my anxiety. I dart from desk-to-desk in a frenzy, sorting through everything I can get my hands on like an auditor with a chip on his shoulder.

Some desks have paperwork on local companies to help secure their assets and keep their employees safe. There are plenty of summaries for upgraded software packages, cyber protection, and fine-tuning building security.

Other desks, well... they have coded lists that confirm my suspicion about Sinro's true activities. The beating heart of its operations.

I raid the break room next. Nothing's safe from my manic investigation. I find Steve's green lunchbox in the back of the fridge with an untouched peanut butter sandwich and a pudding cup. I devour both.

"Sorry, Steve," I mumble, shoving the empty lunchbox back in the fridge. Immediately after I close the fridge door, I reopen it and decide to clean the interior until it's spotless.

Fighting back yawns—the clock now reads 3AM—I try out the fancy espresso machine. I end up breaking it, unleashing steam that burns the back of my hand when I try to unplug the stupid thing.

Now what?

What time does Cain arrive at the office in the morning? I feel like he's the kind of guy to follow a strict routine. Heavy work-out regimen. Probably cooks all his meals.

It hits me that Cain's going to be pissed when he sees what I've done to the office. Will he kill me for the intel I've gained on his company? I doubt he keeps the city informed of all of his business activities.

Should I try searching for the drive? Or would that earn me some torture? What if this is a test?

I comb both of my hands through my wild hair, yanking at my roots. Shit, I've definitely failed. *Shit. Shit. Shit.*

Well, if I'm already doomed, I might as well keep letting this madness reign free.

I stroll past Cain's office. Once. Twice. My fingers trace over the etched gold nameplate on the wall by his door. I picture his dark hair and rich brown eyes and cut jaw and strong hands.

Blood surges to my cock. I sigh. He is a bit dreamy, if not for the whole simmering temper and murderous tendencies.

This infatuation is completely foreign to me. I usually don't think too much about other people. They exist around me, but the only time I take notice is when my brain warns me that I'm in danger.

Giving in to temptation, I break into his office with my handy dandy makeshift lock pick. I drop into his plush chair. Lights from the city spill through the floor-to-ceiling windows and blur in my tired vision as I spin around and around.

When I scramble his mouse to wake up his computer, I'm prompted for a password. I'm no hacker. My failed guesses lock up his dual screens.

I notice the lack of family pictures and mementos in his office. There are no glimpses into Cain's life within these walls. Does he even use his office? Or is it kept for appearances as he stalks the city with vengeance?

Settling deeper into his plush chair, I must keep my eyes closed longer than planned because soon I fall asleep.

CHAPTER EIGHT

CAIN

I startle awake in a tangle of sweaty sheets, convinced I heard the lock on my front door click open.

Leaping from my bed, I reach for the loaded gun in my nightstand drawer and storm through my apartment in nothing but my boxer briefs. My rattled brain tells me there are enemies everywhere. Hidden behind closed doors. Storming the floors of my building.

And the corpses. They always pile up behind closed eyes. I get to watch bullets rip through their flesh in my sleep each night.

Finding nothing amiss in my dark, quiet home, I lean my weight against the wall in my entryway and just... breathe.

It's rare that I dream, but when I do, it's always of my failures. Before I was a businessman and a mercenary, I was a soldier. The first time I killed, yeah... it sat heavy in my brain for a while, but once I was weaned of that horror, I became good at taking lives. Good at compartmentalizing my emotions, too.

Until Aiden.

He unraveled everything inside of me. Lifted the seals on the darkness I'd kept hidden when my service came to an abrupt end.

I'd met him at some local restaurant bar shortly after I'd started up Sinro Enterprises. The stress of my new business, combined with PTSD, led me to drink a bit excessively. He'd called me an Uber to get me home safe that night, his number tucked into my back pocket.

I ignored the temptation for a while, but then we kept meeting up at that same bar. It was easy to believe I'd found my forever wrapped up in his arms. One second in time—a single blast of a gun—changed that. Changed the entire trajectory of my life. Left me with gaping holes where unwanted emotions sometimes bled out.

I knead my fingers along my tense brows. Maybe I need to have a talk with my middle brother, Isaac. Clear my head. He'd have sage advice on what to do with Ezra.

As our client relations specialist and staff therapist, Isaac has always been the most level-headed of us Vincent boys. Though I do question if he does more than take people out to eat.

My phone buzzes from the charger on the granite kitchen counter. I pad over to it, still clutching my gun, and check the time. Just after 6AM. The sky is dark, but it's past the time I normally head into work.

And there's a good fucking reason I'm always the first one in the office. Dozens of missed calls and texts from my staff alert me of something wrong.

Instead of wasting time trying to read all of them, I suit up and exit my apartment, striding for the elevator.

I've converted the seventeenth floor of Sinro's high-rise into four spacious apartments, one of which I've claimed, the other three occupied by my brothers and Rev. The rest of the floor is dedicated to shared common areas—a kitchen and living room with a giant TV and sectionals, a library, a massive gym, and a large outdoor balcony with an infinity pool.

All floors above mine house staff, to make it less suspicious to the public when we come and go at all hours of the day, and all floors below are dedicated to specialized departments, training spaces, storage for vehicles, equipment, and armories.

My blood pressure spikes as soon as the elevator doors open on the thirteenth floor. What could have prompted a freak out this morning? Honestly, it could range anywhere from a broken computer to someone shooting the wrong target, and now, we're under scrutiny from the government again or about to blow up in the media.

"What's going on?" I demand, glare cutting to Gwen behind the front desk. She's a goddess—the front-face of my company, handling calls from all manner of clients. Today, her tawny hair is more frazzled than normal.

"Ah, sir? Everyone's been complaining about their desks being touched. It's turned into a finger-pointing contest, and Rev's not here with his team to deal with it."

I'd dispatched Rev and his squad of ten professional mercenaries last night to scope out Gabriel's warehouse hideout, certain Ezra had set us up. I had yet to receive updates, but I wasn't concerned. Rev knew how to take care of himself.

Only that now left me to deal with this internal mess.

A vein throbs in my temple as I look out at the unrest among the cubicles and offices. I kept our business professionals on my floor, not keen on filling it with our elite killers when I often brought clients in here for sales pitches.

I would chalk this up to normal petty office behavior, but this tips the scale more toward a break in.

Or maybe someone looking to steal that fucking hard drive back.

I growl, my feet carrying me toward the little thief I'd locked away. Probably should have told Gwen about him. I should have done a lot of things differently with Ezra.

"Sir?" Gwen calls out.

I pivot on a heel. "Yes, Gwen."

"Well, it gets a bit stranger. Nothing has been reported damaged or missing, with the exception of Steve's lunch, but no one gives a fuck about Steve."

Her eyes cut to the portly man occupying a cubicle by the windows, fingers tearing over his keyboard like he's got something to prove. Steve *is* a bit of an asshole, but he's extremely good at financial analysis.

I grip the handle of my briefcase tighter, never caught at the office without my guns and knives.

"Not sure I fully understand, Gwen."

"Everything was organized, sir. All files in every desk. Someone cleaned the breakroom, too. Although, the espresso machine won't turn on now, so that's unfortunate." She grimaces. "Gonna be a rough day for everyone without caffeine."

Speechless, I stare back at her. Why would someone rummage through everyone's stuff just to organize it? I'm convinced this has something to do with Ezra, but now I'm questioning his intentions.

"Order everyone coffee from across the street. I'll have Rev hold a meeting to calm everyone down when he gets back from his operation."

I stalk toward the corner office. When I don't find Ezra sprawled out on the desk, I slam the door so hard it rattles on its hinges. "Motherfucker!"

Seth, the mail guy, jumps and lets out a yelp. "Sorry for sneezing, sir."

"No, you're fine, Seth," I grumble, giving him a lazy wave of my hand. "Carry on."

Striding for my office, I catch mutterings from my staff.

"My files were alphabetized."

"...keyboard's been sprayed clean..."

"...thought Jen stole my credit card machine, but it was on my desk this morning, right where I had it a week ago..."

I call Alaric on my cell, getting him on the first ring. "How the *fuck* did we not get security footage of the thief escaping? I'm beginning to think *you* hired him to drive me to madness."

My brother fails to stifle a yawn. "Who? Ezra?"

"Yes," I hiss. "The thief I asked you to research last night. You never got back to me."

"I got busy, okay?" Alaric complains. "I would have been alerted if he escaped. Trust me. Let me do a sweep on him."

He hangs up on me, and I'm left slack-jawed in the middle of the office. The thief is lurking somewhere in the building and neither my brother nor Rev seem to be concerned that he's a threat.

Do I need to reevaluate Alaric's workload? It's this type of careless behavior that leads to data breaches or people dead. I know for a fact the government likes to sniff around, eager for a reason to shut me down. While I'd like to believe people would agree that we're doing the world a justice by wiping out high-profile scum, that wasn't always the case.

Fuming, I stride to my office and unlock the door, only to be stopped short by Ezra curled up in my desk chair like some sort of street cat.

For a few ragged breaths, I just stare down at him. My brain can't process what the fuck is happening. I feel like I'm being tossed around on a broken down fair ride, hurtled this way and that. And all by some rough-around-the-edges kid.

Part of me is still convinced he's a traitor, allied with Gabriel to ruin me or ordered here by the government as an undercover operative. The other part can't help but be intrigued. Ezra snuck into my building, broke out of the corner office, organized the entire floor, and ate Steve's lunch.

I almost want to snort. It *is* kind of fucking funny.

Maybe he was searching for the drive. But why would he put so much effort into cleaning? Why wouldn't he try to escape?

It seems more like he was... bored.

Ezra stirs and blinks up at me with those pretty hazel eyes. I clench my jaw. *No, not pretty.*

"Oh, shit. Guess I fell asleep," Ezra says, popping out of my chair. "Should I go back to my corner room now?"

I want to correct him that it's not *his* corner room. And this isn't *his* office to upheave. I'm in control here.

Instead, I pinch the bridge of my nose. I'll be fighting a headache today, no doubt. "What in god's name are you?"

"Could be a changeling."

"A what?" I ask, cutting him a glare.

Ezra fiddles with his lip ring. "A mythical creature swapped with a human baby at—" He drifts off as I stalk over to him, forcing his smaller frame back against the glass windows. His Adam's apple bobs under my hand as I wrap it around his neck.

"Is all of this your doing or not?" I demand, finding that I'm more curious than aggravated. I do my best to ignore the twitch of my cock in my slacks, though I can't help my leg from pushing between his, sealing our bodies closer together.

Defiance lights up his eyes. "Hey, you act like I made a mess. I put shit back in order. Jen totally stole that credit card machine, and Steve had a receipt for that taco shop instead of eating the lunch his wife probably packed for him. And that stupid espresso machine needs instructions. All the hit lists in people's desks are a little questionable, though." He furrows his brows, and that heat I felt the other night trapped in a small room with him rushes through me, overwhelming all reason.

My gaze drifts down to his pouty lips. His skin is flawless and smooth under my touch. I loosen my grip on his neck, letting my thumb drift down to his pulse point. I stroke over it a few times, satisfied when I feel him responding with enthusiasm.

Do I make him nervous? I *know* I turn him on. How fast could I get his heart to beat?

Fuck these thoughts.

Ezra shrinks under my intense stare. "I'm sorry. I didn't mean to cause trouble. I just really don't like to be locked up."

I fall victim to the captivating swirl of vibrant green and light brown in his eyes, desperate for a sign that he's manipulating me. I can't stand betrayal. Won't tolerate it from my staff or contracted killers. They all undergo interviews with Rev and his team before they even have a chance at meeting with me.

Ezra's body slumps, and I hook fingers through his belt loop to help keep him upright, fighting the urge to tug him closer. His slipping confidence is throwing me off center.

"You can hit me if that would make you feel better," he murmurs. "I don't mind the pain. I think I need it."

What the fuck?

Unable to stop myself from testing him, I pull out my knife and press the cold edge just under his chin. A single bead of blood bubbles from his skin. He doesn't so much as flinch.

Why am I a little desperate to bring his sassy edge back to the surface?

My fingertips brush lightly over his neck once more. I stop breathing as his dark lashes flutter and his mouth parts. It makes me want to close the space between us and claim his lips with my own. Makes me want to reach down to stroke a hand along his length, curious if I could draw a moan from him.

I back the fuck up and flick my knife closed before I do something stupid. "I honestly have no idea what to do with you."

Breaking eye contact, he swallows. "Most people don't."

My desk phone rings before I can craft a response to that. Not wanting an audience for this call, I grip Ezra's arm and haul him back to the corner office. I give him one more hard look. "You will wait for me here until I figure out what the fuck I'm going to do with you. Do you understand?"

Ezra saunters over to the desk and plops down on it in dramatic fashion. "Just don't leave me too long, please. I get antsy."

His admission brings another pain like heartburn to my chest. I slam the door, lock it, and head back into my office to hit redial on the most recent missed call.

"Alaric," I say forcefully.

"Yeah. I can't find a single piece of information on this thief, Cain. I swear he doesn't exist," Alaric says, his tired voice cracking in frustration. I'm starting to think I should force him to take some time off.

"How can that be?"

"No matches with any Ezra's that live in the city. No other name he could go by that would fit his profile. No birth records anywhere close to his assumed age range. No arrests. No ties to Gabriel or any organization we've taken down or gathered intel on. Nothing in government files I skimmed through, either. It's like he's been purged from the system."

I drop into my chair as my composure begins to unravel. "I need you to keep digging."

"Of course I'm going to keep digging. It's like you don't even know me."

I rub at my brows. Sometimes, it's hard fighting the urge to father Alaric. No one expects him to work around the clock. I'd rather he take care of himself. But he does whatever he wants, so I don't waste my breath on lectures.

"While we're on the phone, any updates on the drive?" I ask.

"The drive is encrypted with a 32-character password. Something *that* protected has to be important."

"So what, you need a few more days?"

Again, another pause and the rapid firing of computer keys. "You have too much faith in me. Fastest solution would be to find one of Gabriel's guys and force him to talk. Someone higher up."

I hang up on him, more irked by the lack of knowledge on Ezra than the hard drive issue.

Pressing the heels of my hands into my eyes, I try to piece together what I've observed of Ezra's behavior. His cockiness yesterday would have fooled me into believing he was a street thug, desperate to prove himself. But his concern for his friend and the vulnerability he's showing me now have me questioning everything.

I march for the corner office, finding Ezra perched on the desk, crafting snowflakes out of scavenged paper clips. Realizing I've just been staring at him from the doorway, I ask the question that's been burning a hole in my brain since I learned that he snuck out of the corner office. "Did you come into my apartment last night?"

His eyes shoot wide. "*What*? No. I didn't leave the building, I swear. I don't even know where you live."

My nostrils flare, but I give a tiny nod. "Okay, Ezra."

Walking over to the desk, I wrap a hand around his wrist and pull him to his feet, being more delicate this time. Fuck this irritating prickle of concern. I want to turn him inside out. Learn all of his secrets. Check him for internal wounds.

Guiding him into the elevator, I disregard the confused look I receive from Gwen. I press the button for my apartment floor. This better not be a huge mistake.

"What are we—"

"Shut up," I say. "Just... shut the fuck up."

He purses his lips. "It's a caffeine headache, isn't it?"

My gaze snaps to him, but he appears genuinely upset. *Jesus Christ.* Is this what whiplash feels like? A concussion? A hemorrhaging in my brain? Maybe I should go to the doctor and get a check-up.

The elevator doors open, and I usher him into my apartment, watching for a giveaway in his features that he was lying about sneaking into my private space last night.

Ezra takes in the clean lines of my minimalist, sleek apartment in awe. "Woah. This might be the nicest place I've ever seen."

The comment pisses me off. I'm not angry at him. I'm angry at his situation. If he's been truthful with us, how long has he been out on the streets? Does he have a safe place to stay? Does he sleep in shelters like his friend? He's definitely lean enough for me to be concerned that he's getting enough to eat.

Ever the CEO, I bark out orders. "You will stay here. You will not leave this building for your own safety. Go ahead and snoop all you want. You'll find nothing of interest here."

Ezra turns to face me, his eyes wide. "I don't understand."

"Consider my apartment an upgraded cell until I deal with Gabriel and you can return to whatever you were doing before you broke into my company. Take what you want from the fridge. Go ahead and shower, too."

Shutting the door, I don't bother locking him in this time.

Right now, I'm the only thing keeping Ezra safe, and for some fucked up reason, that makes my stupid internal animal rumble with satisfaction.

CHAPTER NINE

EZRA

I'm stunned in place as Cain leaves me in his home.

Why would he ask me if I broke in here just to give me free rein of the place?

Once I shake off my confusion, I don't waste time settling in. These are new waters to explore, and Cain's apartment is beautiful. A bit cold like him, with concrete floors and exposed ceilings and no real personal touches.

I get the feeling that he keeps everything and everyone closed off. He's probably never had to deal with someone so faulty like me.

Sweeping from the entryway to the living room, I put my hands on everything. I try on his glasses sitting at the edge of a granite island, checking myself out in the bathroom mirror. I flip through the business books stacked on a circular gold end table beside a cream plush couch facing a glass wall of windows.

Naturally, I snoop in his bedroom. Excavating a black ring from his dresser, I hook it on the inside of my pants pocket with a safety pin tugged free from my ear. It's all I find for valuables.

I take a long shower in the glass and stone enclosure, humming in satisfaction at the punishing water pressure. Then I steal one of Cain's t-shirts and a pair of sweats from his large closet. I have to tie the strings on the pants extra tight to keep them up, which makes me giggle.

After cooking up a meal with items I scavenged from the fridge, I manage to make a cup of coffee without breaking anything and sink into his couch, pretending like I'm actually going to read one of his books.

A knock from the front door startles me upright. I jog over to the front door, checking the security monitor beside it. The camera reveals Rev standing on the other side with his hands tucked loosely in his gray slacks. He paired them with a pastel geometric sweater that would look ridiculous on anyone else.

I crack open the door. Will Cain be notified somehow through the security system that I opened it? How much trouble will I be in later when he sees what I've done to his apartment?

Rev looks me over with a cocked brow. Leaning sideways, he peers into the kitchen where I've caused absolute chaos. I think I dirtied up every pot and pan, making an omelet and potato wedges. At least, that's what I was shooting for. I've only watched a few cooking shows in shelters. If Gordon Ramsey were here to judge me, he'd be screaming, "This is fucking raw!"

"Oh, Cain's going to have a fit when he sees you."

"Shit." My face crumples. "I'll clean everything up. I promise."

"I said when he sees *you*. Not the kitchen destruction."

I glance down at myself. "Should I change out of his clothes? I didn't have anything else..."

Rev chuckles. "You are too cute, you know that? Completely innocent. When Cain finally accepts that, you're going to set fire to his world, pretty boy."

I blink back at him, kneading the loose fabric of Cain's soft t-shirt in my hand. "I don't know what you mean."

Rev just cracks a sly grin and struts into the apartment. "Cain ordered me to question you about some things. Apparently, he believes this is adequate revenge for him having to deal with the HR issues you caused this morning."

I run my hands up and down the fabric over my thighs. "Ah, yeah. Sorry about that."

"No worries, Ezra. The drama was very much welcomed after a disappointing mission last night. Our boy Gabriel abandoned his warehouse."

My shoulders droop. I can't help the hitch of panic in my voice when I ask, "Is my friend safe?"

"We have security detail on him. We'll put a bullet in Gabriel and shut down his business soon enough."

I trail him into the kitchen like an eager puppy. "Can I help?"

"That's what I'm here to find out." Rev moves over to the stove to examine my food concoctions. "What is this supposed to be?"

I cringe. "Breakfast?"

He shrugs and pops a raw potato into his mouth before plopping down on the couch. "Minus one for cooking skills. Okay, Ezra with no last name. Let's get a feel for what you're good at, other than the obvious thievery and ability to get under Cain's thick skin. You educated?"

"Um..." I hesitate, breaking eye contact to look out the massive windows. Why'd he have to start there? My last foster parent didn't care to enroll me in school. Another red flag, but I assumed I just lucked out with the no more homework thing. What kid would complain about that?

"I maybe only finished the third grade," I admit.

Cheeks flushed, I perch on the other end of the couch and pull my legs up against my chest. This only seems to further amuse Rev. I get the feeling that I'm becoming more of a science experiment they want to poke at. Guess that's better than a criminal they want to torture and kill.

When I glance back at Rev, his smile falters. "Don't be ashamed, Ezra. Degrees mean very little to us."

"Okay," I say quietly, nodding.

"You obviously know how to read from your organizing of files," he notes.

"Yeah, I know math, too. Basic security systems and computers are a breeze for me. and I can memorize strings of data pretty easily."

"Mnemonist, huh?" Rev's eyes shine with what looks like hunger. "You ever shot a gun?"

I rub my palms over my knees. "No, but I don't think the idea scares me."

If I'm on Gabriel's radar, who knows who else has eyes on me? On Jakey, too, just for being acquainted with me. I should probably learn how to shoot. I can't rely on Sinro's protection forever.

"Good answer. Ever been in a fight? Killed someone?"

My brows raise and my stomach twists. "Wow. These questions escalated quickly."

"Does that surprise you?" Rev asks, toying with a dangling chain earring threaded a couple of times through his ear.

"No. I saw the paperwork in your desks. I saw Cain kill a guy, too."

"Do you think taking a life can be justified?"

My breath hitches as memories threaten to flood my brain. Behind closed eyes, I see the reflection of a single lightbulb in the lenses of a man's glasses. He's wearing one of his starched white shirts. I can still smell the sour tang of his breath. Still feel the warm gush of his blood over my skin.

I jolt up from the couch and pace the living room, desperate to settle the churning bile in my stomach.

Rev's eyes stalk me. "It's okay if you can't answer that question, Ezra."

Pausing in the middle of the room, I carefully assemble my answer so I don't give away too much of myself. "There are certain people in this world who deserve something worse than death. I don't think I would have a problem delivering it to them."

Rev is quiet for a while, and when I turn toward him, he's got a pensive look on his face. "I appreciate you being so open with me. I know you've had it rough these last couple of days. I'm sorry Cain messed up your face."

I shrug, feeling a bit choked up all of the sudden. This attention is messing with me. The interest in my life and my skills. I'd never experienced it before. Sure, I put on a show of being cocky and carefree, but it was a defense mechanism to keep people from digging deeper.

"S'okay. You all haven't been... horrible to me."

Rev nods. "Now, I'll give you some information to process. You gonna keep pacing like that?"

I hadn't realized I'd started back up. "Probably. I struggle to sit still sometimes."

"No desk job for you, then. Alaric will be disappointed to have lost you to field work."

"Wait... are you talking about... hiring me?" I ask, spinning my lip ring around.

Did I want that? Could be a good thing for me and Jakey. After this shit with Gabriel, I don't know that I should keep stealing.

"It's a possibility, Ezra. As you may have figured out in your thorough investigation of our office, Sinro Enterprises offers a very broad range of services."

"You're mercenaries," I reply without hesitation.

Rev shrugs. "We prefer the title private military contractors. People hire us for a number of reasons. Protection, cyber security, penetration testing—don't giggle at that—surveillance, and breaking up criminal organizations."

Intrigued, I plop down on the floor, cross-legged.

Rev smiles at me in approval. "Cain screens all of our clients. He wouldn't accept a job that would result in innocent lives being taken. He doesn't lean that way. Servitude to humanity runs through his veins. Military guy." Rev winks.

It's not hard for me to imagine Cain in a uniform. He's built like an experienced soldier.

"So Cain takes contracts from who then? The government?"

"Sometimes. Sometimes politicians. They like to claim they're cleaning up the streets. Sometimes it's local police when a situation is too dangerous. Sometimes he runs his own jobs, funding them with money he's earned through the consulting side of the company."

"Modern day vigilante, huh?" I crack a nervous grin, though I do feel better about what's going on here. It's more noble than I expected from a big corporation.

Rev nods. "Now you're getting it."

"Your website is very vague about your services."

"Not everyone is sold on the idea of PMCs. We stay out of the media. Disclosing our true mission to the public would put all of us at risk, including the clients that bring word of evil to our desks."

I process this for a few minutes, running my fingers over the rug beneath me.

Rev checks his expensive watch. "Unfortunately, that's all I have time for today. You're welcome to use the gym or pool on the balcony. I'm sure Cain didn't offer those facilities to you, but I think he'll understand if you need to burn off some energy."

My chest tightens. "Ok."

"You might want to try cleaning up the kitchen if you don't want him to be overly testy tonight."

"Rev?" I call out before he retreats through the front door. "Thank you. For being so—"

"Don't say kind," Rev says, dropping his smile. "I'm not kind, Ezra. I play a role, and sometimes I get lost in it. That's all."

His phone rings, saving me from having to respond to his odd admission.

"Yeah?" Rev answers, propping his shoulder against the door. "Surprised you're letting me take the lead on this one. I'll finish up here and head out with my team."

Rev's pale eyes cut to me, the corner of his mouth lifting. "Yes, he's still here. No, you'll have to come up here and check on him yourself."

He hangs up and pockets his phone. "Hey, Ezra?"

My spine straightens. "Yeah?"

"Cause some more chaos for the bossman tonight, okay?"

I glimpse a true smile from him as he leaves, and it's better suited for a demon in hell.

The front door clicks open as I'm elbow deep in soapy water. The sink overflowed while I got distracted playing dress up in Cain's closet. He has all the same style suits in shades ranging from black to navy to gray. Everything not business formal ranges in shades of the same colors, which is incredibly boring.

I had no idea how much dish soap to use. Judging by the spillover in the kitchen and Cain's slack-jawed expression, it's definitely not half the bottle. Slowly, he places his briefcase on the shelf by the door, water rippling on the polished concrete floors beneath his leather shoes.

"Explain," Cain orders, stripping off his jacket and rolling up his shirt sleeves to reveal heavy ink covering his veiny forearms. A ring of black encompasses both wrists, gradually fading into a forest scene, and ending in sharp pines at his elbows.

My heart leaps into a sprint. "God, I just felt bad about all the dishes from breakfast, and Rev mentioned you'd be pissed. Something about setting fire to your world. But I've never done this before." I tangle a bubbled hand in my messy hair. "Didn't know how to work the fancy dishwasher, either."

I let out a frustrated breath as my cheeks heat, irritated by my inability to do anything but steal shit and aggravate people.

Why am I even doing his stupid dishes? He choked me. Zip-tied me. Cut me with a knife. And he's technically holding me against my will now, right?

But for some reason, I trust that he doesn't actually mean me harm. Isn't that fucked?

In my short life experience though, it's the nice ones that are un-predictable. They often turn out to be the worst creatures to walk this world.

Shoes splashing through water, Cain hurries over to shut off the running sink.

"I leave you alone for eight hours and you trash my home," he complains, but there's no real fire behind his words. "Between the office and this, I should throw you out."

"If that's what you want," I say, backing away from him.

He grips my forearm, and I brace for a hit. Which is stupid, because I know I wouldn't hate it.

It's just… after Rev's kindness, or whatever I'm supposed to call it, and Cain's shifting moods, and knowing Jakey's out in the world alone, I'm feeling weird. Off.

I feel weak for the first time in a long time.

Cain and Rev said they would deal with Gabriel, but how long would this drag out? How long until I got to see Jakey again?

"I said I should," Cain emphasizes, his tone softer as he draws me close. "Doesn't mean I'm going to."

"Oh." Goosebumps rise on my flesh, and I forget to inhale as he stares down at me, something swirling in his sultry brown eyes. My heart takes notice, thudding hard against my ribs, sending hot blood racing through my body.

His eyes move over the healing cut on my cheek, then drift to my temple where there's a nearly hidden yellow and purple bruise from Alphabet Soup smacking me in the head. He did that earlier, too. Almost as if he's checking on my wounds.

I shove down the urge to close the small gap between us. Features scrunching, Cain releases me and steps back. "Grab a mop from the closet. Let's get this cleaned up."

Darting over to the closet, I retrieve two mops and a bucket. Cain keeps glancing over at me as I work furiously to soak up water.

"At least your floors will be clean," I comment.

He shakes his head, and I swear I hear him give a low chuckle.

Once the floors are dry and he's tackled the bubble mountain in the sink, he loads up the dishwasher and glances at the clock on the wall.

"You hungry?" he asks, turning to where I'm curled up on a stool at the kitchen island. He seems thrown off by my position. A bit irked, too. Wouldn't be the first time someone didn't like me. Cain definitely doesn't like me, regardless of this change in his behavior, and I don't blame him.

"I can always eat."

He calls in an order for Chinese food before retreating into his bedroom. When he comes out, dressed down in a black henley that clings to his chest and sweats, his eyes rake over me.

Spinning my lip ring, I wait for his anger over the clothes I stole from his closet.

Cain just ruffles his damp hair. "You're a bit of a tornado, aren't you? You definitely need something to do until we can get rid of you."

I try to hide my grimace. Here I thought Rev was going to set me up with a permanent job. Maybe they don't think I'm qualified.

Cain leans over the kitchen island, bringing his face so close to mine that I forget how to draw in air.

"Something's not sitting right with me." His voice is soft, but his gaze is deadly. "Why can't we find anything on you in the system, Ezra?"

Panic slams into me, and my hands clench the fabric of my sweatpants. I drop my chin to my knee. The buzzing beneath my skin is back, convincing me that I need to move my body.

"Because I shouldn't exist," I whisper.

Cain's mouth turns down. He doesn't break eye contact with me, almost like he wants to sear through all of my defenses. But I'm real good at keeping people out. No one knows about me.

No one but my foster parent and *him*. The man I killed.

I climb out of the chair, unable to stay seated. Back and forth, I roam the length of the kitchen under his scrutinizing gaze, hands curling and uncurling at my sides.

"Could you stop doing that, please?" I say.

"Stop what, Ezra?"

I spin on him. "Looking at me like that. Like I'm some puzzle with missing fucking pieces."

The permafrost in his dark eyes melts as they hold me. There's a flash of lust, too. And I can't help it. I have no control over my body when I dip into these destructive moods. No fucking restraint on my impulses.

As I walk slowly over to Cain, he drags his massive body off the counter. A muscle ticks in his jaw as he clenches it, but he doesn't back away from me. If anything, he leans closer, his body heat seeping under my skin and setting me on fire.

My pulse races as I reach out to grip his nice shirt, suddenly desperate to ruin it. The bob of his throat fascinates me. I undo the first two buttons at his collar, revealing a glimpse of his silky, perfect chest.

Cain doesn't move a muscle. He lets me handle him, no complaints. Or maybe he's in shock. I mean, I'm probably in shock at this point, my brain saturated with too much desire.

Unable to stop pushing my fucking limit, I take a fistful of his shirt and use it to help raise up on my toes. I slip my other hand around the back of his strong neck, tangling my fingers in his soft, wet hair. A breath away from his mouth, I hesitate. I watch his nostrils flare, allowing him the chance to shove me off. When he doesn't, I brush my lips against his in the softest kiss.

Electricity jolts through me, shocking enough to wipe away my panic and make me crave more of him.

Only, Cain doesn't kiss me back.

Shit. I'm so stupid. I definitely misinterpreted what happened in the office. Maybe he isn't attracted to me. He just got turned on by the idea of carving me up.

My heart sinks as I let my hands fall away from him, though my head rests on his solid chest for a few disappointed breaths.

"Ezra," he warns, creating space between us. Never once touching me. "What are you doing?"

"Causing trouble, I guess," I whisper, fighting to pull myself together. At least the madness inside of me is calm now. It's been replaced by fiery embarrassment.

I ease away from him, hating this newfound tension growing between us. Cain doesn't seem to know what to say. His mouth opens and closes a few times. Then his phone rings.

"Food's here. Gonna go grab it," he mumbles.

Left alone, I work to seal up my battered emotions. Why the hell did I do that? Why isn't Cain raging at me? He doesn't even seem mad. He'll probably lay into me tomorrow after some sleep.

An uncomfortable fog settles over the apartment when he returns, all buttoned up and put back together. I channel my unrest into viciously winding chow mein noodles around my fork as we sit down at the dining table.

Cain doesn't ask me any more questions. He doesn't comment on the kiss. It's actually starting to piss me off. Was it not even worth getting mad over?

"So, what's on the hard drive?" I ask in a sharp tone, shoving another bite of noodles and cabbage into my mouth.

Cain sets his fork down on his cleaned plate. "It's none of your business, Ezra."

I stab my fork into my food loud enough to clang on the ceramic plate. My embarrassment has now mutated into an attitude, which isn't okay, but I can't seem to adjust it.

"Considering I was threatened into stealing it, I *do* think it's my business, Cain."

He assesses me with menacing, icy eyes until I'm squirming in my chair.

"Sorry for asking," I mutter. "Wait, I'm not sorry. I rescind my apology."

"What has gotten into you?" He sighs, shaking his head. The ends of his drying hair have started curling over his forehead, distracting me from my next bite of food. "We don't know what's on the drive yet, but I'm hoping we'll have answers tonight."

Frowning, I remember the phone call Rev took before vanishing. Was he headed back to Gabriel's warehouse?

I want this ordeal with Gabriel over with, but I don't really want to leave Sinro without learning how to properly defend myself. Rev dangled a carrot in front of me with talk of a job. They wouldn't just rip that away, would they?

And I have to admit that I'm desperate for a kernel of Cain's affection. The man has me all tied in knots, desperate for release.

Silently, Cain picks up our plates and washes them in the sink. He disappears into his bedroom for a few minutes, returning with a handful of bathroom supplies. "Spare stuff you can have."

I stare down at the toothbrush, toothpaste, and deodorant he laid out on the counter. It shouldn't make me emotional. They are such basic essentials.

Suddenly, I feel guilty about the ring I jacked from his dresser. But he's obviously not using it, and something about having a piece of Cain settles right inside my fucked up brain.

Clinging to my anger, I cross my arms over my chest. "Cool."

Cain's deep brown eyes bore into me. "Second bedroom's yours. I'm sure you snooped in there already."

He strides to his room, hesitating at the door. "Any more funny business, Ezra, and I'll be forced to keep you in much worse conditions."

The threat is weak, though, leaving me feeling messy on the inside.

CHAPTER TEN

CAIN

As soon as I close myself in my bedroom, I have to brace my weight against the door.

God, please tell me why you sent this guy into my life. I haven't been perfect; I get that. Murder is a sin. But I thought maybe I was doing the work that needed to be done.

Why did he have to kiss me? Ezra was just a cocky little thief, not someone I could ever care about. Now I'm feeling uneasy about the thought of releasing him back into the world when all is said and done with Gabriel.

How did I go from wanting to throw him out a window to wanting to provide for him in the span of a day?

Ezra puts on a strong face. He pretends like he's not scared, but that destructive energy vibrating under his surface concerns me.

I keep circling back to the lack of information about him, trying to come to a different conclusion. If he is some sort of deep operative spy who's flying under our radar, I suppose we'll find out soon. All I can do at this point is keep him under watch.

And with the way he tore through the office and my apartment? I need to keep him busy before he burns the entire building to ashes.

Withdrawing my phone, I shoot a text to Rev, knowing my chances of getting a response are slim when I sent him and his team out to infiltrate another one of Gabriel's operations at some shipyard.

You working or slacking?

Rev's surprisingly fast to respond with a selfie in tactical gear, posted up on a roof. I make out silhouettes of his team behind him.

How did the chat with Ezra go today?

A little depressing, to be honest.

I clutch my phone tighter, dropping onto my bed in the dark. Rev rarely shows compassion for others. He's skilled at hiding the fact that he doesn't give a shit about much of anything.

I take the bait anyway. *Why is that?*

My blood pressure ticks higher. I'm not usually this stressed or wound up. Irritable almost always, but that's just how I'm wired.

Barely educated. No experience with weapons. He's definitely been through enough shit to see things from our unique perspective.

I grit my teeth and let my phone fall onto my chest. This suffering that seems to cloud over humanity fucking digs at me. Why is it necessary? Why do people treat others so horribly? It makes me wonder if evil is an infection that can be spread.

My phone buzzes again.

Surprised you're not complaining about him. You'd kick my ass if I touched your clothes or destroyed your kitchen.

I stare at the message for a while. My brain replays the vision of Ezra in my t-shirt and sweats, covered in soap and looking too damn cute. I close my eyes, imagining his hand gripping me by the shirt again, his mouth pressed against mine in a kiss that had alarm bells blaring in my head as all systems went into failure.

My cock strains against my sweats. Groaning, I set my phone on the nightstand and shove the waistband of my pants below my heavy balls. I fist my cock and give it a few tight pumps from root to tip.

I try not to think about Ezra, but it's impossible when he's burrowed his way so deep into my brain I don't think I'll ever erase his presence there.

Accepting that this is going to be a disappointing orgasm, I don't even bother with lube. I spit into my palm and jack myself in quick motions until I'm spurting thick ropes of cum onto my tensed abs.

I lie in bed until my breathing returns to normal. Then I wipe myself clean in the bathroom and storm into the kitchen to grab a bottle of water from the fridge.

At least, that's what I tell myself I'm doing. I can't help a detour down the hall. The door to the other bedroom in my apartment is cracked, but the light is off and it's dead silent.

I hover there for a few moments, beginning to feel like a creep in my own damn house. But I have a right to make sure he's not fucking anything else up. If he didn't want me to check in, he would have locked the door.

I push the door open wider. My eyes sweep from the empty bed to the floor where Ezra's curled up with the throw blanket from the back of my couch, the one meant for decoration, not keeping a body warm.

I sigh, dragging a hand through my hair. I give the guy a perfectly good bed, and he chooses to sleep on the floor. He's going to wake up with cramped muscles.

Carefully, I scoop him up in my arms. His hand grips my t-shirt, right over my sternum, but he doesn't seem to wake up. I pause to assess that flutter of something in my chest as I stare down at him.

He looks so... soft. So precious.

How did I not notice the first time I saw him? Maybe because my callous nature automatically categorizes everyone as a criminal to start. Hard not to when I've witnessed so many horrors in this world.

Add in the fact that I'm nearing my limit with Gabriel's ability to avoid our bullets.

I draw back the blankets and tuck Ezra in. Hovering longer than acceptable, I'm unable to stop my thumb from tracing the line I carved into his otherwise unmarked face. A scar that will always remain.

I did that.

And I regret it. I know better than to strike first without good reason. The Special Forces trained me to assess situations first. My lack of control is just further proof that I'm out of practice, more businessman than soldier now.

One thing is for certain. I'm no good for someone like Ezra.

Assured he's still asleep, I sneak out of the room and prepare for a restless night in my own bed.

CHAPTER ELEVEN

CAIN

I get a text from Rev the next morning before my second cup of coffee.

Shipyard was overrun with roaches. We'll need more teams to successfully infiltrate, but we did manage to return with cargo.

Before anyone can slap early meetings on my calendar, I stroll to the elevator, coffee in hand, and ride it all the way down.

Deceptively big, the lower levels of Sinro Enterprises span two blocks underground, all the way to the edge of our parking garage.

Stepping off the elevator on lower level two, I press my thumb to the security pad on the wall. When the door swings open, I find Rev still in his fitted black tactical gear.

Gabriel's crony is duct taped to a wobbly stool in the middle of the room over a drain in the concrete floor. I know it upsets Henry to have less of a mess to clean up, but I don't need the guy occupied with bleaching floors. I need him out running body retrievals.

Our captive quivers with fear, and I smell the disgusting stench of piss on his clothes. He's rambling, promising us money if we let him live.

Disregarding him entirely, I aim my attention at Rev. "You shooting for a promotion or something?"

Rev cracks a grin while I sip at my coffee–no sugar or cream to cut through the bitter taste. I don't drink it for pleasure. I drink it to wake my ass up, another checkmark on the rigid routine I'd developed after I got out of the army.

Plus, there's something so human about brewing a cup of coffee in the early morning. And most days, I needed a reminder that I am, in fact, human.

"Nah. Told you. My sights are set on that corner office. There's a surprise on the table for you, too. You're welcome. After this, I'm taking the day off. Tired of doing all your work. I've got a hot date tonight."

Shaking my head, I walk over to the table and find a manilla folder waiting there for me.

"What's this?" I ask.

Screams erupt as Rev begins his work. I sip my coffee as I flip open the folder.

"Shut the fuck up. Businessmen are talking," Rev says to his captive, and I hear a smack. "It's my onboarding plan for Ezra."

I let the folder fall open in my hands, not at all surprised to see that Rev wants to move forward with training Ezra to join his team.

After some back and forth over text last night, because sleep is for the weak, Rev decided Ezra was better suited for elimination than extraction, intel, basic security, or paperwork. He's far too wound up to sit still.

I don't mind the thought of Ezra learning how to defend himself, but I'm a little concerned about absorbing him into our dark world. Surviving on the streets is one thing, but becoming well-known to more high-profile criminals is entirely another, especially when he isn't even trained with weapons.

And I'm not set on placing him with Rev's team. Despite Rev's seemingly warm personality, he can be pretty damn cold. Colder than me.

I set the folder down and turn around, leaning my weight against the table. Blood drips from the criminal's wounds I can't see from this angle. Rev likes to start with removing fingernails.

"What the fuck do you want from me? I don't know anything, I swear!" the guy cries.

"Yeah?" Rev stabs his dagger into the guy's thigh. Howls erupt. "Then this is really going to suck for you."

Leaving the blade there, Rev perches on the guy's other thigh to face me. "Well? It's quite thorough, right?"

"It is," I agree. "But we barely know anything about this guy. Alaric couldn't dig up anything on him. He could be some deep undercover operative, and you're pitching the idea of taking him under wing and training him to kill."

"If he's undercover, he already knows how to kill," Rev counters. "Are you honestly doubting my intuition?"

I sigh. The screams of Gabriel's guy are starting to irritate my eardrums. "Can you hurry up with him, please?"

Rev hops off his lap and slaps the guy in the face again. "Look here, shitbag. You tell me what your boss would be hiding on encrypted hard drives, and I'll make the pain go away, I promise. You keep spewing lies about not knowing shit, and I'll start sawing off fingers and toes with a fucking plastic knife."

The guy turns into a sobbing mess, struggling against the duct tape until the stool tips over. He crashes into a puddle of his own blood.

"I don't know anything, okay?! They only pay me to check in deliveries."

Rev squats down next to him. He pulls out his gun, resting it against the shell of the guy's ear. "Deliveries of what?"

The guy lets out a tortured wail. "I don't know. They never tell me what's inside the shipping containers. I just record numbers and assure the right people come to pick them up for transport. Please don't kill me."

"How are the containers transported?" I ask.

"Ships bring them in from the gulf. Semis and trains haul them across the country."

I frown. We don't have eyes on the river or the gulf it spills into. Maybe it's time to invest in boats. The mention of a countrywide operation has me questioning if I shouldn't reach out to my government contact, too.

Rev looks at me, and I give a disappointed nod. This guy's a nobody, but he's still actively engaged in criminal activity. It's inexcusable.

Plus, Rev needs the kill. Last time I deprived him of one, he was testy with me for two weeks. I need him firing on all cylinders right now. Especially since I'm not.

Rising up, Rev shoots the man in the head, unfazed by the blood splatter. Behind closed doors, without an audience, this is his true nature. He is the shadow following you home at night. The demon lurking in your nightmares.

If I wasn't so immune to death from my time serving, Rev might have terrified me. Now, I don't blink twice at his viciousness.

"I'd like to start training Ezra tomorrow," Rev says, tucking his gun back in his belt holster.

"We need to meet with teams to plan out a strike, Rev."

Rev cocks a brow. "I get lunch breaks, don't I?"

The fact that he's pushing this so hard has a spark of anger igniting in my chest.

"I don't know. I don't have a good feeling about this," I say, envisioning the vulnerability that sometimes slips through Ezra's sassy facade. Red flags wave in my brain that this will only end in ruins.

Rev smirks. "You trying to protect him now?"

I grip my coffee cup tighter. "We don't even know if we can trust him."

"I know your issues run deep, but are you really not seeing this one clearly? Or are you still mentally comparing him to Aiden—"

"We're not fucking going there," I snap back, fury running my blood hot.

Rev doesn't bat an eye at me, awaiting the full loss of my temper. I just sigh and drop my head into my hand, rubbing at my brows.

"This guy's really messing you up."

"He's my own personal nightmare." And before I know what I'm doing, I confess, "He kissed me last night."

Rev's brows shoot up as he plops down on the floor next to the dead body, settling in for a juicy story. "No shit? Didn't think the little thief had it in him. How was it?"

I try to sear Rev with my glare, but it backfires, lost in the depths of the depraved creature that lives inside of him.

Rubbing fingers over the bridge of my nose, I shake my head. "I didn't kiss him back. Then he got all short with me."

"You asswipe."

"What?" I exclaim, head jerking up.

"You hurt his feelings. He's probably all knotted up on the inside because he's got a crush on you, and you fucking turned him down. You've been nothing but mean to him."

"He tried to steal from us, Rev." My heart beats a little harder. "Wait, a crush?"

Rev nods like it should be obvious to me. "Good lord, have you been with anyone since Aiden?"

The casual way he keeps throwing my previous lover's name out there stems from a deep understanding that I've gotten over Aiden's death. Spent enough time spilling my guts to professionals, only because I was desperate to move on and forget the whole fucked up situation.

How the hell did this conversation flip from professional to pointing out my relationship failures and insecurities?

But it's true. I haven't been with anyone seriously since Aiden. Just a few random hook-ups outside of work. Never in my apartment. Never more than once with the same guy.

"Too busy working," I reply lamely.

Rev doesn't buy into my bullshit. "We're both workaholics, and I still manage to sneak in a good fuck a couple of times a week."

I stare back at him, mentally trying to cleanse images of Rev in precarious positions fighting for attention in my brain. "I don't know what you want me to do with that information."

"First of all, apologize to the guy. And then, maybe think about why you have him living in your apartment, when if it were anyone else, they'd already be dead." Rev peels himself off the floor. "We're not done talking about him, but I need to make some calls and hit the gym before my hot date."

"Forget it," I say. "I won't turn him into a killer."

"Your expression tells me a different story. Would you rather him tail Seth in the mail room than learn to protect himself?"

"No." I huff. "But I'm not sold on him reporting to you."

Rev's piranha smile returns in full effect. "Territorial."

I fight back my anger, pretending to get distracted by an email that just came through on my phone. "I just don't know that you have the right... skill set to handle him."

"Because I'm so villainous."

"You said it. Not me."

"Okay. How about I teach him some things to start? See if he's even cut out for this. And if he is, we'll both take him out on a run to decide who would be better suited to keep him."

I grit my teeth, hating the idea of Rev ordering Ezra around and spending more time with him. Fuck. Why am I getting so worked up about this? Is it because I know Rev is gay, too?

My brain circles back to Ezra's kiss last night. The potent need that had coursed through me when his soft lips pressed against mine was unmistakable. Even now, my dick grows hard at the memory.

Would Rev even be Ezra's type?

I bite back a growl. "He's just..." *Fuck.* What is he? "Sensitive."

"Ah, yes." Rev nods. "That he is. But I think a little gunfire will help him along beautifully."

I swig at my coffee, trying to maintain an air of calm. "I don't know, Rev. Let me think about it."

Rev's grin doesn't shrink an inch. "Yeah, go ahead and mull it over. Maybe get a nut off while you're at it."

"Fuck you."

He winks. "Don't think we're compatible, bossman."

Ignoring his comment, I check the time on my phone. Noon already, which means it's lunchtime. Has Ezra eaten? When have I ever noticed the time while working? I'm usually too busy to care about breaks. I rarely acknowledge my hunger until the sun sets and the office falls silent.

The thought of Ezra all flustered while he destroyed my kitchen has me striding for the elevator. Why does the idea of his hurt fucking feelings bring discomfort to my chest?

I'm really not cut out for dealing with people. I've never been good at being considerate or showing affection. With Aiden, I went through the motions. Yeah, I loved him, but I didn't care for any of the normal checklist items. Moving in together. Marriage. Kids. The only reason I'd even bought him a ring was because he expected it.

Rev catches the elevator doors, climbing in with me.

"Lunch date?" he asks, raising a brow.

I roll my eyes. "Quit it."

Rev feigns innocence. "What? You have to admit, he *is* dangerously cute. Hard not to notice. Even if you fucked everything up last night."

My eyes flash with murderous intent as I stalk off the elevator toward my apartment, Rev's mad laughter sounding behind me.

I won't entertain this with him. Rev thinks I'm growing sentimental for the thief. That's not even a possibility. The organ in my chest is long dead, blackened by the amount of souls I've collected over the years.

I press my thumb to the security pad outside my apartment door, on edge over what chaos will reveal itself inside. It's much easier to crack a grin at the image of pretty Ezra elbow deep in bubbles now than it was yesterday when we had to clean up the disaster.

When I step inside, my apartment is clean. No fires. No alarms. No bubbles.

It's too quiet, and that kicks my heart into overdrive, fear sparking through my nervous system.

"Ezra?" I call out.

Why isn't he answering me?

I scour my apartment. Beds are still made, and nothing seems to be out of place. Charging into the common areas, I breathe a sigh of relief when I discover Ezra on the treadmill in the gym. He's wearing another t-shirt of mine and a pair of my black briefs that show off his full ass and toned thighs.

My dick starts to thicken. He doesn't notice my approach, too focused on keeping stride. My brows raise at the hour and a half time on the treadmill. Does this guy ever tire?

He startles when he sees me, missing his footing. I lurch to grab him in an outstretched arm as he stumbles off the treadmill.

"Shit, sorry." Ezra's wide eyes flick up to meet mine.

"No. My fault," I say, finding it hard to uncurl my arm from his trim waist. I clear my throat and let him go, putting some space between us. Unable to make eye contact, I force out more words. "Want to get some lunch?"

God, why am I being all awkward about this now? Fuck Rev for getting in my head, like always.

A slow smile eases onto his face, and yeah... I'm momentarily stunned by him. To my relief, he doesn't seem upset about my overthinking last night. Maybe we can move past this and forget the kiss.

Although, I know I won't be able to. Not in this lifetime.

"Lunch?" Ezra's brows lift as he mulls over my offer. "Like both of us together? You and me?"

"Never mind. This was a mistake," I mutter, heading for the door.

"Wait!" Ezra's hand wraps around my wrist. I frown at the contact, surprised by the stutter of my heart. "Please. I want to get lunch with you."

My chest puffs up. *Take that, Rev.*

I swallow a groan. This is not some competition to win over Ezra. The guy shouldn't even be here.

So then, where does he belong?

"Whatever," I say, failing to sound menacing. "Get cleaned up and we can go."

"Are we leaving the building?" he asks.

"Planned on it, unless you don't tone down that tornadic energy."

Ezra vibrates with hyperactivity all the way to my apartment door. He seems to be back to his normal self today. Or is the vulnerable side the real Ezra?

I fight the urge to look at him again, knowing it would be a bad idea. Lunch with him is a bad idea.

When I open my front door, he darts inside. He skids to a stop. Frowning, he rushes back to me, nearly colliding with my body. "I don't have any clean clothes."

I create some distance between us. For good measure. "Just borrow more of mine. We'll pick up a few things for you when we go out."

His lips purse, and his eyes grow big. He looks too fucking delectable. Why didn't I kiss him back last night? I can't deny that I wanted to. Still want to as I stare down at his beautiful face.

No. *Fuck*. I know why I didn't reciprocate. I don't get caught up in this kind of shit. I have a business to run. Hundreds of criminals to take down. Criminals who would take advantage of anyone close to me.

Internally, I'm torn between wanting more of these expressions from him and wanting to slam him up against the wall and demand that he stop fucking with me.

I'm going to beat the living daylights out of Rev the next time we step into the boxing ring for putting these toxic thoughts in my head.

If I find out that Ezra's been playing us this entire time, I won't hesitate to kill him with my bare hands.

Christ. Maybe I do need to get laid. It's been... what? Over a year since that dancer in a club? That's why I'm wound up too tight. I've had nothing to fuck but my own fist for too long.

Ezra bolts into my closet, completely at ease tearing through a mercenary's apartment. He's surprisingly brave. Has he found all my guns yet? I almost want to laugh at the thought.

Maybe he *would* make for a good mercenary.

I give him space to rinse off, white-knuckling the kitchen counter when the little shit leaves the door to the bathroom wide open like an invitation.

He rushes out dressed in one of my dark t-shirts, another pair of my black joggers, and his combat boots. Wild, damp hair falls into his face.

Brain malfunctioning, I watch in horror as my hand reaches out to brush a lock behind his ear. His eyes nearly double in size, and his full lips part.

"Cain?" he asks hesitantly, tongue darting out to flick his lip ring.

I almost come unglued, desire slamming into me so strong, I have to rip myself away from him.

"Your hair's a mess," I mutter, striding for the door. "Hurry up. I don't have all day."

But for him, I think I fucking do.

CHAPTER TWELVE

EZRA

Cain's acting weird.

He retrieved me for lunch, pretending to be all huffy about it, when he made it clear this morning that he would be gone all day.

Which means he's *choosing* to spend time with me and trying to appear pissed off about it.

Cain guides me out the front doors. Bitter cold wind strikes me, shocking my body and reminding me this is where I belong. Out here on the streets, uncomfortable and driven by a constant need to survive. Not holed up in Sinro Enterprises, offered a fluffy bed and eating takeout with trained murderers.

Is Jakey doing alright? Can I trust that Rev is taking care of him?

"So, are all your employees... you know?" I ask, jogging to catch up to Cain's long stride.

"No. Some just wanted desk jobs, but all of them know what we do. Most were hand-selected. Given a second chance out of the military when they couldn't fit in with the real world."

I offer him a smile. "That's really fricken noble, Cain."

He whirls on me, shoving me up against the bricks of a store. People turn their attention on us but speed up their pace, not eager to jump in on a fight with him. Cain's over six feet tall and solid muscle.

"This is not an opportunity for you to pick your way further under my skin. You're lucky I'm allowing you out of that building. Your last breath should have been in that alley."

I slump in his grip, letting him hold some of my weight, a little bit turned on by his closeness. He smells like his body wash. *Eucalyptus.* I know because I used it. There's a dark shadow of stubble on his face today, which isn't helping dial down his sex appeal.

For once, I keep my sass bottled up. I don't want him to change his mind about our arrangement. Don't want him to view me as someone trying to destroy his business or his personal life.

But if he was doubting my intentions, why would he take me to lunch?

He releases me with a scowl and stalks off. I struggle to keep pace as he cuts into a mom and pop sandwich shop. The front is all glass windows, and there's a red and white awning that blocks out the sun, keeping the interior chilly.

"My man, Cain," the burly man behind the counter bellows. He has dark hair, a beard, and tattooed arms that clash with his red polo and white apron. Instantly, I'm put at ease by his personable smile. "Good to see you, Mr. Vincent. How's business in that ivory tower of yours?"

"Lenny," Cain greets with a nod. "Steady as usual. You doing good?"

Lenny waves a giant bread knife. "Never been better! How's the crew? All their parts and pieces still intact?"

Cain offers the first smile I've seen touch his eyes, and I'm captivated by it. Rendered speechless as my heart chugs heavy beats and my breath hitches.

He's beautiful all the time, but when he's not trying to hide his warmth under scowls and shadows, he's stunning. More brilliant than the sun.

I ache to have that smile directed at me.

"Doing good," Cain replies, resting a hand on the deli counter. "Rev's still a thorn in my side. Salem's a godsend. I can't get Henry to take a day off. And my brothers are the same. Isaac's booked up most days, and Alaric's content to lurk in the blue light of his tech dungeon. Wish he would socialize more."

"And you?" Lenny asks, cocking a bushy brow. "Find someone to dull that razor-edged nature of yours?"

I creep around Cain's side a bit more, not wanting to miss anything in his expression. "No time for that, Lenny."

Satisfaction fills me. Does that mean Cain's not seeing anyone? Shit. I didn't even think about that when I threw myself at him last night. Filled with shame, I drop my head.

Lenny chuckles. "One day you'll regret that. Don't come crying to me when you're lonely. But I won't keep pestering you about it. What'll you have today?"

"You know my order, Lenny. Make it a double."

Cain steps away from me, putting me in full view of the shop owner.

"Oh." Lenny's smile grows. "You recruiting young now? What's your name, kid?"

Again with the kid shit. Does Cain think I'm a child, too? Is that why he rejected me?

There are plenty of other reasons why he would turn you down.

"Ezra, sir," I say, figuring it's best to charm the large man waving around a knife. If he's friends with Cain, I don't doubt this guy knows how to use it.

"Well, Ezra. Consider yourself blessed. Cain has brought you to the greatest sandwich shop in East Bank! What can I get for you?" He carves into a loaf of fresh bread baked with savory herbs.

"Two orders of the same, Lenny," Cain cuts in with his firm, business voice.

Lenny points his serrated knife at Cain. "Oh, no, you don't. No bossing us around. What if Ezra doesn't care for pastrami? I'm not about to let him have a bad experience in my restaurant."

Cain frowns, and Lenny waves him off. "Always with that temper. Never frightened me."

"I'm honestly good with what he orders," I say, hoping to keep Cain from sinking into a foul mood before I have to sit at a table with him. Or maybe he'll walk us back to the apartment and ditch me for work.

It should worry me that I'm craving his attention. That's not okay, right? My little attempt at being upset last night after I tried to seduce him fizzled out too quickly. It's so pathetic.

Lenny nods me over to the counter, and I lean against it, overwhelmed by the selections on the menu.

"I can do a hot sandwich or a cold cut. What's your preference?"

"I don't really know." I look to Cain for advice, but he gives me nothing in his cold gaze.

"No worries, Ezra. I'll take care of you." Lenny gives me a wink, and I give him my best smile, heart thudding extra fast when I notice Cain watching me.

People like Lenny and Jakey are a rare breed. They need to be treasured.

After Cain pays, he leads us over to a red plastic booth. His mood has shifted darker, if that's even possible.

"I'm not trying to be difficult," I mumble, hoping that will suffice as an apology when he was the one who brought me here with him. I knead my hands together under the table.

Cain lets out an aggravated sigh, but his features soften. "No, it's not you. I actually have something important to discuss."

I perk up. "Okay. Shoot."

"I'd like you to train with Rev while you're under our... protection."

My brows raise. "Verses what? Killing me or releasing me into the wild so Gabriel can kill me?"

Cain's nostrils flare. "If that's how you want to see things, then yes. Consider it a trial run. You prove yourself, and there could be a potential job offer in the future with good pay and solid benefits."

"Benefits?"

He leans back in the booth, eyes narrowing at me. "Ezra, have you ever held a job before?"

I suck at my lip ring. "If I say no, are you going to change your mind about hiring me?"

I've never worked a day in my life, only stolen to survive. And before roaming the streets...

There is nothing. Nothing but fucking nightmares.

Fighting back the sickening emotions thrashing in my chest, I manage to hold his gaze.

Cain shakes his head. "No, I won't change my mind. Long as you're not a spy."

What if I suck at the job? What will Cain do with me, then? With insider information on Sinro, I feel like the end result has to be a bullet between my eyes.

I bounce a bit on my seat. Catching the impulsive movement, I channel that energy into picking at my painted nails under the table instead. Would it be weird to ask Cain for another bottle of it? I'd left my backpack at the shelter with Jakey. Chances of getting it back were slim. Which really fucking sucked because that meant I'd lost the scarf Jakey had made me.

"Do you think I can do it?" I ask quietly, shrinking under his intense brown eyes.

I don't know why I need his opinion. Unless he's not talking about hiring me as a killer.

Muscles in Cain's jaw work as he glances away, taking in the other patrons chatting. "Honestly, I'm not sure. But we can figure out what works for you. I'd just feel better knowing you'll be okay on your own."

Lenny interrupts by dropping a tray of sandwiches on the table between us. Cain's pastrami and swiss monstrosity, and mine—a grilled chicken, bacon, and swiss on the softest bread I've ever touched. My stomach rumbles in satisfaction, and I tear into my sandwich, forgetting all about Cain's offer.

"Good lord, is it possible to orgasm from a meal?" I moan into another bite.

Cain's eyes flick up to me, churning with something dark and seductive. My heart leaps in my chest. My dick gives a twitch, reminding me that I'm very much attracted to this man.

Lenny pats the edge of the table. "Glad you like it, Ezra. Next time, we'll hook you up with the meatball sub."

After we finish our meal in silence, Cain throws a twenty-dollar bill on the table and walks away. I scramble to follow him.

"Keep an eye on that one, Ezra," Lenny calls out with a wave as we reach the front door.

I wave back, grinning. "Will do! Nice to meet you."

Cold air rattles my bones outside the shop, and my arms snap over my chest. With all the chaos of the last few days, I didn't have time to stock up on thicker clothes for me and Jakey. Was he a popsicle right now? I like to imagine he's right where I left him, safe in that shelter, knitting away, now under the guard of mercenaries.

Stopped at a crosswalk, Cain looks down at me and matches my pained expression. He sheds his long peacoat to drape it over my shoulders.

"Put it on," he orders.

I blink up at him, confused by this entire fricken day.

"I swear, Ezra," he grumbles, reaching to shove my arms through the holes of his warm coat. "How did you survive on the streets?"

I wince. "I'm not helpless, okay? I did just fine for myself. Jakey and I know how to get by."

His eyes cut to mine, anger flashing in their depths. What crawled up his ass today?

"Who the fuck's this Jakey to you?" he demands.

I don't back down, keeping my chin high. "Told you, he's my friend."

He's quiet for a few strides before saying, "Rev had someone pick him up and take him to a senior living estate."

"What?" I stop in the middle of an intersection. The light changes and cars honk at me. Cain grabs me under the elbow to usher me across the street.

"He's safe there, so don't worry about him, okay? He's under constant care and our protection." When we make it to the other sidewalk, he lowers his face to mine, causing my pulse to quicken. "But I swear, Ezra, if I find out that you're double-crossing us—"

"I'm not! Jesus!" I fire back. "I may be many things, but I've never been a liar."

Cain holds my stare. Seemingly satisfied with what he finds, or doesn't find, he keeps his hand around my arm, tugging me along to a men's apparel shop.

A thin man with blonde hair greets him when we enter. "Mr. Vincent. Pleasure to see you again so soon."

I shouldn't be surprised that Cain has so many connections. He's a CEO running a successful business just down the street.

"What can I do for you?" the employee asks, hips swaying as he approaches Cain.

"I need a full wardrobe for my new intern."

My eyes dart to Cain. "But I didn't accept—"

"Hush, Ezra."

"Asshole," I mutter, to which I earn a low chuckle from him. Is that what he wants from me? My sass? If so, then I'll do my best to keep it flowing all day.

The store employee looks me over from head-to-toe with disgust. "I suppose I've worked magic on worse."

He saunters off, and flames burst to life in my chest. "I don't think I like him much."

Cain moves to drop onto a low velvet couch in the fitting room area. "You will after Drew's done dressing you."

"I'm guessing he's dressed you?" I mouth off.

Cain raises a brow at my sharp tone, and my fingers twitch with that churning, destructive energy. "He has."

I shove down my irritation as Drew returns. But after an hour of being around the man, between putting his hands on me and picking apart my every flaw, he has me so riled up I'm ready to burst.

Too slim around the waist. Bony hips. Strong jaw, but a little bit too crack whore chic in the face, don't you think?

That comment has me bristling. Hands balled into fists, I step up to Drew until chests are pressed together. Cain slips between us, facing me. His eyes sweep over me as his brows furrow.

"Just a minute please, Drew," Cain says, keeping me shielded from the view of the aggravating twig of a man. Drew scoffs and wanders off in search of more clothes.

"What's wrong?" Cain asks.

I'm still huffed up like a frightened cat. "I don't like the words he's saying."

Cain's eyes narrow. "They're just words, Ezra. You'll have to learn to shut down those emotions if you ever want to work for me."

My head snaps up to him, stupid hot tears filling my eyes. "Yeah? My mother was addicted to drugs. I. Don't. Like. His. Words." I stand up taller.

Most people think I'm hooked on something, too, bouncing from shelter-to-shelter. I assume the woman who birthed me is dead by now. Wouldn't know. I was too young to even memorize her face when she left me at the police station. Not sure who my father is, but I'd put money on him being an addict as well.

When Drew comes back carrying a new suit, Cain lifts a hand. "You're dismissed, Drew. Get someone else to help us."

Drew's face turns beet red. His gaze drifts between us, our bodies leaned in toward each other, attracted like magnets. Cain never stops looking at me. His eyes are surprisingly warm, more burgundy than brown under my examination today.

Slamming the suit hanger on the rack, Drew vanishes. He's replaced by Eduardo, who is kind, but I still instinctively pull away from him when he fixes my collar and measures my inseam.

Cain pretends to read emails on his phone, though I catch him scrolling mindlessly, too fast to process anything. I feel his gaze on me every time I step out of the dressing room in a new outfit. He checks my expression first before letting his eyes drift down my body.

It feels... intimate. Which is wild because two days ago he wanted to kill me. He still probably wants to kill me.

We end up with four bags of clothes. I'd expected to walk out with suits, but Eduardo had a different plan for me, and Cain hadn't protested anything he dressed me in—chunky sweaters, long cardigans, oversized stylish shirts matched with fitted jeans and ripped pants that hugged my ass and thighs. Eduardo gave me a wink and said he'd have someone drop my things off for me.

I'm bundled up in my new fleece coat when we exit the shop. It makes me a bit sad that I don't get to wear Cain's coat anymore.

Soon as we make it back to Cain's apartment, he wraps a hand around my wrist and pulls me tight against him. We're pressed together everywhere it counts. My breath catches as I tip my head up to look at him.

"Ezra." His tone is soft but commanding. "Why do you react like that?"

Blinking up at him, I do my best not to let my eyes fall to his tempting mouth. "What?"

"You don't seem bothered when I... handle you, but when other people touch you..."

Shit. I shake my head under his scrutinizing gaze. "I don't react in any sort of way."

"Did someone hurt you? Is that why you're homeless?"

Heart sputtering in my chest, I back away from him. "If you're planning on psychoanalyzing me, I'd rather take my chances on the streets with Gabriel."

Cain doesn't seem keen on letting the matter go. I don't understand why. Why would he care?

He releases a heavy breath and drags a hand through his hair. "You're right. I'm just... never mind. I'm sorry."

My jaw drops. "Did you just apologize?"

Ignoring my question, Cain hangs up his coat. "Rev will have your bags brought up. I set a security badge on the counter for you. It accesses only the necessary floors, so don't think you've got free rein of the building."

Cain's out the door without another word, phone already pressed to his ear.

I push out a sigh as my body sags. How long will I be left alone this time? It scares me, especially when I'm already feeling emotionally battered after the day with him. Were my demons that easy to see? Or was Cain looking for a reason to confirm that I am damaged goods?

CHAPTER THIRTEEN

EZRA

R ev surprises me by hanging out long enough to walk me through weight machines in the gym. He shares a photo of Jakey that brings hot tears to my eyes. My old man's sitting in a recliner at the senior estate they put him up in, drowning in multi-colored yarn.

"Quirky friend you got there, Ezra," Rev says, cracking a grin. "Wouldn't expect anything less from you."

Too soon, our session ends though, and Rev walks me back to Cain's apartment to suffer in boredom. The silence picks at me like a vulture on roadkill. I've become attuned to the constant noise of the streets. The snores and squeaks of bed frames in shelters. Jakey's humming or elaborate storytelling.

Spinning my lip ring, I check the clock. Just after 5PM.

I know Cain's not on a set schedule. He's the CEO of a very demanding company. One mess up could tank his reputation. He has clients to answer to and special teams to lead, and the last thing he probably wants to do is come back to me lurking in his home—the street kid who tried to kiss him and he now feels obligated to protect.

But what the fuck am I supposed to do?

My head fills with too many anxious thoughts, like why Cain would take an interest in how I react to physical touch. Why is it that I desire him when I've never wanted anyone intimately before? What would happen if he put his hands on me? Would I freak out or give in to pleasure?

I tug at the ends of my hair. How the fuck do I shut my brain off?

After a long shower, I slip on a pair of his boxers and the softest heather gray t-shirt I can find in his closet. I move from the couch to the kitchen stool to his bed. I roll around in his perfectly made sheets, frustrated with my body when I get hard from the lingering smell of Cain there.

In an attempt to distract myself from this consuming need, I rearrange Cain's bathroom drawers. Mostly, I do it out of spite. I move his toothpaste into the toiletry closet and his toothbrush into the shower. Then I stack the toilet paper on the bottom shelf where I know he'll have to bend his tall frame to reach it.

Touching his things only makes me think about him more. His looming, dark presence and inked arms, and intense eyes that seem to shift colors with the emotions he strives to bottle up.

I groan, palming my stiff cock.

When it hits 10PM, I start to worry that Cain's either avoiding me or he's in some sort of trouble. What if Gabriel got to him?

Great. Now my brain's in panic mode. I don't even put shoes on as I head for the elevator. The thirteenth floor is empty when the doors slide open, and I practically sprint into Cain's office.

His tired expression flips to irritation immediately, and it makes my chest ache.

"Ezra," he says darkly. I don't miss the way his eyes flick to my crotch before finding their way back to my face. Thankfully, my dick went soft in the middle of panicking.

A muscle in his jaw twitches. "Why aren't you wearing any pants?"

"Forgot," I murmur.

"You... forgot pants."

I don't shy away from his glare, though my heart is beating too fast. "Happens to the best of us."

When he doesn't speak, I can't help but add, "I got worried about you."

I mean, it's either poke the bear until he plays or find some other way to bleed out this pent-up energy. And I've already been to the gym twice today.

He watches my fingers tap on my thigh for a few strained minutes. "There's no need for that. I often work late hours."

I shift my weight back and forth, expecting him to dismiss me. At this point, he's going to have to put his hands on me to get me to leave. I don't want to go back to his apartment alone. He can fuck me up if he wants. Yell at me. Toss me out. I really don't care.

Other than Jakey, Cain's the first person whose touch hasn't made my insides shrivel up, and I have to wonder why that is. I want to test this out. Push both of our limits. Because Cain has limits, too. Internal defenses that want to keep me away.

Cain leans back in his chair, his focus solely on me now. "What do you need, Ezra?"

God, those words trigger my heart into a chaotic rhythm. Hot blood shoots through my veins, directed straight to my cock. What *do* I need?

I brace against the doorframe, my breaths falling short. I shake my head. "I don't know. I'm all riled up with no good way to chill the fuck out."

He hooks a finger in his tie to loosen it. The little action, though not meant to be sexual, has my body taking notice. Vexed Cain, with his dark hair and dark eyes, dressed to kill in his black suit, is a vision of beauty.

Fantasies run rampant in my head. I imagine him stalking over here to pin me against the wall. Maybe he would scoop me up into his arms. Press his solid body against me. Ease my boxers down and sink his hard cock—

"Ezra." Cain growls.

I become starkly aware of my erection, but I don't cover it up. No point when it's already pushing against the fabric of his clothes I borrowed.

"I can't help it," I whine. "I'm lonely and all horned up. And if I keep touching shit in your apartment, I guarantee I'm gonna break something."

A spark of amusement cuts through his frigid mask. "Horned up?"

I nod innocently, aching to grip my cock and stroke it. Give him a show. See if I can tempt him into action. I *know* he looks at me. It's why I didn't back down from kissing him the other night.

I've never been this way with anyone, but Cain doesn't frighten me. Something in my fucked up brain likes his aggression. I like that he doesn't hide his rough edges.

Is it my personality that turns him off? I know I'm a lot. A collection of jagged, mismatched parts and pieces.

Scrounging up my confidence and the flagging need for him to hurt me, I move around his desk. He watches my every move, his tongue slipping out to swipe over his bottom lip.

"Ezra," he warns, but his tone has dipped into something low and rumbly and sensual. His dark gaze caresses me, urging me to climb onto his lap. I slide my hands around his neck as my pulse throbs beneath my skin.

I know I'm playing a dangerous game, but I fucking get off on it. Is that what this is? Another way to satisfy my addiction to adrenaline?

To my frustration, Cain doesn't touch me back. Doesn't move me. Just stares into me with those soulful eyes, burrowing deep in search of my truths.

"Please don't turn me away again," I beg, sucking at my lip ring. My courage wavers, despite my knees sliding deeper into the chair. My dick grows painfully hard.

Just when I think it's clear that he's not into this, Cain rests his palms on my thighs. He grips them tightly. His voice is a rumbled whisper. "Is this how I need to touch you?"

Breathless, I nod, and we both watch his hands as they graze up my thighs to wrap around my hips.

"This should not be happening," Cain murmurs, but he makes no move to release me.

Braving rejection, I lean forward to rest my forehead against his collarbone. "Can't help it. You're just so... ugh."

He chuckles. "Ugh?"

"Yeah. Ugh. Sexy. Commanding. Vicious. Can you be rough with me? Please," I plead. "Either that, or I'll have to take a blunt object to your mirrors."

"What the fuck." But Cain lets out another low laugh. "Are you threatening vandalism to get me to hurt you?"

I swallow, fighting that chaotic energy heaving inside of me. This was a piss poor idea, but I couldn't stand to be left to my own devices for another second.

My fingers curl into the fabric of his dress shirt. "I just need…"

He shifts my body, tilting my hips to press my cock against his own hard length beneath his slacks.

"Oh, God." I jerk upright to take in his expression. Lust-filled, warm eyes stare back at me as his hands clench me tight enough to bruise.

"Need what, beautiful boy?"

My eyelids flutter. "Need you."

One of his hands runs up my spine, wrapping around the back of my neck and tugging me until our mouths collide.

I groan against his lips. This has to be a dream. How else could this be happening right now?

Cain's hand slides around to the front of my neck, squeezing hard enough to force me out of my head. My body melts into him. Dissolves beneath his rough touch as his other hand slips beneath the waistband of my boxers to grip my bare ass.

"Fuck. Ezra," he murmurs against my lips.

His tongue claims my mouth, stroking my own in a slow, mind-numbing rhythm. He licks and sucks at me as I grind on his lap, chasing pleasure I never thought I would find in this lifetime.

When my movements become frantic, he deepens our kiss, seemingly ravenous for the little whimpers I can't help but release.

Cain drags his mouth down to my neck. His teeth sink into my throat, painful enough to leave marks. The loud moan that comes out of my mouth could definitely be heard outside his office.

But Cain doesn't stop. His hand tilts my jaw, giving him better access to drag his hot tongue over my Adam's apple. His grip is punishing, and our slotted cocks provide enough friction to build pressure at the base of my spine.

"Fuck, that's so good," I mumble.

With the hand around my throat, Cain tips my upper body back enough to bite my nipple through my shirt. I spill hot cum unexpectedly, hips jerking for several frantic heartbeats afterward.

When the pulsing of my orgasm stops, I crack my eyes open. Desire burns in Cain's brown and gold-flecked eyes. I take that as a sign to return the favor, skimming my hands down his solid chest and abs to unhook his belt.

Cain lifts me off his lap. Breathing heavily, he holds me by the hips until I find my balance.

"I want to," I say, pouting.

Cain shakes his head and replies, "No more of this, Ezra. We can't do this. No more seduction games, understood?"

Oh. Well, now I feel even more like shit, despite the fact that I just got off.

I frown. "So... pants are essential?"

"*Yes*. I bought you clothes, Ezra. The least you could do is wear them. Now please go back to the apartment. I'll be there shortly."

I can't believe he's kicking me out. He can't lie and say he's not into this. I felt the evidence. Does he not want me to touch him? Does he not think I'll be good? I can be good for him.

Shame washes through me over my desperate behavior. I turn and march from his office, but not before dropping a "fuck you" at his door.

Maybe I'll break something after all. Set fire to his bedroom. Run out the front door and scream at Gabriel to come pick me up. Blast holes into me and hang me on his wall of guns like a trophy.

I rinse off under a stream of hot water, replaying what happened. Shit, I came just from grinding on Cain's lap. No wonder he put a stop to this. I couldn't even fucking last.

Heat rushes up my neck and cheeks, and I get a bit light-headed with the steam curling around me. Slamming off the shower, I dress in comfortable layers and hide under the throw blanket on the spare bedroom floor, worried I'll fall into too deep of a sleep and never resurface if I curl up in the soft bed.

Cain kissed me back. I didn't make that shit up. He can't deny it. So why did he turn me away? Why doesn't he want me?

The lock clicks on the apartment door. I hold my breath as his footsteps thud across the floor. Listen to the thunk of his briefcase, the suction of the fridge door opening, and the crack of a water bottle lid.

I squeeze my eyes shut when his bedroom door closes, leaving me to my misery.

CHAPTER FOURTEEN

EZRA

Rev promised to meet me at the gym daily on his lunch breaks. The repetition is giving me purpose, something I desperately need. He told me when I show enough discipline, he'll take me to the lower level gun range.

I can't lie and say the idea of shooting a gun doesn't make me nervous. I've never held one before. Been shot at plenty of times. Had I lived a different life, I might not have believed myself cut out for any of this.

But that's not my reality. I can visualize all too well who I would hold a gun against. I know I could kill that man a thousand times over, which makes me believe I'm right where I'm meant to be.

"How's it going being locked up with the CEO?" Rev asks, sprawling across one of the weight benches. He props his chin on one hand, lazily playing with a dumbbell in the other. He's not built like Cain, but no amount of weight seems to phase him. I couldn't even lift the bar he'd set up earlier for his final round of bench presses.

I drop onto the squishy black and gray speckled floor, water bottle dangling from my hand. The smell of plastic and old sweat hits my nose, making it scrunch up.

Rev smirks. "That good, huh?"

I unleash a groan from my soul. "I got antsy and kissed him. And, to make things worse, I did something naughty in his office. I have no self-control."

"Wow, you don't make me work for answers, do you?"

I frown. "I don't think he liked any of it."

"Nah." Rev flashes a sinister grin. "He liked it."

I shake my head, rolling down to lie flat like a starfish on the floor. "Sometimes I get that feeling. Mostly, he's just indifferent and cold with me."

Rev shrugs. "He's a bit fucked up, but aren't we all?"

"I... suppose so."

"Let me clue you in on a little secret. There are spare apartments in the building he could have put you up in. Instead, he chose to keep you close."

"Because he doesn't trust me."

"Cain doesn't trust anyone. But that's not the reason he's hiding you away."

My brows furrow. "I don't understand."

Rev flashes perfect white teeth. "He's staking claim on you, pretty boy. Can't stand the thought of someone like me swooping in to ruin your life."

"Oh." I spin my lip ring, replaying my interactions with both Cain and Rev to try to find my way to the same conclusion.

Rev tips his head in curiosity. "So, is it just guys for you, too, Ezra baby?"

I swallow and stare up at the ceiling. I guess I've never really paid attention to gender. Never invested thought into relationships, either.

But I *want* Cain. And I definitely didn't dream about coming on his lap last night. The embarrassment and regret from that are too real.

I slip a hand in my hair and pull at it. "I don't really know. I don't have much experience. Not like that."

Every encounter I've had with someone physically has been against my wishes, except with Cain. Which makes me question how I could be so fucking needy for him. So turned on by the idea of him doing more to me. So trusting of him when I barely know him. It's like some primal part of me has assessed him and refuses to categorize him as a threat. I feel safe with him, and that makes me very, very stupid.

"I can prove to you that he's interested," Rev says, hanging over the weight bench far enough to block my view of the ceiling.

I blink up at him. "Um..."

"Come on, get up." He pulls out his phone as I struggle to roll onto my feet, muscles screaming in protest. He moves close enough to snap a picture of both of us. "We can do better than that. Look like you're having the time of your life."

Catching on to Rev's games, I lean into him for the next picture and stick out my tongue. Cain probably won't give a shit, but it's still fun to pretend like our little game will drive him into a jealous rage.

Another hour into our workout and photo session, which has turned quite dirty, I'm convinced Rev is a villain. Together, with my chaos and his lack of remorse, the two of us borderline on a national threat.

I'm not sure how many half-naked, sweaty pictures of me he's sent to Cain, but I'm too high on the thrill of it to care. Worst-case scenario, Cain will punish me, which doesn't have the effect he thinks it does on me. Best case, he'll change his mind about wanting to fool around with me.

"Another set of burpees, pretty boy," Rev hollers, squatting down to slap my stomach. It makes a hollow sound, and he lifts a brow. "Need to get you eating more protein."

By the time Rev's done with me, I'm worn the fuck out. Everything in my body feels shaky and weak. I wrap the damp towel he hands me around my neck and ask the question that's been nagging me since my lunch with Cain the other day. "Has he... been with anyone?"

"Cain? He had a long-term partner. Guy named Aiden swept him off his feet. Moved in with him. Cain even bought him a ring."

My stomach twists as I recall the ring I'd snatched from his dresser. Was it Cain's or Aiden's? And if he'd kept Aiden's ring, what did that mean? That Cain wasn't over his past relationship?

"Day after they got engaged, they ran into one of Aiden's old coworkers. Apparently, Aiden worked for the government, not in catering like he'd told Cain."

"Oh shit," I mumble.

"Yeah. That whole house of cards bullshit. One lie unraveled a bunch of other lies. Aiden confessed to infiltrating Sinro to keep tabs on Cain. He was instructed to make sure we were operating in a gray area. Never dipping into dark dealings. The government was right to fear us. Sinro is teaming with ex-soldiers."

I frown. "Why would Aiden trick Cain that way? Why not come on as an employee at Sinro or something instead of playing with his emotions?"

Rev scratches his chin. "Aiden claimed he fell in love with Cain. He was fighting to keep Cain from breaking things off on the walk home from the coworker incident when he was shot."

"Holy shit." I rub a hand over the sudden pain in my chest. I mean, I'd seen people die out on the streets, but never anyone I'd really cared about.

If that had been Jakey, I don't think I'd ever be the same again. I've put all the love that should have been shared with a family into that old man. And while he often confuses me with his son, I know in my heart that he loves me for who I am.

"Don't let it deter you," Rev says, rising up from the bench. "That happened twelve years ago. But if you tell Cain I told you about it, he'll make both of us suffer."

"Got it." I pretend to lock my mouth, knowing I'm probably going to blurt it out the first time I see Cain. "Actually, I'm really bad with secrets."

Rev laughs. He gives my hair a playful ruffle, and surprisingly, I find that I don't mind his touch, either. "You're so innocent. Why can't I find a guy like you?"

My cheeks heat, my stomach dipping at the thought of someone like Rev being interested in me. I feel like he would devour me alive.

Rev checks the clock on the wall. "Any minute now, Cain's going to barge in here in a rage over our spicy pics. You best run and hide. The bloodshed might scar you."

A smile creeps on my face as my gaze drifts to the boxing ring in the corner. "Or we could mess around in the ring."

Rev chuckles. "Now you're speaking my language."

CHAPTER FIFTEEN

CAIN

Letting Ezra grind himself to orgasm in my office was wrong.

So why can't I get it to stop replaying in my head? I don't have time for a relationship. Don't like the idea of the messy emotions that come with it.

But I *do* want to fuck Ezra.

The moment the elevator doors dinged closed last night, and I found myself alone in the office, I took out my aching cock and jacked off, coming in record time and hard enough to nearly black out on my desk.

I'd jacked off again in the shower when I got back to my apartment, too wrapped up in the thoughts of all the depraved things I wanted to do with Ezra to go straight to bed.

Ezra likes it rough. Needs it that way. And I enjoy dominating my partner. We'd be an electric match in bed. Doesn't mean we should end up there.

Sitting behind my desk the next morning, my focus is still absolute shit. The ticking of my watch has me biting through the skin on the inside of my cheek, a habit I haven't given into in years.

Aiden used to scold me for doing it in public, especially when he would drag me out to ridiculously expensive restaurants to "show me off". The clinking of silverware and the banging of doors was enough to set me on edge, tricking my brain into thinking we were surrounded by threats.

I was fresh out of the military. I hadn't been prepared for the fair-haired, fit guy across the bar to make a move. But Aiden had been incredibly charming and talkative. He made me feel alive, when most of the time, I felt empty. And when I wasn't empty, I was angry.

Gripping my pen tighter, I tap the end on my desk. Work needs to get done. We need to track down Gabriel. Figure out what he's selling in those shipping containers and what he's hiding on that drive that's taking Alaric far too long to crack.

I've dealt with crime lords before. However, this all feels above Gabriel's level. Thugs like him don't hide things well. They get off on spreading fear, working in such large numbers the police prefer to avoid involvement. Hell, he wasn't even on our radar until recently.

My phone buzzes on my desk. I ignore it to finish up an email to a new client, but whoever is texting me is persistent. I pick it up and swipe through my lock screen, nearly slamming my phone down on my desk when I scroll through the pictures Rev's been sending me.

The first one is of him and Ezra together. Rev's holding up his hands in a peace sign, and Ezra's got his tongue sticking out. I stare at Ezra longer than I should, thrown off by how truly gorgeous he is.

The second picture... did they fucking cut up one of my t-shirts? I bought Ezra a whole new wardrobe. Why does he continue to wear my stuff?

Although, I can't really complain about glimpsing more of Ezra's flawless, tan skin. Half the length of the shirt is missing, showing off his toned abs in mid-crunch on the gym floor. He's in fucking boxers, too.

He doesn't fucking listen.

Gonna work this pretty boy into a sweat, Rev's text reads.

Immediately, I swipe into my contacts to call Rev and bitch him out, but that would just play further into whatever game Rev thinks he's winning.

I set my phone down and dig into studying financials. But that bubble of irritation keeps interfering with my ability to process anything I'm looking at on my computer screen.

My phone continues to rumble. I glare at it as if that will make it stop. Should I appoint someone else to train Ezra? All Rev seems to be doing is snapping indecent photos of him. I could use Rev out in the field. Sometimes I feel like I rely on him too much, though.

I make a mental note to pick up athletic clothes for Ezra. If I keep buying them, maybe he'll cover up for once.

Maybe he needs to be punished.

I pinch the bridge of my nose, willing away the scenes playing out in my head. Ezra on his hands and knees, naked in my bed. My fingers hooked in his pretty mouth, pressing down on his tongue as my hand strokes his hard cock. He'd moan and whine like he did the other night when he came on my lap.

Another buzz from my phone. I snap my best pen in half, ink leaking over my hand and onto my desk, staining the polished wood.

I can't help but peek at the goddamn pictures. Ezra, shirtless, doing pull-ups. The angle does nothing to hide the outline of his dick in his boxers or the surprising cut of his arms. He's lean in the waist, but he's definitely in shape. I suppose his lifestyle requires it.

The next picture is on a glute machine. Ezra's laid out, round ass on full display. I clench my teeth together as my hard cock fights against the confines of my slacks. I had my hands around that soft flesh.

Fuck. I want to sink my teeth into him.

My fingers fly over my phone keyboard. *Quit it, perv.*

I can hear Rev's laughter echoing in my head. *He's a natural athlete. Pretty boy can throw a punch, too.*

At least Ezra's got something going for him beyond stealth and his wits. Has he had to fight someone before? Worry sluices through me. After discovering his aversion to physical touch, I want to dissect his brain.

My phone buzzes again. *Oh, and don't worry. He's twenty-three. Not underage.*

Don't care.

Not going to admit to Rev that I actually *do* care. It wasn't far off from what I'd assumed, but I had hoped I hadn't let a minor grind himself against my cock last night. That thought had haunted me all night. Which is another reason I'm in a rare fucking mood today.

Age shouldn't matter, but at thirty-six, I've moved through so many different phases of my life compared to Ezra.

Though, that thought isn't enough to shut down my desire to claim him.

Another text from Rev. *If you won't play with him, I will.*

My blood pressure skyrockets as my fingers type away. *Touch him and I'll string you up by your toes for a week.*

Don't threaten me with a good time.

By 4PM, I'm white-knuckling my briefcase and my phone, rushing out of my office without looking back. Curious eyes blink at me from cubicles. Gwen seems to be the most concerned by my early departure.

"Headed out for the day," I grumble. "Forward important calls to my phone—"

"Sir? I just got an important call."

I pivot, catching Gwen's down-turned expression. The only time she speaks in that tone is when something's gone terribly wrong.

I stride over to her desk. "What's going on? Who is it?"

Mentally, I sift through employee names and their assigned operations. Thank God Rev was distracted with the little thief today and not out in the field like the last couple of days. And my brothers hardly ever leave the building. I rarely have to be concerned about their safety.

But Henry's almost always out. Same with Salem—my victims expert. Rorik, too.

"Maybe it should wait until tomorrow," she says, picking up her stress rock painted like a smiley face.

"Tell me the name."

"It's Lenny. He's... he was murdered, Cain," she says, failing to hold back the quiver in her voice.

Her words trickle through my brain, ice cold. "What. That has to be a mistake. Ezra and I just had lunch at his place."

She shakes her head, eyes filling with tears.

Gwen and Lenny were two of my first hires. Lenny had just retired four years ago to open his shop. Every week since, I'd made sure to check in on him and drop a tip on his table. Lenny was happy running his business. Happier than when he was working for me.

I understood. This job isn't for everyone. The ones that hang around are often veterans that are denied jobs elsewhere because of their military experience. They're judged and labeled a liability.

Guilt crushes my lungs. The emotion is quickly replaced with uncontrollable, roiling fury. Lenny would have lived to an old age if not for his ties to my company.

"What information do we have?" I ask through clenched teeth.

"Clean shot to his temple. Cameras caught one of the masked guys. No serial number on the gun or identifiable features."

"God dammit." I fight the urge to smash my fist through a wall or rip her entire desk from the floor. All the guns we'd confiscated from Gabriel's dock operation were ghost guns, missing serial numbers.

This crime lord was turning out to be a real pain in my ass.

Gwen sniffles. "I'm so sorry. I'll contact Salem and have her reach out to Lenny's wife."

My stomach heaves as memories of Aiden hit me like a suckerpunch. Meeting his family for the first time at his funeral and having to explain my connection to their son because he'd never even told them about me. How much it fucking rained the day they lowered his body into the earth. The emptiness of my apartment. And the simmering anger at being left with his unraveling secrets.

Thinking about Lenny's wife having to go through that horrible pain makes my vision swim and pulse race from a burst of potent adrenaline.

Why would Gabriel's men target Lenny? It was possible they were keeping tabs on Ezra, but why shoot the guy behind a deli counter? Were they trying to send a threatening message, or was this an Aiden situation all over again and I'd fallen into trust with Ezra too quickly? Wouldn't be the first time a beautiful face and the whole innocent act fooled me.

I'm so stupid for believing anything Ezra told me. Everything he made me feel.

I'm not fucking doing this again.

Storming from Gwen's desk, I take the stairs to my apartment floor. Muffled voices and grunts echo from the gym, which only further riles me up.

I walk in on Rev and Ezra tangled up on the boxing ring floor. I realize they're just wrestling, but all control over my temper snaps.

"You're fucking done," I shout, jabbing a finger at them.

Rev immediately picks up my unhinged fury. He releases Ezra from a chokehold and helps him to his feet.

"Hey, don't be too hard on Ezra. I'm the bad influence."

Ignoring Rev, I stalk over to Ezra and grab him by the arm, hauling him toward the door. "We're going to have a serious fucking talk, little thief."

CHAPTER SIXTEEN

EZRA

Cain slams my head onto his desk after dragging me down the three flights of stairs to the office. Pain flares through me, but not enough to make me scared for my life.

Cain won't hurt me.

"You've been working for Gabriel this whole time, haven't you?" Cain roars. "You preying on us? Passing information back to your murderous fucking friends?"

He's putting so much pressure on my skull that I'm starting to believe it might crack.

"What! Where is this coming from?" I grit out, struggling against his hold. My muscles are complete goo after my extended time in the gym. "What are you talking about?"

"Lenny!" Cain shouts in my ear. "How come he ended up with a fucking hole in his head? Who's next, Ezra? Rev? Gwen? Fucking Seth, the mail guy?"

Lenny's... dead? No, that can't be right. I just met him hours ago. He served me up one of the best sandwiches of my life. Treated me like a friend.

Panic creeps along the edges of my mind. Cain believes it was Gabriel's guys. They must be stalking me. Waiting for me to fuck up. Hurting anyone I come into contact with.

It's definitely a threat, and that makes me worry for Jakey more than ever. Rev said he would take care of him. Will that change now that Cain seems to think I'm a traitor?

"Gabriel must have eyes on me," I say, fingernails digging into the surface of Cain's desk as anger and fear tangle in my stomach. "Jakey. I need to make sure Jakey's alright."

"Your little homeless friend?" Cain chides.

To my embarrassment, hot tears spring to my eyes. "Please," I beg, thrashing under Cain's punishing hold, terrified by the idea that someone else was killed just because they were seen with me.

Without Jakey, I have no reason to exist. No support. No backbone.

Cain scoffs. "Is that all a fucking lie, too? A way to win sympathy? I bet he's just some fucking rando you had us pick up from the shelter."

"Fuck you, Cain!" I yell. "I don't give a shit if you kill me slowly or do it fast! Just... just let me make sure he's okay first. None of this is his fault."

Cain's grip on my head loosens. His rough hands snatch me off the desk and shove me into his chair. An inferno burns deep in his brown eyes when he stares down at me. Hellfire on a level I've never seen before. Lenny's death has him fucking rattled.

My own temper bubbles in my veins, and I can't help but taunt him. "Thanks, but I don't want your job."

"Quit with the smart-ass remarks, Ezra," Cain spits out. "I'm not in the mood."

We stay locked in a glare for what might be an eternity until Cain's chest stops heaving with breaths.

"I want to crack that head of yours open and see what's inside," he admits. "I *want* to trust you, Ezra."

His words dissolve my own anger, leaving me feeling paper thin.

"I'm not lying to you." I swipe at the stupid tear that rolls down my cheek. "I'm really sorry about your friend. Really fucking sorry."

His jaw remains clenched, but I catch his throat bob. "You think crying is going to make things better?"

I shake my head. "It never makes things better."

No, my tears never stopped anything.

Cain kicks the armrest on the chair, spinning me until I'm facing his computer. He clicks open an unmarked folder on his desktop. He points a finger at his screen as horrifying images reveal themselves, better suited for nightmares. "You want to run around with crime lords? This is what you're in for. This is what they do in the shadows. Why we work tirelessly to purge them from the world."

Most of them are photos of crime scenes. Bodies missing pieces, some almost unrecognizable as human, laid out in public places and dark rooms in homes.

They grow increasingly more disturbing.

There are pictures of hostages, heads covered in burlap sacks, skin burned and cut, hands bound. And then children. Dirty. Shackled. Too skinny. Crammed in bedrooms and closets and... basements.

Oh, god. My heart stutters, convincing my brain it's going to give out.

"What's on the hard drive, Cain?" I ask in a shaky tone, already feeling disconnected from my body. It's like my soul has been punched out of my body, but it doesn't seem to know what to do or where to go.

"We don't know. But we're going to find out."

If Gabriel's involved in selling more than weapons and drugs...

My stomach tightens like someone's wringing me out. I drop my head into my hands, tugging my hair at its roots to keep me present. The past slams into me, anyway. The stench of sweat. The cold press of iron against my bony ankles. The pain of cracked calluses on my bare feet. The itch of my skin in filthy clothing, hanging off my too-thin frame.

No. No. No.

Suddenly, I can't get rid of *his* touch. The stroke of light, cool fingers all over my body. Whispered instructions in my ears.

I shove back from the desk, knocking the chair to the floor with a loud thud. My head is dizzy from the onslaught of unwanted emotions rushing through me, and my lungs ache for air.

Cain's brows furrow as if I shouldn't have been surprised by what he was showing me.

Because he assumed I was betraying him, just like Aiden.

It's too late to worry about what Cain thinks. Panic's charging for me like a fucking freight train, about to hit so hard I know I'm going to be down for a while.

Senses overloaded, I drag my nails up and down my sweatpants, wishing I had something rough to break them on.

Fuck. Fuck. Fuck.

Screams claw their way up my throat, and before they can escape, I throw myself over the top of Cain's desk and bolt for the stairwell.

Footsteps thud behind me, and true fear slithers down my spine. Will Cain put a bullet in me this time? Throw me out onto the streets? Present me to Gabriel in pieces like I'd seen on his computer screen?

"Ezra!" Cain calls out before the heavy stairwell door slams shut behind me. I leap down the center, dropping several floors before my hands catch on the railing and lurch my arms so hard, I think I might have dislocated one of them this time.

The pain only helps focus me, and I'm able to climb back over the railing and escape through the door to the ninth floor. I search for a place to hide. I can't let Cain see me like this. I just fucking can't.

Most of the ninth floor is locked up, but I find a closet with janitor supplies to hide in. Slumping down on my butt in the cramped space, I fight against the overwhelming pressure in my chest telling me I can't breathe. That there will never be enough air to refill my lungs.

God, I'm going to fucking die.

I'm dying.

I shouldn't be scared, but I am. I'm so fucking scared.

I close my eyes, but all I see is *him*. Soulless eyes behind black-framed glasses. The smell of cat piss seeped into the concrete where he ripped up the carpet. A boxy, windowless basement that became my cell. My dirty, shaking hands and bloody fingernails.

Am I screaming or is that only in my head? I suppose if I were making noise, Cain would find me.

I start to rock against the shelves, finding solace in the rhythm of my back bumping against cleaning supplies and buckets, and the pain in my throbbing shoulder.

I'm not sure how much time passes. Sometimes these attacks feel like they go on for days when they're only minutes long.

And when the rocking isn't enough because my mind is too filled with horrible memories, collected from fucking years of abuse, I pluck a safety pin out of my ear and spear it through my forearm next to hundreds of pale scars. Thread it countless times through my skin until I'm only focused on the hot pain and the beading of blood and nothing else.

My pulse settles.

The pounding in my ears fades.

I fill my lungs with air.

Then I stumble out of the closet, mind numb and body drained. I climb into the elevator, bracing against the wall. When the doors part to the seventeenth floor, I move into the common living area. I collapse onto the rug in front of the large sectional. Dragging a throw blanket over my body, I close my eyes and pray for sleep to claim me.

I don't bother cleaning up my bloody wounds. Don't even bother planning an escape from Sinro Enterprises.

What does it matter?

Why does any of it matter?

CHAPTER SEVENTEEN

CAIN

Am I no better than the monsters I hunt?

Often I fall down that wormhole of toxic thinking, and tonight is no different. Blinded by rage and determined to make Ezra my enemy, I hadn't thought twice about showing him the horrors we confront.

He wants to play thief to criminals? Then he should understand the full consequences of his actions. He wants to work for me? Then he can't be so fucking weak.

I drag a hand down the side of my face, overcome with regret. I let things get out of hand. Fuck. I'm not even immune to those pictures after all these years.

Knowing evil like that exists in this world is why I work overtime. It's why I joined the Special Forces, letting them scrape out my insides and rebuild me. It's why I sacrifice my sleep and personal life now.

But Ezra's reaction? No one could fake that fear. I may not have Rev's intuition for what lies beneath the surface or Isaac's intellect on human conditions. However, I've seen that terror reflected back at me too many times from the eyes of victims I've rescued.

The impact of this newly gleaned, jagged piece of Ezra hits me hard enough to throw me off balance. All of my doubts about his innocence in Lenny's death go right out the window.

Were we wrong in thinking he could handle a job as a contracted killer? Was he abused? Or is he just sensitive by nature?

The idea of me tainting that gentleness... well, I don't fucking like that shredded feeling in my chest at all.

I need to find Ezra. Need to make this right. I need to erase those images from his brain.

What the fuck is wrong with me?

Bolting from my office, I sprint for the stairwell and scour the main lobby. I search the lower levels, harassing Alaric until he checks the security feed. We catch Ezra slipping off the elevator on the ninth floor over an hour ago, but when I race up the stairs, I find nothing amiss except for an opened closet door.

Was he trying to hide?

Charging up more flights of stairs to the seventeenth floor, I bang a fist on Rev's door. I'm not sure how closely those two bonded today, but my gut churns at the thought. If they do end up together, I don't have any right to be upset.

Rev opens the door wrapped in a towel. Water droplets fall from his shag of wet, silvery hair onto his bare chest. His skin is covered in white ink tattoos. They're so faint, I've never actually deciphered all the shapes.

"I have a phone, you know," he says, icy eyes staring back at me. "Why do you look like that?"

"Is Ezra with you?" I demand.

Rev swings his door wide, giving me a full view of his empty kitchen and living room. It's a mirror image of my apartment. "As much as I wish for that, no. I *do* respect your property."

I hold back the urge to snap at Rev about Ezra being property. This is just how Rev's brain operates sometimes.

He mutters insults before shutting his door as I charge down the hall toward the common areas.

Panic wraps cold fingers around my throat. Did Ezra succeed at escaping? Lenny was shot less than a mile from our building. Gabriel would snatch Ezra up in minutes.

I check the gym and balcony area. Both are empty. When I stride past the living area, I glimpse a blanketed lump on the floor. My heart sinks. *Ezra.*

I watch the blanket rise and fall with his steady breaths, no other sounds to accompany it. What do I do now that I found him? Do I let him sleep? Should I call Salem or Isaac to come help me deal with this situation I fucking created, all because I have deep-rooted trust issues?

Both of them are probably visiting Lenny's family right now, something I plan to do tomorrow when I rein in my aggression. Nothing worse than losing my temper in front of a victim's loved one.

On silent feet, I approach Ezra. I ease the blanket off his head. He's curled up in a tense ball, fingers woven through the thick threads of the blanket like he's afraid someone's going to rip it away from him.

It makes me sick to think that I made him feel this way. All because I forgot how to be human. Forgot that others might feel things differently from me. I let my rage over Lenny's death and Aiden's betrayal drive me to cause Ezra true pain.

My gaze moves down his body, spotting dots and streaks of red along his golden skin. A wave of nausea overcomes me as I turn his arm to reveal cuts and punctures. Fucking hell. He still has a safety pin speared through his flesh. I bite back a growl, recalling how many of them he had clipped to his ripped black jeans and speared through his ears in the alley that day.

The couch becomes my support as I drop down next to him on the floor.

"Baby, what did you do?" I whisper.

Forcing deep breaths to keep my head level, I slip my arms beneath him and lift him. I start toward my apartment door, but I hesitate halfway there, gaze cutting to Rev's door across the hall.

Would Ezra do better in Rev's care tonight? Who am I to play doctor when I was the one who hurt him?

But I know I won't be able to settle without Ezra close to me tonight. I carry him inside my apartment and place him in my bed.

After retrieving supplies from my bathroom, I clean and bandage his wounds, biting into my cheek as I drag the safety pin out of his skin.

Thankfully, he never stirs. I don't have the words necessary to comfort him if he did wake up.

I watch him sleep for a while before giving up on the idea of crawling into bed with him. I'm still too keyed up. Slipping out my front door, I head to the gym.

With only the glow of the city lights through the windows to illuminate the equipment, I blast heavy metal from the sound system to drown out my thoughts. If I let them linger, I'll need to find someone to kill.

That's what I'm made for, after all. It's the only thing I'm good at.

I move toward the punching bag in the corner of the gym and slam my fists into it, over and over again. I don't bother wrapping my hands. For every fucking wound Ezra carved into his flesh, I'll tear the same into my knuckles and elbows on the bag.

Well into burning off steam, my music cuts off. I spin around to find
Rev leaned against the wall behind me, dressed in only his black pajama
pants. He takes in the beads of blood rolling down my fingers to plop on
the floor.

"We need to talk," he says in a chilling tone.

Jaw clenching, I turn back to the bag and throw out another series of
hard punches.

"I haven't seen you lose it like this in a while, Cain," Rev says over the
solid thud of my fists. "Is this about Lenny or the pictures I sent you of
Ezra? Or maybe something you're not telling me about?"

I growl in irritation, giving my throbbing hands a shake. "Can't I just
work this shit out of my system without needing to talk about it?"

"Yeah, sure. Whatever you need," Rev replies with sarcasm, moving
into the boxing ring and motioning me over. "You might actually stand
a chance tonight. I worked out too hard with our pretty Ezra."

Gritting my teeth, I take the bait. We square up in the ring and circle
each other like sharks, two predators out to see who is the better killer.

I'd feel bad for beating on Rev, but the guy's mastered some moves. He
spent time street fighting for money after his three tours in the military.
Couldn't find his way back into society after murdering hundreds of
people.

In a way, Sinro has been his therapy. Not only does he meet with Isaac
weekly, but he's worked his way up the ranks in my company, earning
every single promotion.

He's earned his team's respect, too. Rev jokes that he just wants to
keep his scorecard clean. Doesn't want any company deaths tarnishing
his perfect record out on operations. But I know that some part of him
does actually care about his employees, however small it may be.

Rev strikes at me without warning, delivering a blow to my side. I grunt against the pain and return a punch, flinging blood everywhere. He blocks it and swings at me with his other fist, taking advantage of the fact that I forget he's left-handed. The successful blow knocks the air right out of me.

"Fucker," I wheeze, pacing around him in the ring to catch my breath. We continue this back and forth until we're both dripping sweat and panting. I manage to catch him in the ribs a few times. Twice in the cheek. But he definitely kicks my ass, dropping me to the floor with a heavy hook to the jaw.

Hovering over me with a grin, Rev asks, "Ready to talk, big boy?"

I rock up to a seated position and peel off my shirt, using it to soak up the sweat dripping down my face and the blood still oozing from my split knuckles.

"You already know what's up," I mutter, tossing my ruined shirt aside. "Lenny's death fucking set me off."

Rev mimics my position, plopping down on his butt a few feet from me. "Lenny knew the risk he took settling down in the city with a record like his. He wasn't afraid of death."

I sigh. "No, but he shouldn't have faced it this early."

After a few minutes of silence, Rev asks, "Did you think Ezra was to blame?"

The slight downward curl of my lip gives me away.

"Oh, Cain. What did you do to him? Is he tied up somewhere? Don't tell me you finally decided to kill him."

"How do I constantly want to punch you in the face?" I mutter, shaking my head. I clutch at my hair. "Ezra's... not good. I fucked up. I showed him some of our files, thinking I could catch him in a lie about working for Gabriel. It really messed him up."

Rev mulls this over. "Did you call Isaac?"

"No, but I plan on it." I smash the heels of my hands into my eyes, hissing when the sweat makes them sting. "My day is already booked up."

"Drop some of your meetings on my calendar. I'll handle them. Hell, why don't you take the day off to make it up to the thief? Spend some time with Lenny's family, too."

I comb over my mental calendar and find nothing that Rev couldn't deal with on his own. Cracking my neck, I reply, "I'll think about it."

Rev holds out a bottle of water for me. I gulp it down, spilling droplets on my bare chest as I walk to the trash can. When I toss the drained bottle, I spot Ezra reflected in the mirrors, lurking in the doorway.

His haunted eyes meet mine. He shifts his weight back and forth, seemingly uncertain about his place in this world. It fucking guts me.

"On that note," Rev says, slinging a towel over his shoulder. "I'm going to shower for the second time and pass the fuck out for real. Still slow on the left arm, boss. Ezra, I'll see you in the gym tomorrow."

Rev lingers until Ezra acknowledges him with a dip of his chin.

I can't stop my feet from carrying me over to Ezra to better assess him. I wish I could rewind this entire day. He's got dark circles under his eyes. His hair is sticking up higher on one side, in desperate need of a wash, and his shoulders are so tense, I ache to knead my fingers into his muscles to loosen them.

"I'm sorry." I push out the words.

"It's okay," he whispers. "It's not your fault."

My hand raises, hovering just beneath his chin. I wait, searching his eyes. I need evidence that my touch isn't going to break him.

He lowers his chin to meet my fingers, and I stroke them along his silky skin.

"I am not a good man, Ezra," I admit, hating the tightening in my throat. "I don't have many morals. I don't trust easily. It has only managed to burn me. I've spent half my life killing people for our country and the other half fumbling through it, trying to pretend to be normal."

Eyes wide, Ezra tilts his head up to look at me. I wish I could dive into the well of pain he keeps hidden away and figure out who hurt him. That was what I was built for. Hunting.

My other hand curls into a fist at my side. "You can leave here if that is what you wish. I'll have security on you until Gabriel is dealt with, I promise."

Ezra's face scrunches up. "You don't want me here?"

My heart thuds hard against my ribs. I swear he was designed to destroy me. I slide both of my hands into the soft hair at the back of his neck, tilting his head so our eyes are locked. "That's not it at all. I just don't want you to lose yourself if you decide to stay with me."

Ezra's brows furrow as he processes my words. I'm giving him a choice. Giving him an out from my dark world and messed up methods and unnecessary, violent moods.

His hand comes up to cuff my wrist. "I was already lost, Cain."

My arms wrap around him before I can think better of it. Ezra nuzzles against my sweaty chest. We stand like that for a while, just holding each other up. Fighting to keep even breaths. To stay together.

"I don't see an easy life for me or Jakey," Ezra says. "At least with you, I can learn how to protect him. Maybe I can become strong enough to help those kids. I would never hurt them, Cain." His breath hitches as he fights back a sob. "I would have never gone along with that job if I'd known that was a possibility. I... I think I hate myself for it."

I bury my face in his hair. I like that he smells like my shampoo. I like him in my clothes, too, regardless of the fact that I bought him his own.

I clutch him tighter, desperate to meld him to me. To shape him back into a whole human after I took a sledgehammer to his foundation.

All the little pieces of Ezra I'm collecting are adding up to something completely fucked. As if I'm standing in the eye of a storm, I can only prepare for the approaching devastation, unable to escape it now.

Part of me hopes Ezra will change his mind and leave Sinro Enterprises, knowing I'll only manage to hurt him again. Selfishly, I want him to stay.

Ezra's fingers curl into the muscles along my back like he can hear my thoughts.

Without hesitation, I press a kiss to his hair. "You hungry?"

He pulls back and sniffles. When he starts kneading his bottom lip between his teeth, I reach out and gently pull his lip free. I stroke my thumb over the bloody spot he created and fix his lip ring.

"No more of that," I say firmly.

I fucking despise this entire situation. His self-inflicted wounds turn me inside out because I can't slaughter those demons. They exist in his head, not out here in this fucked up world. No bullet or blade can penetrate them.

His throat bobs. Sensing he needs more from me, I gather him up in my arms, wrapping my hands around his thighs as he secures his legs around my waist. I carry him into my apartment. Then I set him on my couch and tuck him in with a blanket.

"Stay."

For once, Ezra doesn't argue or throw back sarcasm. Ezra sits. Ezra blinks back at me with nothing behind his gaze. Ezra needs me to take charge tonight.

I retrieve a new shirt to throw on. After I wash my hands and wrap my bloody knuckles, I prepare giant salads for us. I toss on sliced chicken and walnuts to boost his protein intake.

We eat on the couch in silence, looking out at the golden lights of the city. Only when our bowls are empty do I speak the words that have been circling my brain since I cracked open that file on my computer. "I won't ever expose you to something again without warning or consent."

Ezra makes a face like he's going to brush me off again but thinks better of it when I cut him a glare. He nods. "Okay."

"You will tell me when something becomes too much. Your training here. My affection."

He gives me another nod, and I collect our dishes to wash in the kitchen sink. When I walk back over to the couch, I can't help but give in to the pressing worry in my brain. "Are you okay to sleep by yourself?"

What I really want to know is if he feels the need to harm himself again. I want to ask him why he sleeps on the floor. I want to know why those photos troubled him to the point of self-mutilation. I want to ask him so many troubling things I know will wreck me.

Mostly, I *need* him close to me tonight.

His brows raise. "As opposed to what? Sleeping with you?"

Blood rushes to my cock, but my head is too bogged down with stress and frenzied emotions to let anything happen between us.

"You can. If you want. Just... just for tonight."

What the fuck am I doing?

But I can't take my words back. Not when Ezra's suddenly overcome with demonic energy, leaping over the back of the couch and bolting for my bedroom. I hear the headboard rattle as he dives into my bed at full speed.

When I reach the doorway, I catch him rolling around, messing up my perfectly made sheets. His shift in behavior summons a relieved laugh from me. I lean against the door frame, crossing my arms over my chest. "Weirdo."

This pretty little thief is going to kill me.

He hums and rubs his cheek against my pillow, looking far too cute to be legal. Rev told me his age, but I still haven't processed how I feel about the gap between us. Still don't know why I'm hung up on it, or the fact that I want to keep thinking about him and me like we could be something. I don't even know what that something is.

I let my eyes appreciate him for a moment. He really *is* beautiful, in a feral animal kind of way. I want to delve my hands into his chaotic blonde waves. Run my tongue over his plump bottom lip and suck it into my mouth. Trace my hands over his lean, tan skin and seal our bodies together.

I want to fuck him hard and raw, but I think I'd like to take my time with him, too. Work him into delirium.

"How about you rinse off before you get sweat all over my bed?" I say, padding in to turn on the shower for him. Away from his eyes, I adjust my erection.

I leave him to shower, fetching us both bottles of water. Then I set my alarm and browse through a few emails in the kitchen. Soon enough, Ezra's back in my bed after a shower, dressed in only his boxer briefs.

"Thought I told you pants are necessary," I mutter, strolling past him to take my turn in the shower.

I don't bother closing or locking the door, knowing Ezra will just pick it if he wants to. All privacy has vanished from my life since he's snuck his way into it.

At this point, even if he is somehow fooling all of us, I know I wouldn't be able to put a bullet in him. Hell, he can snap naked pictures of me and post them on billboards all over the city if he wants, I still won't be the one to kill him.

Sure enough, when I step out of the steamed up glass enclosure and wrap a towel around my waist, I find Ezra curled in a ball on the bathroom counter. He's not peeking at me, just lurking there like a cat in need of attention. That's what he reminds me of. A stray cat, claws and all. Sometimes sweet, and other times sassy. Hot and cold. All frenetic energy and then vulnerability.

After slipping on a clean pair of underwear, I scoop him off the sink, fighting a quiver at the corner of my mouth. This sudden desire to console and protect him isn't an uncomfortable feeling. In fact, I feel the most centered I have in a long time.

My plan was to dump him in my bed and do some laundry until he fell asleep, but I find it physically impossible to unwrap my arms from his body when I lay him down.

Carefully, I sprawl out beside him. I keep him tucked against my side, my gaze hooked on those emotive hazel eyes. If I hold on to him tight enough, maybe he won't be able to hurt himself ever again.

"Beautiful boy." I lean in to place a kiss on his forehead. "Sleep. Tomorrow I'll take you to see your Jakey."

I know my calendar is overloaded, but I want to be the one to take him. Maybe it's guilt. Maybe it's something more expanding inside my chest.

Ezra's smile returns, and my weak heart skips as he snuggles his body closer to mine.

CHAPTER EIGHTEEN

EZRA

I wake up sprawled in the center of Cain's massive bed, the sheets tangled around my feet, and drool crusted on my face.

When I roll off the mattress and burst into the kitchen, I find Cain leaned up against the counter, reading something on his phone and sipping a cup of coffee. The sight of him makes my heart leap and my nerves twinge.

"Are you not working today?" I ask, eyeing him suspiciously.

He takes a long swig from his oversized #1 Boss mug. "Told you. We're going to see your friend."

I march over to him and position myself between his arms. Tilting my head up, I narrow my eyes at him. I don't want things to be weird between us, but I also don't want to give words to what happened last night. I don't really know how.

Cain's anger doesn't scare me. If he thinks that's enough to drive me out the front door, he's dead wrong. Yeah, what he showed me last night threw me for a loop. But I'm going to let it fuel me through training. I'm going to prove to Cain and Rev that I can handle this. I'm going to free Jakey from this mess.

I want to save others.

Cain sets his phone and coffee mug on the counter behind him. Gently, he takes my arm and examines my scabbed wounds. "Why do you do this?"

Wincing, I fight the urge to rip my arm away from him and hide.

"Ezra." His voice is a smooth order, his eyes ablaze with barely contained rage.

Tears sting my eyes, and it makes me more aggravated. "Whatever the fuck this is inside of me... sometimes it needs to be calmed, okay? I don't know what to feel or how to just... be."

Cain pulls me into his arms. I close my eyes and nestle in tighter. He rests his chin on the top of my head. "Anytime you feel like that, you come to me. Do you understand?"

I shake my head, my cheek brushing against his firm chest. "No. Not really. This is a me problem."

Easing me back, his fingers nudge my chin higher until our mouths meet. I have to lean my weight against him as my legs go weak from his kiss.

When he breaks away, he cradles my face in both of his large hands, those deep brown eyes striving to convey everything we can't seem to vocalize. Or don't want to.

"Do you get it now, Ezra? Your pain is my pain, too."

He gives me another soft, lingering kiss. I have to grip his shirt in both of my hands to stay upright. Cain kisses me like he cherishes me. It makes my stomach all fluttery and my eyelids almost too heavy to open.

His laugh is low as his thumb brushes over my lip ring, giving it a little flip. "Can't leave my shirts alone, can you? Is that punishment for how I behaved last night?"

"I'd rather *you* punish *me*," I admit, giving him a sly grin before bounding off to get dressed, satisfied now that I know things are going to be okay. I didn't fuck shit up with my meltdown last night.

Add that in with the anticipation of seeing Jakey, and I'm on another level today.

Dressed in warm clothes, I come out to find Cain bundled up in his coat and a scarf. He holds a second travel cup of coffee out for me. "Decaf. Otherwise you're going to be too hyped up. We'll be stopping by Lenny's house afterward."

I frown. "Can we pick up some flowers for his wife?"

A muscle in Cain's jaw flexes. "Of course."

I sip at the hazelnut coffee as we ride the elevator down into the parking garage. When the doors open and the cool winter air hits me, I freeze up.

Cain glances back at me, brows furrowing. "What's wrong?"

"Last time you took me out, someone was murdered." My fingers reach to flip the safety pins I usually keep on my pants. Only, I'm wearing the clothes Cain bought me, fitted black jeans and a knitted cream sweater.

Picking up on my habitual movement, Cain frowns. "Ezra, we're taking a bulletproof vehicle and security this time. I have a team assigned to watch over Lenny's wife and your friend."

I push out a breath, encouraged forward by his steady gaze. He leads me over to a sleek black Mercedes Benz. As soon as he turns the key, heavy bass vibrates the speakers. His hand snaps to the volume button, and I snicker.

"What is this, Mr. Vincent? You listen to the rap music?"

He gives away nothing in his face. "Hush, little thief."

"Careful. Someone might think you're a normal man under that beautiful, stone-cold exterior."

Cain drives us out onto the streets. We're followed by an unmarked black Sinro vehicle which I try to ignore as I tap my fingers on the window to the beat of the music.

Thirty minutes outside of the city, we cross through the gates of a sprawling estate. It's the fanciest place I've ever seen. Several cottages line the curving road toward a massive three-story building with balconies and dormers. It looks like some sort of holiday resort.

There's a pond with a fountain, surrounded by willow trees and a walking path, and a giant front porch along the main building filled with rocking chairs occupied by elderly people. They greet us as we walk to the automatic front doors.

"What fine-looking men have come to entertain us today!" The tinier of the silver-haired women calls out. This is followed up by a whistle from her friend beside her, wrapped up in a knitted pastel blanket.

I can't help a surprised laugh, and when I look up at Cain, he's fighting back a smile.

"Ladies," he greets.

We leave them chattering like squirrels as we stride through the doors. The manager, a kind woman named Janice, comes out of the office to take our names and guide us through the long halls to a community center.

"This is great. It's so rare that our residents get visitors," Janice says.

I reach to squeeze Cain's hand. I'm too choked up with emotion to speak when I get my first look at Jakey on one of many floral print couches positioned in a large circle, surrounded by other seniors all knitting away. His hair has been washed and cut neat to his scalp, and he's dressed in a clean sweater, blue jeans, and new sneakers.

I don't think I've seen him look so happy since I met him in that scrapyard when he invited me around his bonfire. He worked so hard to earn my trust. Made me feel needed. Safe. Loved.

My body locks up on the spot. Do I have a right to be in his life anymore? He's obviously well cared for now. Am I better left forgotten?

"Is it expensive to keep him here?" I ask.

Cain strokes warm fingers along the back of my neck. "Don't worry about it. I have more money than I know what to do with."

With hesitant steps, I move closer to the couches.

"Jakey?" I say, to which several curious heads raise.

As soon as Jakey's watery blue eyes meet mine, he cracks a heart-wrenching smile. "My Ezra! I told you old farts he was real. My boy has come to visit me."

I drop down between his legs and wrap my arms around his waist. "I'm so glad you're okay. You're okay, right?"

He pats my hair, trying to smooth down a wave determined to escape my head. "You kidding me? I schooled everyone in bingo yesterday. I've got a little side business going on for my knitting, too. Seventeen orders already. Can you believe it?"

A nurse enters the circular ring of couches. "Are you Jacob's grandson?"

Jakey scoffs at her. "Told you he's my boy. How old do you think I am?"

I don't correct him. Jakey *is* old enough to be my grandpa, but I quickly learned never to correct him. It only serves to make him distraught.

The nurse gives him a warm smile. "So sorry, I'll do better to remember next time."

She holds out her hand to me, and I shake it. "I'm Isabel."

"Ezra," I say, feeling weak all over in the best way possible.

She looks at Cain, eyes going a bit wide. Yeah, he's a lot to take in. If his impeccable taste in clothing wasn't a sign of his elite position in life, the icy expression on his unholy beautiful face was.

"Cain Vincent." He offers his hand, which she clutches a little too long.

"Well, Ezra and Cain, I'm so glad you stopped by. Jakey's charmed us all with his elaborate stories. You're welcome to stay for lunch if you'd like."

We end up sharing a table with five other residents in a formal dining room. When the guy sitting at Cain's other side learns about his service in the military, they start swapping stories.

While I'm doing my best to shower Jakey with my attention, I can't help but tune into pieces of Cain's conversation, rattled by the different layers and experiences of humans in this world. It makes my heart ache.

Then there's that barb of sadness again over the fact that Jakey doesn't need me in his life. I mean, I'm happy. So fucking happy he's here. But I can't lie and say I'm not heartbroken over what feels like the loss of the only constant in my life. The only soul that has ever cared for me.

A hand squeezes my knee under the table. My eyes dart to Cain as he leans in, his breath warm against my ear. "You okay?"

"Yeah." I nod furiously. "Maybe. Probably not. Let's not stay for dessert."

Cain's eyes circuit my face in assessment. He gives me a tight nod.

After our plates are cleared, I wrap my arms around the back of Jakey in his chair. "I'll be back to see you soon. I promise."

Tears burn in my eyes, and I know I'm at my limit for the day, overloaded with mixed emotions.

Jakey pats a hand over mine. "Love you, Ezra. My precious boy. I'll be counting down the time until I get to see you again."

Shit. This old man is my Achilles heel, I swear it.

Back outside, I suck a big gulp of icy winter air into my lungs. I revel in the chill that spreads through me.

Cain moves in front of me, close enough to reach out and touch. "What do you need, Ezra?"

I keep my fingers from seeking out safety pins. "I'll be okay. Need to hit the gym when we get home."

Home. My throat tightens.

Cain doesn't seem to notice. His body is turned away from me now as he watches a platinum blonde woman—the one I saw in the elevator the day I snuck into Sinro—striding toward us from the parked SUV that followed us.

"Hello, Cain," she acknowledges, then turns her attention to me. She radiates a kindness that soothes my prickling jealousy over whatever relationship she has with Cain. "Ezra. I've heard quite a bit about you."

"Good things, I hope," I say with a lopsided grin.

"Salem leads my extraction team," Cain explains. "She helps get victims out. She works with our contacts to get them into protection programs and placed in safe homes."

My eyes go wide, and Salem gives me a warm smile. "I've been checking up on your friend. He's an absolute joy, Ezra."

"I know. He's pretty great, isn't he?"

"Anytime you need some company that isn't so murderous, feel free to give me a ring." She leaves us, greeting the rocking chair patrol squad by names.

I'm stunned in the middle of the parking lot. *She helps victims.*

Cain's palms come to rest against my cheeks. "Before you even think of asking to work with her, you need to understand. Salem sees the worst of our operations. What you witnessed on my computer, that's her everyday job, Ezra."

I wince, knowing Salem's work would set me off. I'm so fucking pissed off over what was done to me to make me this fragile. Some days, I want to blame God. How could he sit back and watch the suffering of his creations?

But if there was a God, then wasn't the devil real, too?

Cain guides me back to his car. As soon as we're seated, I lean over the console to place a kiss on his warm cheek.

"Thank you."

His hand tightens on the steering wheel. "You're welcome. I'm glad you're okay with him being here. I didn't think he'd do well in an apartment at Sinro."

"It's perfect. He's so happy. I'm happy, too."

"Good. After stopping by to see Lenny's wife, I'll need to go into the office. Unfortunately, I'll be home late tonight."

"Thought you had the day off?"

He sighs. "The CEO never gets a day off. I have a few meetings this afternoon I need to attend."

My heart sinks, but I can't start being too needy with Cain. One orgasm and a few kisses doesn't mean I have a right to demand more from him. He runs a huge company. I don't want to push this and make him question taking me in.

But I do want him. In any way he'll let me have him.

An afternoon of meetings turns into a solid week of Cain working over-time.

We're long past my job due date with Gabriel, and I'm constantly nagging both Cain and Rev for updates on Jakey's safety.

I can't help but feel a bit unglued. I can't just sit back and wait for others to deal with threats, hoping everything will work out for the best. Nothing ever does in my life.

In my time pacing his apartment, working out, and swimming laps in the heated pool on the balcony, I've noticed changes to Cain's apartment. More food in the fridge, mostly protein. Cans of watermelon sparkling water, which makes me smile because that meant Rev talked to Cain about how much I loved it after buying me a can a few days ago.

But it's the glass bottles of nail polish in the bathroom that really do me in. I clutch them to my chest as I sink down onto the cold tile floor, trying my best not to cry. The fact that Cain's so attentive makes my chest ache like it's caving into a hollow part of my soul.

It makes me nervous, too. Eventually he's going to figure out how blighted I am. I'm not worthy of this level of thoughtfulness. I don't think I'm worthy of anything, really.

After coating my nails in a thick layer of black, I notice doubles of everything in the bathroom, fluffy blue towels included. And his closet keeps magically expanding with items in my size. Though I'll never stop strutting around his apartment in my boxers. Not only do I get enjoy-ment out of it, I'm also hoping one day my body will be tempting enough for him to pounce on.

He can't hide his stolen looks. I know his eyes follow me. It's his self-control that's driving me up a fricken wall. I want him to play with me. I thought maybe something would change between us when he decided one night of sleeping in his bed wasn't enough after finding me curled up on the floor in his guest bedroom again.

You sleep with me now. Unless you don't want that.

No part of me wanted to argue and tell him he didn't need to take pity on me. He pretends to be this callous businessman. Underneath, I think he really likes to take care of people.

That evening, I toss restlessly in his bed, surprised I haven't woken him with my movement. I've never been one to sleep for too long, constantly in a state of survival on the streets. Before that, too, I was never certain when I would be in danger.

Rolling over, I scoot close enough to soak up Cain's body heat and breathe in his scent. I spend far too long staring at his exposed back, trying to keep my gaze from dipping to the swell of his ass beneath the silk sheet. There are two scars that look like bullet wounds near his shoulder blades, and a four-inch scar near the dimples on his lower back.

His tattoos surprisingly only cover his arms. My fingers twitch with the urge to trace them, but I feel like he wouldn't appreciate me touching him while he sleeps. He's barely touched me when he's awake, and I'm literally half-naked in bed with him every night.

Overcome with the need to run this energy out of my system, I creep out of bed and pull on comfy clothes. Then I sneak out the front door.

Quiet moans reach my ears before I make it to the common area, accompanied by the sound of slapping skin. My stomach dips.

I peek around the corner and spot Rev on the couch. His hands are buried in some guy's dark locks. A guy who happens to be completely naked and rocking up and down on Rev's lap.

Rev's gaze flicks to me and he grins, slamming his hips up to make the guy riding him drop his head back and moan.

Oh, shit. I flush with heat from head-to-toe. Here I am, trying to avoid dirty thoughts, and this scene has my dick hardening.

Dropping my gaze, I rush for the gym and pull the door closed behind me. I brace against the wall, practicing some deep breaths to get my head level and my body calmed down.

Three miles of running on the treadmill isn't enough to get my mind off the topic of sex. I imagine Cain in Rev's place and me riding him. He'd be rough with me, just like I need. His slicked up cock would thrust into me at a punishing pace, driving me over the edge into blissful pleasure.

I groan and hit the stop button on the treadmill. *Fuck.* I need to come. It's not fun running with a stiff cock bouncing around in my sweatpants. Maybe I could just jerk it in here real quick and continue my workout.

Cracking the door to the gym, I peek my head out. When I don't hear any more obscene sounds from the living area, I move to one of the weight benches.

I stare at myself in the mirror. I've been here nearly two weeks, and there is new definition carved into my body. I'd say the street rat is gone, but there are still dark circles under my wild eyes, and my blonde waves are a tangled, sweaty mess.

Should I ask Rev where I can get a haircut? Or would things be awkward now that I caught him with his dick buried in someone?

I reach down to palm my erection, hissing at how painful it's already become. My hand snaps off my dick as Cain appears in the mirrors, stepping through the doorway.

"Ezra?"

Shit. I try to shake the dirty fantasies from my mind. Cain wouldn't be into them. The incident in his office was a onetime thing. Another way for him to mess with my head.

"Couldn't sleep," I mumble, hoping that will be enough to get him to leave.

I'm so fucked up over this shit. That trip to see Jakey and the stupid bottles of nail polish exposed me to too many sides of Cain, and now I can't get rid of this deep, foreign pain in my chest whenever I look at him. I finally met someone I want, but he doesn't want me back.

Broken. Defiled. Tainted.

I startle as Cain kneels between my legs. Too stuck in my thoughts, I hadn't noticed him approaching. His hand carefully tips my chin up until our eyes meet. "Are you hurting?"

I can't help a wild laugh. *Am I hurting?* Jesus, I've been imagining getting fucked by this guy since I met him. I've slept next to him in bed. I'm left alone to pine for his attention and crave him in ways I can't put into words because I've never felt this way about anyone. I didn't even know it was possible. It shouldn't be for me, right?

Spinning my lip ring around, I squirm on the bench. "Yes, I'm hurting. But not in the way you think."

Stupid, big mouth.

Cain's brows furrow. I scoot away from him, and my dick decides to shift from where I had it tucked under my waistband, now noticeably stretching the front of my sweats.

His gaze drops there, and a muscle in his jaw leaps. Heat rushes through my face, all the way up to the tips of my ears. Dark eyes flick up to meet mine, so rich and brown and... suddenly ravenous.

"Oh god. This is so awkward," I mumble.

He locks a hand behind my knee and tugs me to the edge of the bench. "No. I've been depriving you."

His other hand grips my hair at the base of my skull to drag me into a kiss.

A gasp slips from my parted lips when he palms my cock through my sweatpants. He kisses me hard, dipping his tongue into my mouth. He strokes it against my own tongue in a slow rhythm, matching his hand sliding up and down my shaft through the material of my pants.

I shudder and moan, and this sets him off. Cain scoops me off the bench, spinning me around so my cheek and chest press against the cold mirror. He keeps one hand gripped in my hair and his other arm wrapped around my stomach, pulling me tight against his own erection. It feels unreal pressed against my ass.

"Oh, shit." I groan, struggling to stay upright.

"What do you need, beautiful boy? You need to be unwound?" His voice is a low rumble, raising goosebumps on my sweat-slicked, too-hot skin.

His hand on my stomach drifts lower. Hooking a finger in the waistband of my pants and boxers, he drags both down below my heavy balls, exposing me. "Need me to take you apart?"

"So bad. So so bad."

His hand wraps around my dick, squeezing my crown hard before stroking me from root to tip. I try to thrust my hips forward, drowning in pleasure just from this touch alone, but he grips my balls and gives them a painful tug.

He chuckles darkly. "Greedy little thief. Trust me to take care of you, okay?"

My body trembles. "Okay."

He goes back to stroking me, swiping his rough thumb over the precum beaded at my slit. The sounds escaping my parted lips should embarrass me, but I'm too far gone to care.

"Fuck. Cain," I whine. "I want it. Please."

He presses open-mouth kisses to the back of my neck. "I know, baby. I'll get you there."

When he removes his hand from my cock, I can't help but groan in frustration. I hear him spit, and then his slick hand returns to stroke me, his fast pace driving me to madness, so smooth and wet and tight around me.

Pressure builds at the base of my spine. I'm whining and mewling and fighting to take control, but loving the grip he keeps on me, his other hand still fisted in my hair like he hates me, smashing my cheek against the mirror.

Fuck. This is better than I imagined.

"Gonna come. I'm—" My whole body tightens up, and then explodes when he punishes me with a final, tight stroke. Warm cum pulses out of me, spilling over his knuckles and onto the floor. My body continues to shudder even after he drains me.

We both watch in the mirror as he smears my cum across my quivering, sweaty abs. After snapping my boxers and pants back into place, he uses a rag to wipe the floor.

"Don't stay up too long. Lock on the door will recognize your thumbprint."

My eyes go wide. "Wait. When did you program my thumbprint?"

Cain gives me a quick kiss on the back of my neck, silencing me, and then walking away.

I stare at my blissed-out face in the mirror. How do I already want more of him?

Shit. I don't know that I'll ever satisfy my desire for this man.

CHAPTER NINETEEN

CAIN

I don't like that I had to ditch Ezra for work the next morning.

But I don't want to let important operations slip just because I'm falling into something addictive with him. I can barely keep my fucking hands off him. Forget trying to push him out of my head at this point.

Rorik's made good progress at the shipyard, covertly setting up a deal with Gabriel's guys to get us access through the north gate this evening. He's an irreplaceable asset to my company. His skeletal tattoos and natural scowl have allowed him to meld seamlessly into numerous criminal organizations.

I have three teams set to deploy. Mine, Rev's, and Rorik's. That's thirty-three people. Should be a slaughter.

I text Alaric to send the teams detailed layouts of the property in time for our meeting.

Remember not to kill all of them. We need that encryption code.

I sigh, hating the idea of having to haul scumbags back into the building. I hate the idea of leaving Ezra alone tonight even more. I don't even want him in the same city as Gabriel. Don't want anyone to ever lay hands on him again.

Except for me.

My fingers hover over Salem's number, but I know she's on protective duty watching over Jakey. I dial my brother, Isaac, instead.

"Hey, Cain. What can I do for you?" Isaac's cheery voice sounds. He's the only one around here besides Salem who has any fucking manners. Gwen pretends to be polite because she gets paid to act that way, but I've heard the shit she calls people behind closed doors and under her breath.

"Do you think you could entertain a friend of mine this evening?" I ask, loading into the elevator with two of my guys, Forest and Nick, who double as accountants during the day.

They both peek over at me as I hit the button for lower level one, and I fight the urge to tell them to mind their own business. I suppose it is a bit of a shock to learn that their workaholic, anti-social boss might have friends.

Although, I don't categorize Ezra as a friend. My thoughts involving him are far too devious.

"Sure thing," Isaac replies. "Is this *friend* your pretty little thief?"

Fucking rumor mill around this place. Then again, no one has seen me with a partner in over a decade. And after the office rearranging incident, I have to wonder what Rev disclosed to everyone to calm them down about their shit being touched.

Last time Rev held an informative meeting I couldn't attend, he told everyone that I had explosive diarrhea. I knocked out one of his teeth in the boxing ring that night. Cost him ten thousand in dental work.

"Don't start with me," I warn. "Can you take him to dinner at Madora Estates? He's got family there. Salem's posted up on watch."

Getting to meet Ezra would have been enough of a temptation for my overly curious brother, but I know Isaac would never turn down an opportunity to spend time with Salem. They're a good fit for each other. Not sure why either one hasn't made a move, but that's none of my business.

"Sounds wonderfully entertaining. I'll take care of him. Oh, and Cain? You really should consider going home for dinner soon. Mom and Dad miss you."

I hesitate, trying to remember the last time I visited the farm. Has it already been three years? Fuck. I'm a horrible son.

But being back there only reminds me how much I'd changed after my time in the military. That realization first sank in when I was granted leave from service to attend my grandfather's funeral. I'd stayed with my parents, helping them keep up with their commercial dairy business while they sorted through my grandfather's substantial finances, padded by dozens of successful hotel properties.

Normality felt wrong. Like an itch in my brain I couldn't reach. I struggled to ease back into the simple life. Chores I had once relished felt pointless, and home-cooked meals didn't hold the same magic when I knew good people were out there suffering.

My ability to hold conversations had withered beneath a storm of horrors playing out in my head like an endless film strip. Hard to talk about the weather when your brain is stuck on visuals of humans being blown apart.

"Cain?" Isaac says.

As the elevator doors ding open, I reply, "I'll think about it."

Stepping into the armory with my teams of mercenaries gearing up, I know this right here—the company I've built on the bones of criminals—will forever be where I belong.

And if the government ever decides to shut me down, if they teeter more to the belief that my business is a threat to them or to the public, I still don't think I could ever give up this lifestyle.

I am a killer, and I will be a killer until the day I'm dropped into a grave.

The assholes put up a fight, I'll give them that.

We stormed the rain-slicked shipyard, pouring in through the north gate like a mutating virus as soon as Rorik gave the signal. While Gabriel's cronies matched us in firepower, we outranked them in experience.

The only reason it took so long to clean house was because we had to identify who was running the show in Gabriel's absence. The fucker knew how to keep his head underground.

We wasted hours prying open shipping containers, too, only to discover ungodly amounts of drugs and a few decomposing bodies. I had to call in Henry's team to dispose of both.

We ended up with two shitlords tossed in the back of one of our windowless bulletproof vans. I had to call Isaac back to the office to keep one of them from bleeding out after Rev shot him in the kneecap.

Isaac might not be a practicing doctor, but he had enough knowledge to keep the guy conscious and out of death's hands as we tied him up in the interrogation room.

"You can kiss the corner office goodbye," I mutter to Rev as I circle our two restrained prisoners.

"He was about to throw a fucking grenade! I should have shot him in the head."

I strip off my jacket and bulletproof vest, eager to get answers out of our prisoners and check on Ezra now that he's back in the building. Did he have a good dinner with Jakey? Did Isaac ask him too many questions?

Pulling out a pair of latex gloves, I tug them onto my hands.

Rev gives his prisoner a slap on the cheek. "Hey there, shitbag. Let's you and I have some fun."

I lower myself down in front of the other guy. Their chairs are pushed back-to-back so they can't see each other. Makes it more intense for one of them when their buddy starts screaming.

The guy curses at me in a language I don't recognize, so I jab my fist into his teeth, breaking two of them.

"You talk when I tell you to, understood?" I speak slowly.

He spits blood onto the floor, and I remove my knife, flicking the blade out. There's a flash of fear in his eyes before he scowls at me.

"Here's how this is going to go. The quicker you offer up information on the encryption key to that drive, the less I carve you up. I want a password or the name and location of the person who can provide them."

When my guy doesn't respond, I slice through his shoelaces and rip off his shoe. Screams erupt from the other prisoner, a sign that Rev's in his element as well.

Moments like these make me want to laugh at the idea of us pretending to run a normal business, sitting behind desks and spending hours in meeting rooms. Wearing suits and ties and strutting around like we're normal fucking business men.

We're nothing short of fucked up, deriving pleasure from torturing bad people.

My captive spits blood again. "Kill me. No information to share."

I sink my blade clean through his little toe, severing it. He howls and thrashes, and I just grin back at him.

"Fucking hurts, doesn't it? I'm going to be real with you. You're not walking out of this building. Now, the level of pain you experience on your way out of this life? That depends on what you tell me."

I let my gaze drift up to Rev standing across from me, hair a bit messy and blood on his favorite silver button-up shirt. He looks lit up from the inside, like Christmas came early.

My captive starts rambling in his other language, so I sever another toe. "I don't like to repeat myself."

Blood slithers toward my boots as the door to the interrogation room swings open. I have my gun in my hand, aimed at the intruder, before I can even think.

"Ezra." I push out a hot breath and lower my weapon.

He fiddles with the sleeves of his sweatshirt. "Sorry. You left the door open. I hadn't seen you since Isaac said you returned."

"Now's not the time for this." My protective instincts flare up, determined to hide this darkness from him. I don't want him to fear me.

But at the same time, I do think I want him to know the *real* me.

Of course, Ezra doesn't listen. He takes slow steps into the room, head tilted as he looks over the guys we're torturing. Rev's victim is in a much bloodier state, missing fingernails and an ear.

Ezra halts his perusal, a finger reaching out to touch the ink on the guy's neck. "I know this guy. Alphabet Soup. He was with Gabriel when I was threatened into stealing from you." Ezra frowns. "He kept hitting me in the head."

The guy looks up at him, panic transforming his features as Ezra keeps his fingers on his throat.

Rage floods my system. I have my knife pressed against another toe, eager to draw this out as long as possible. This fucker will be praying to the devil to take him into the lowest ring of hell to escape me.

"You want to play, too, Ezra?" Rev asks, grinning like a maniac.

Ezra remains focused on the captive he recognized. "It's such a strange tattoo."

Interest piqued, I rise to my feet and move behind Ezra, letting my body press into him.

"Could be some sort of code, don't you think?" Ezra peeks up at me, a brow cocked.

"Fucking hell," I utter, heart lurching as I glimpse another string of numbers and letters on the other prisoner's neck.

I call up Alaric. "Yeah, I think Ezra may have found your key. I'll send pictures now."

"Oh, good. I just ordered a large pizza."

"Hey, do you not see him on the security cameras, or do you just not care?" I chastise.

Ezra stares up at me in shock, but I soften my features to let him know I'm not actually upset about his sneaking around.

"Oh, I see him," Alaric says. "Your thief is cute."

I growl and hang up. When I raise my phone to snap a shot of the first prisoner's neck, he starts flailing. Gritting my teeth, I pull out my gun and fire a shot into his skull.

So much for torturing him all night.

Rev gasps. "Our hostage! No corner office for you!"

I roll my eyes and send off pics to Alaric. Then I turn to Ezra, grimacing at the blood splatter on his sweatpants.

Fuck. How is he feeling about all of this? Overwhelmed? Panicked? Frightened?

How am I so fucking turned on by the fact that everyone recognizes him as *mine*?

I *want* to claim him. More than I want to protect him from myself.

Closing the distance between us, I snake my hands around Ezra's waist and back him out of the room.

"Do what you want with the other one, but keep him alive for now," I tell Rev, kicking the door closed behind us as chaotic laughter ensues.

Shoving Ezra up against the hallway wall, I cage him in with my body and search his expression for fear. Gazing up at me through those sinful dark lashes, he doesn't appear shocked or disturbed by what he just witnessed. Quite the opposite, actually.

His pupils blow wide as his tongue flicks out to play with that sexy lip ring I've imagined sliding along my cock too many times.

"What are you doing?" he asks breathlessly.

I lower my mouth to his neck, running my lips over his warm, soft skin to make him shiver. I nip at his earlobe.

"Beautiful boy, I'm going to take you home and devour you."

CHAPTER TWENTY

EZRA

Cain mauls me as soon as we enter his apartment. His kisses are deep and hungry, his hands grabbing at my clothes to rip them off. I'm naked by the time the backs of my knees bump against the edge of his bed.

He pushes at my chest to drop me on my ass as he comes to stand between my spread legs. I fight the urge to cover my erection, even though he's touched me there already.

Thankfully, my workouts and proper meals have helped put more mass on my bones. At least I don't have to be self-conscious about that anymore.

Cain's dark eyes glisten down at me with lust. "Don't fucking move, Ezra. Touch yourself if you need to, but you're not allowed to come until I'm out of the shower, got it? I'm not playing with you when I have some shitbag's blood on my hands."

Swallowing, I nod, already reaching to take my cock in hand. He watches me stroke myself a couple of times, letting out a low, predatory growl.

He disappears into the bathroom, and the thrum of anticipation has me clambering to my feet to give chase. I want to be good for him, I do. But sometimes the urge to misbehave wins out.

I suck in a breath at the vision of Cain standing naked under the rainfall shower, dark hair slicked back and perfect, round ass on display. When he turns toward me, head tipped back and eyes closed, I watch the water run down his sculpted body, over the hills of his pecs, slithering down his eight pack. Down to his massive, half-hard cock.

Good god. I bite down on my bottom lip, a hand still gripped around my dick.

I'm able to slip into the shower without alerting him of my presence until the glass door snaps closed behind me. Cain's brown and gold-flecked eyes, tinged with anger, land on me. He spins me around, forcing my front against the cold tiles. One hand pins both of my wrists above my head. The other grips my hip.

"What do you think you're doing?" His low voice against the shell of my ear sends a shiver through me. Pretty sure my dick's already leaking.

"Begging," I admit, squirming in his hold. "I'm not scared of you, Cain."

He pushes his hard body against mine, the hand on my hip sliding up to grip my jaw and tip my head to the side. "You should be."

He sinks his teeth into my neck, and I cry out in painful pleasure. I rock my hips back, eager for more, but he moves his cock just out of reach.

Cain runs his hot tongue along my neck. He licks and nips and sucks his way down my body, letting the hand pinning my wrists trail the same path as he lowers to his knees. Biting down on my ass, he slaps my other cheek, and I gasp.

"Turn around, Ezra," he orders.

All too eager, I spin for him. In awe, I stare down at the beautiful, powerful man on his knees for me. He nuzzles against my shaft, pressing kisses to my hips and thighs. Everywhere but where I need him most.

I groan in frustration, my hand gripping his dark, wet locks. I curl them tighter as he continues to tease me, sucking and licking at my cock, but still not taking me into his mouth.

Shit. I love him unleashed. I think this might be the true Cain. The man under the cold mask and all the anger. The one who gives space for harder emotions. Who cares about pleasing me.

I might want to rush this, but I love that he wants to take his time with me.

Cain runs his tongue along the vein up my shaft. When he reaches the head of my cock, his lips part. I suck in a breath, and then his mouth closes over me.

He sucks me deep into this throat first thing, and my head slams back against the tiled wall. I'm trembling uncontrollably when he starts to bob up and down my length. He's drawing the soul from my body, dragging his tongue over me, flicking it over my slit and around the head of my dick.

"Fuck." I don't even have a chance to give him a warning. I cry out as I spill into his mouth. He swallows every drop of my cum without complaint.

Cain rises up, towering over me. He spins me around to press me against the tiled wall again. His hand tangles in my hair to hold me captive.

"You like me like this, don't you?" I tease, pushing my ass against his impressive length. He's so thick and hard, I can't imagine it'll feel good the first time he fucks me.

But I want it. I need it. Only with him.

Cain runs a hand down my ass. A finger brushes against my hole. I hiss, but it turns into a moan when it starts swirling it around, just enough to drive me crazy.

"Mmm, I do, Ezra. I like you grinding that beautiful cock against me. I like your defiance. Like you curled up in my bed." He presses a kiss behind my ear as one finger starts to push inside me. "I like the sounds that pretty mouth makes. Like the way your eyes watch me."

I whimper. "Can't help it. Every part of me is drawn to you."

Cain slowly pushes another finger inside of me. "I like that I can set you off, too. I want you moaning and rambling nonsense every time I pleasure you."

"Yeah?" My dick starts to stiffen again.

"Yeah. My needy little thief."

I cry out when his fingers press against the most sensitive part of me. My fingernails claw at the walls. "Fuck. Fuck. Fuck."

He plants hot, open-mouthed kisses along my throat as he keeps hitting that spot inside of me that has pleasure sparking through my entire body.

"You hard for me again?" he murmurs, dragging his flat tongue from the base of my neck to the top.

"Always," I whisper, pushing my hips back. His fingers sink deeper. Fuck, I'm losing the ability to think. I'm all nerves. All sensation.

Cain reaches for a bar of soap. "Let's go for two then, baby."

He slicks up my dick, sliding his hand along my length, his grip tight enough to have my eyes rolling back in my head.

"Jesus Christ. Cain, you're... ah, you might be killing me."

"Good way to die, no?" he teases. "You going to come for me this way, or do I need to suck you off again?"

"Yes," I whine, squeezing my eyes shut.

He chuckles. "Yes, to what?"

With his fingers stroking in and out of me and his other hand slipping along my hard length, I come violently, shuddering as I unload hot strands onto the shower wall. When my orgasm recedes, my knees go weak. Cain catches me around the waist.

"My bones don't work anymore," I complain.

He kisses the back of my neck, and I feel his hard length slide between my cheeks. Before I can overthink what I'm offering, I push against him. "Take it. Fuck me, Cain. Please."

Cain groans, rocking against me a couple of times as his arms snake around my chest. His fingers flick over my nipples. "Fuck. You're so deep in my head."

"Please, Cain. I'm clean, I promise. You can fuck me raw."

He spins me around, shoving me to my knees. My eyes flick up to him, momentarily in shock, and then I drop my gaze to his thick cock.

"I want you to show me how good that pretty mouth can be, Ezra," he says, diving a hand into my hair.

Eager to please him, I flick my tongue against his crown. Finally, he's letting me touch him, and I'm going to make it good for him.

I run my tongue along his shaft in long strokes and run it over his slit like he did to me. I moan at the salty taste of pre-cum. Trace his prominent veins down to suck his heavy balls into my mouth.

"Fuck. I love this," I say, then draw his cock into my mouth. He groans. Both of his hands grip me by the hair.

I work him over slowly, more concerned about technique than speed. I want to please him. Need to satisfy him.

I suck his cock hard enough to hollow out my cheeks. Then I take him as deep as I can go, still leaving several inches exposed. I wrap my hand around him too, stroking in sync with my movements.

Cain soon takes control. He holds my head firmly as he fucks into my mouth. "That's it, beautiful boy. Take me deep. Look at you. Fucking perfect on your knees for me. Do you want my cum?"

I moan on his cock. My hands grip the back of his thighs, his powerful muscles flexing with every thrust.

"Fuck. Ezra." Cain groans. "You were made to ruin me. Swallow all of it. Not a drop wasted. Need you filled up."

He comes in my mouth, and I struggle to drink all of him down. My fingers dig into his skin as his cock pulses on my tongue. But I take it all before I pop off and sag onto the wet tiles.

Cain leans down to kiss my mouth. He slips his tongue past my lips to make sure I didn't leave a trace of him behind.

"You are perfect," he murmurs. "Perfect for me."

He lifts me onto my feet and washes both of our bodies. I'm already half in a comatose state, my eyelids fluttering heavily.

He laughs and helps me out of the shower to towel me off.

When I step in front of the mirror, I don't recognize the man staring back at me. His tan skin glows over newfound muscles. His eyes are bright. He looks content, the storm inside calmed for once.

Cain dresses us both. He tugs me into his bed, keeping me tight against his warm body.

God, if you do exist, please don't take this good thing away from me. I think I'd be crushed if this ever comes to an end.

CHAPTER TWENTY-ONE

CAIN

It's already 7PM, and I've done little more than read over the same email a thousand times and move my mouse around my computer screen.

I wasn't feeling up to leading a debriefing meeting after our shipyard operation, so I forced Rev to do it. I know I'll get shit from him later. His coy little smile is already pissing me off, like he knows shit he shouldn't. Which is impossible because he hasn't seen Ezra today.

Can Rev sense when someone got off? Wouldn't surprise me if that was his super power.

Just thinking about Ezra with his mouth around my cock has me half-hard under my desk. I have two choices. Force myself to work or abandon this futile goal and go home to play with him.

It's hard for me to be selfish in this line of work, which is why I keep trying to fall back into my normal routine. This consuming thing with Ezra is becoming dangerous. We need to slow down. *I* need to slow down.

First thing this morning, though, I went and got tested. Not that I had any concern when I've been celibate for too long. Still, he offered up confirmation that he was good, and I want to be able to do the same.

Because I *am* going to fuck him.

Groaning at my lack of focus, I rock back in my chair. I swivel around to take in the view of the glistening city. Cars crawl along the patchwork of streets, crowded enough to alert me that it's past time to clock out.

My desk phone rings. Without looking, I reach for it. "Yeah?"

"Cain," Alaric says, his usual even tone off.

"Did you get in?" My heart lurches in my chest. I spin around to face my computer, scrolling through emails to make sure he hasn't sent me anything, and I missed it.

"Oh, I got in," Alaric says darkly. "Clever thinking on the tattoos. But, Cain? This shit... it's next-level disturbing."

For him to say that, after years of working at Sinro, brings a chill to my bones.

"Send it to me," I order, already bracing for what I'm about to witness. Can't be worse than what I've seen in this lifetime.

An email pops up on my computer. I click into it. My brows furrow at an archaic-looking snapshot of what appears to be a grocery list.

"I don't know what I'm looking at. Explain."

Keys pound in the background. "So, it looks like your standard list of non-important grocery items, right? But each item on the list is coded with details on where to pick up kids, Cain. It's a shopping list for traffickers."

My lungs compress. I hang up my desk phone to video chat Alaric instead, so I can watch him work through his screens at lightning speeds.

He clicks on the first item: Milk $2.96 x 13. Seemingly harmless, but then he clicks on the picture of a milk carton, revealing additional information that has nothing to do with a grocery store:

Mika Williams

296 Lynsey Rd

13 years old

"Jesus," I utter.

There's a folder with images of the child, too. I squeeze my eyes shut, grateful when I hear him click out because some of those pictures had to have been taken by family members.

He moves on to the next item: Wine $24.09 x 10

Wade Henderson

2409 Winston Ct

10 years old

"Alaric. How many?" I force the words through my teeth.

"I've opened up thirteen different lists, all with over a hundred names. This list dates back fifteen years. This operation has been around for a while, Cain. There's no way Gabriel's been dealing in this shit for that long. We would have caught it. Someone else is pulling the strings. I think that someone gave Gabriel the drive and instructed him to start collecting."

My vision swims with fury, blurring the screen in front of me. How could this have been going on so long in my city? We should have caught wind of this shit. Unless someone powerful was involved, helping with cover up.

"See if you can find any current records or names that haven't been crossed off a list. We could use them to head Gabriel off."

"I'll do my best. I need a fucking raise after this shit," Alaric mutters. "Or a gallon of bleach for my eyes."

Both Alaric and Rev deserve raises. Honestly, all of my staff deserve more than monetary compensation. They've stared evil in the face and never once backed down from it.

Head spinning after my call with my brother, I can't help but continue down the list, horrified by the amount of items crossed off. Kids taken from their lives, some willingly sold by the people they trusted most.

It tears my insides apart to think of the outcome for these kids, but I know the statistics. I know how many don't survive. And the ones who do? Spend their lives in slavery or in prison or on the streets addicted to substances to help them forget.

My hand hovers over Lemons, brain snagging on the lack of listed price, just an Out of Stock x 8.

Leo James

185 Northwind Ct

8 years old

The break in the pattern has me clicking on the image. Instantly, I regret it. The revealed photos crush me because I recognize that face. Know those hazel eyes on an intimate level. His bone structure has sharpened, but it's nearly impossible not to identify him.

Ezra.

I stare at his hollow expression in that first picture for what feels like years. Decades. Centuries. Time has no value anymore. I don't know if I'm blinking or breathing. Do I even exist?

Leo James.

And out of stock? What the fuck does that mean? Do I even want to know? Too many venomous emotions are already flooding through me when I type the address into Google. A tiny, worn Victorian home pops up, and when I dig into the homeowner listed, I come to learn that she's a foster parent. Which means she's had access to other kids.

I slam a fist down on my keyboard, cracking it in half. Scooting my chair away from my desk, I surge upright and pick up my thermos. I hurl it at the wall. Coffee splatters over the paint, dripping down onto the carpet.

What the *fuck* have I done?

Ezra. *My Ezra.* His name is on that *fucking* list. There's no way. This has to be some sick joke.

Rev peeks his head into my office. I had no idea he was working late, but it shouldn't have surprised me. "Routine evening meltdown? Is this a solo thing, or can I start throwing shit, too? I've always hated that potted plant in the walkway."

His eyes cut to it like it's plotting his murder. With as many times as he's tripped over it, I'm beginning to think it has a conscience.

"Ezra was a victim of trafficking," I blurt out, feeling my breath getting away from me. "He's on that fucking drive."

Christ, if Gabriel had cared enough to dig through old records on the drive, would he have recognized Ezra, too? It makes me sick thinking about how close these monsters were to him.

I rip my hands through my hair as Rev's expression crumples. With silent movements, he comes around my desk and takes in the photo of young Ezra on my screen, perched on a stained velvet couch like he was posed for fucking holiday pictures.

"Oh, shit."

"Yeah. Oh, shit," I retort. "I... we... we've been messing around, and I shouldn't have... I should have never touched him, Rev."

Rev struggles for the right words to fix this, but he's the wrong person for the job, never one to be able to calm me when I spiral out of control. He's always just let me rage. "You didn't know. Ezra would have told you if he didn't want that."

"Would he?" I snap back, needing Rev to be mad at me. Needing someone to punish me for what I've done. Ezra was a fucking *victim*. "Or was he brainwashed into submitting to monsters like me?"

"He trusts you, Cain."

"And I've done nothing but hurt him!" I shout back.

"If that's what you want to believe." Rev's bright eyes drill into me. "What do you need, Cain? You need me to call up Isaac? I don't know what to say to make it sink in that nothing you did was done maliciously. Ezra had a choice. Ezra *wants* you. And you flipping your shit because you found out something from his past, is only going to upset him in the worst way possible. You're going to convince yourself to create distance, and it's going to upset him. He *needs* you."

Rev's speaking words that make too much fucking sense for someone clinically diagnosed as a psychopath. I can't stay in this office any longer knowing what's on my fucking computer. That Ezra might be alone right now.

I storm out of the office, headed for my apartment. I find Ezra curled up on the couch, reading a book about travel I bought him because I know he dislikes my books about business.

I drop to my knees in front of him, emotion strangling my throat.

"Cain? What's going on?" Ezra asks, brows furrowing.

"Can I hold you?"

I need the warmth of his skin to know he's alive, but I hate myself for asking to put my hands on him.

"Always." He draws me into his arms, and I bury myself against his chest. He strokes a hand through my hair. "You're scaring me."

"Sorry, I just need to do this for a while. Is that okay?"

Ezra pats a hand on his thigh. "Come up here."

I draw back only to remove my suit jacket and shoes. Then I plop down on the couch with my head on his lap like he instructs.

Here I rest. Cain Vincent. Ex-military. Current CEO and mercenary. Calculative and vicious. Snuggling up on the couch like some domesticated animal. Burning up inside because the guy I like was submitted to such a horrible thing, and I can't ever make that go away for him. I can't change what was done to him. Can't change what I've seen or how I feel about it.

"This should be reversed," I say weakly.

"What, I'm not allowed to pet you?" Ezra muses, rustling my hair.

"I feel selfish letting you do it."

His body stiffens beneath me. "Okay, something is really wrong with you tonight. I don't think I can sit here and continue this if you don't talk to me."

I take his hand and bring it to my mouth, pressing a kiss to the scars on his wrist.

"Alaric got into the hard drive. There were... pictures. Old records of kids trafficked. Pictures of... you."

Ezra's fingers tighten around the strands of my hair. I want him to hurt me. Want him to scream and claw and lose his cool.

His voice is terrifyingly calm when he finally speaks. "It's in the past."

"Ezra."

"I don't want to talk about it. I got out. I'm here now. I'm learning how to save others. That's enough for me. You're enough for me."

I close my eyes and practice slow breaths.

"Cain. Please don't make this a thing. I can't have it being a thing." His words are strained. "Do you understand? I need you to keep looking at me. Need you to keep touching me. Grounding me. You take all of that away because of something that feels like another fucking lifetime to me, and I might actually fall apart."

I feel his tears dropping on my head. Clutching his thigh, I give it a couple squeezes. If I look at him right now, I know I'll fucking dissolve.

"Okay," I whisper, closing my eyes as exhaustion sinks. "Just know, Leo did *nothing* to deserve what happened to him."

CHAPTER TWENTY-TWO

EZRA

I rest my head back on the couch, hot tears streaming from my eyes as Cain sleeps on my lap, and the world falls horribly silent.

Pictures of you, Cain's voice echoes in my head.

It's revolting, the whole idea of trafficking. That an entire ring exists here in this city. I thought I was an anomaly, but my time at Sinro has proven that to be a fallacy. I was so wrapped up in myself, scraping through life that first year after my escape, that it hadn't occurred to me there might be other kids suffering.

It just gives greater weight to what I'm doing here, training to hopefully save them from monsters.

Beneath that intense desire to become something powerful, I'm angry. So fucking angry that Cain saw me that way. I don't want this to change how he handles me. How could he not think I'm defiled? Tainted?

Broken. Broken. Broken.

I hold back a groan. I'd done well to keep it all shoved down. The panic, yeah, that's always fighting to break free, and sometimes it does. A lingering side effect of the torture I endured.

I extract myself from Cain on the couch, careful not to let his head plop on the cushion. Then I'm scavenging the kitchen for something sharp to bleed out this awful, sick feeling roiling in my chest.

"Ezra?"

My brain doesn't register Cain's words, only my actions as I yank open drawers. I upheave silverware in search of a knife. I rip pots and pans out of cabinets, hurling them onto the concrete floor. Why does he have so much shit to cook with?

"Ezra. Baby. What's wrong?" Cain demands, pushing off the couch into view.

Everything! Everything's fucking wrong!

I find a knife and press it against the inside of my forearm, lining it up between pearlescent scars. Cain's dark eyes flick to the blade. Fear carves into his normally harsh features, and my heart drops in my chest. Why is he so twisted up over this? Why does he care?

"Ezra. Stop."

I shake my head frantically. "I can't," I whisper, tears blurring my vision.

I'm not in control. Not when I'm a slave to my demons. I ache for relief from everything bubbling and churning and heaving inside of me. Emotions I can't give names to. They don't seem to want to rest. My abuse happened fucking years ago. It shouldn't define me, right? Why can't I just be fucking normal?

My vision is so blurred with tears that I don't catch him moving. His hand ensnares my wrist before I can make the first cut, knocking the knife onto the floor. Cain spins me and hauls my back against his chest, wrapping his long arms around me to keep me still.

I start screaming.

I just want to stop feeling.

I need something to turn off my brain.

Need to focus on the pain and not the things I don't know how to fucking process.

Need to split my skin to bleed *him* all out of my fucking DNA.

He had no right to touch me. To do those awful things to me. No right.

But nobody cared.

I tear into Cain's inked forearms with my fingernails, leaving tracks of blood. He just clutches me tighter as he slides both of our bodies to the floor. I'm blanketed in him, and still I'm fighting against his hold.

I should be embarrassed. This behavior isn't okay. It's childish, fueled by too many explosive emotions warring for attention inside of me.

Cain doesn't waver. He holds me through my meltdown. Holds me until my body finally tires of losing against his iron grip. With heavy breaths, I slouch against him.

He rests his forehead against my shoulder. "What is it, baby? Talk to me. Please. What do you need?"

"I need... I just need..." Words won't even come out right. My brain feels scrambled. Though I'm no longer flailing, I'm still burning up on the inside. "I need to fight."

"Okay. Done. I'll call Rev."

"No!" I jerk away from him enough to meet his pained expression. "I need to fight you."

"Ezra, I'm not going to—"

"Prove that this doesn't change things between us!"

Cain huffs out a frustrated breath. "I wouldn't have fought you before those pictures, okay?"

I tense. "Because I'm weak."

"Because I'm dangerous!" Cain snaps back. "Because I don't want to hurt you. I've never wanted to hurt anyone, and now it's the only thing I know how to do!"

I rest a hand on his sternum, feeling his heart beating rapidly. The gold in his dark eyes looks molten as he stares down at me.

"Please, Cain," I beg. "This is what I need."

Cursing, he rises to pace his kitchen, leaving me puddled on the floor. Just when I think he's going to refuse me, he storms to the front door and slams it open.

"Let's go," he orders. "Before I fucking change my mind."

Silently, we make our way to the gym. We square up in the ring, both shirtless and barefoot. It's way more intimate than I would have expected. Cain is honed in on my every movement, those beautiful, deep, soulful eyes tracking me like a hunter.

The promise of pain to come helps to center me. Makes me feel in control again.

I know this is fucked up, forcing him to hurt me. I know I won't win. But I also can't move forward, thinking Cain might treat me differently. That he might constantly be thinking about those disgusting pictures.

Cain strikes first, landing a shot to my ribs. It's powerful, but I know he's holding back.

I jab at him, skimming his jaw with my knuckles as he ducks to the side. Adrenaline pulses through me, and I swing with my left hand. I hit him in the side, but it barely has an effect.

Shaking out my knuckles, I bite down on my bottom lip and mimic his dance around the ring.

Cain strikes again. This time he hits me twice. Once in the cheek. Another blow to my jaw. Heat rushes to both spots where I can now feel my pulse throb.

Muscles in Cain's jaw flex, but he doesn't lower his fists.

Good.

I send three rapid punches his way, surprised when I make his head crack back. Instinct has me lowering my hands, worry for Cain replacing my anger.

But Cain flashes a wicked grin, all dark and mysterious and sexy. "Fuck, that was a good shot."

I bounce on my feet, unable to stop my grin. "Yeah?"

"Yeah. Do it again, baby."

Overeager from his praise, I rush him and try an uppercut. He dodges and lands a shot to my kidney. The pain is explosive, and I fight to stay on my feet.

I whirl in time to catch a fist to the face, blood spurting from my nose. I'm too focused on this fight and the way his lethal body stalks me around the ring to care.

I charge him, wrapping my hands around his solid waist, determined to take him down. Pride fills me when I drop him to his ass. My body goes with him, plastered against his chest. Cain lets out a full laugh. I don't think I've ever heard such a wonderful sound.

He positions me on his lap. His hands come to rest on my waist, brushing over my skin in a way that lets me know we're done fighting.

He grabs his shirt from the floor to wipe at my nose. "You're a mess, baby."

I brush fingers over the bruises forming on his chin and cheek. "You're looking pretty hot yourself."

His throat bobs. "You good now?"

I nestle my head into the crook of his warm neck. "Yeah, I'm good. Will you do that again if I get like that?"

Cain doesn't answer for a while. "No promises."

After he kisses my temple, he brushes his mouth over my throbbing, bruised knuckles. "Can you tell me why you got so upset?"

My face scrunches up. "It definitely changes things, right? Like, how could you not look at me differently?"

Cain tugs at the hair along the back of my neck hard enough to get a gasp out of me. "It changes nothing. Do I need to fuck you to prove to you how distractingly sexy I find you?"

Straightening up on his lap, I fail to hide a smirk. "You think I'm sexy?"

He leans in to nip at my bottom lip. Then my jaw. "Ezra, I get hard just saying your name."

Wrapping my hands around the back of his neck, I roll my hips against him. "Say my name then, Mr. Vincent."

"Ezra. Beautiful boy. You're playing with fire right now," Cain murmurs.

I tangle my fingers in his dark hair, rooting myself to him. "Fuck me good, so we can both sleep tonight. Please."

His eyes circuit my face. "Only if you promise to tell me if it's ever too much. I need that from you."

I nod. "I promise."

Cain flips us so he's pinning my body to the floor. He drags my sweatpants off, flinging them to the side, and grips my thighs to spread them, exposing me.

I flush with heat. "Shit. Right here?"

He lowers his head to swipe his tongue over my rim without warning, and I hiss. He groans like I'm the best thing he's tasted, sending blood straight to my dick.

Cain works his tongue from my hole up to the tip of my hard cock and back down again. He repeats this path until I'm shuddering with need, and then he spears his tongue inside of me.

"Oh my god. Who came up with this? They deserve... shit, they deserve a medal." I moan as he thrusts his tongue in and out. "If we would all just... Jesus, if everyone ate ass, we'd have world peace."

Cain has to pause to laugh. Quickly, he slips back into a feral state, spitting on my hole and slowly stretching me with two fingers. It burns at first, but I'm too wrapped up in the sight of him between my legs to care.

He lifts up enough to tug his pants down and slick his thick cock with lube from a small packet in his wallet. I'd tease him about having it on him all this time, but that switch in my brain creeps up toward panic at the thought of his intrusion.

I'm not scared of the pain. Never have been. It's my mind that frightens me. What it might dredge up. The chaos it threatens to unleash, winding me up so tight until I become what Cain likes to call me. *A destructive tornado.*

Cain brings me back to a place of only pleasure as he strokes me slow and hard in his big hand. I push out a long breath to further relax my body.

I recognize his touch. His smell. His warmth. His kind soul. I trust him fully.

"You don't want it, we stop," Cain says, fixing his intense, pretty brown eyes on mine. My toes curl as he notches himself against me.

"You know I need it. Need you," I whisper.

Cain eases his tip inside of me. Slow and steady, he works his cock deeper, fighting the resistance of my body. It does burn, but I don't hate the full sensation. Don't mind him stretching me to fit him.

"You good, baby?" His voice is already edged with lust, and it makes my pulse throb under my hot, sweaty skin.

"Fucking magical." I clutch at his forearms, trying to pull him deeper. "No, really. This is good. So good, Cain."

When his hips are flush against my ass, he starts a brutal rhythm. He pushes his cock so far inside of me, I can't help but cry out with every punishing thrust of his body. My hands claw at his chest and his muscled arms as he keeps my thighs pinned against my body.

Cain leaves no doubt in my mind that he's not scared to wreck me. He pulls out of me to flip me onto my stomach, dragging my ass up into the air so he can fuck me from behind. One hand keeps my chest pressed to the ground while the other wraps around my dick.

"Oh, god. Cain." I shudder, my thighs and abs quivering.

He strokes me in rhythm with his thrusts, angling his hips to send waves of pleasure rushing through me, from my dick all the way down to my toes. The slick sound of him moving in and out of me and our skin colliding as he fucks me hard have me at the edge in no time.

"I'm too close," I whine, trying to smack his hand away from jerking me off.

"Fuck no," his voice rumbles. "That cum is mine."

He turns me over and drops down to deep-throat my cock. He suctions so hard, I nearly black out when my orgasm hits. I buck up into his mouth as moans spill from my parted lips.

My body is still tingling with warmth when he finishes swallowing my cum.

"Love your sounds," Cain murmurs, leaning over me to brush his lips against mine as he pushes his cock back inside of my ass. "Tell me this pretty, tight hole is mine."

"Yours." I nod and grab him behind the neck to crush our mouths together, tasting my release on his tongue. I suck it off, and Cain slams his hips against me one last time, hard enough to bruise, groaning as he spills inside of me.

His elbows brace most of his weight when he rests his body on top of me and cradles my face in his hands. We lay there until we both catch our breaths, just staring into each other's eyes.

When Cain pushes up onto his feet, he tugs me with him and helps me slip on my pants. He holds my hand as we walk back to his apartment, shirtless and covered in blood and cum.

I startle at the figure sitting in the common area in the dark. Rev innocently sips at a cup of coffee on the couch, a book held in his other hand.

Cain rolls his eyes. "You're depraved, you know that?"

"What?" Rev says, lowering his mug from his mouth.

"You're holding the fucking book upside down," Cain says, and I giggle when Rev looks at the cover with feigned surprise. Then he breaks into a grin. "Caught red-handed. Sorry, I heard the commotion. Got caught up in the show."

My cheeks heat, and Rev gives me a wink.

Cain flips him off and slaps my ass hard enough to launch me down the hall. "Bed. Now."

"Goodnight, Rev," I call behind me.

His reply floats after us. "It was indeed."

CHAPTER TWENTY-THREE

EZRA

Heavy knocking wakes me in the morning. Groaning, I stumble out of bed and open the front door to find Rev beaming at me. He shoves a giant iced coffee in my hand, topped with whipped cream and drenched in caramel.

"I went easy on the sugar for you. Don't want you shaky on your first day playing with firearms."

"This is easy on the sugar?" I frown, staring down at the drink.

I'm not sure if we should address last night's incident, but Rev doesn't seem the slightest bit embarrassed about getting caught. Suppose if he was willing to have sex in the common area, he really doesn't give much thought to privacy. Or boundaries.

I slip on my combat boots and follow Rev down to lower level two. He presses his thumb against a security pad beside the first heavy steel door. When it swings open, I gape at the bright white interior, teeming with weapons. Three walls house glass cases for guns and blades of all kinds. The other wall stretches about a hundred feet down, broken up by hanging targets.

"It's like a shopping mall for killers," I say, wandering over to an expensive wooden table covered in handguns, rifles, and heavy-duty plastic boxes of ammunition. My fingers trace the curved handle of a serrated blade.

"Cain wants you to learn how to shoot a gun before he shows you how to play with knives. Honestly, I think he's just worried he'll end up fucking you instead of teaching you. Pretty sure knives turn him on." Rev winks, and my brows shoot up into my hairline.

"Um, can I opt for knives first, please?"

Rev chuckles and licks the excess whipped cream from his plastic coffee cup lid. "He that good for you, pretty boy?"

Flushing with heat, I peek into one of the ammunition boxes. My eyes shoot wide open at the size of the bullets. They're as long as my thumb.

Rev shuts the lid on that box. "Outside fun only, I'm afraid. Alright. We'll start with the basics."

He walks me through parts on all the guns. We disassemble and clean a few of them. It's tedious, and I don't always remember where the pieces go, but Rev's a thorough teacher, never once losing his calm.

After I load bullets into a magazine, Rev hands me ear protection. I drape them around my neck as he motions me over to the firing line. Paper targets—black silhouettes of people—dangle from the ceiling about thirty feet away in each individual shooting lane.

Before Rev can get me into position, the door to the range swings open, and Cain strides in, looking like a professional hitman in his navy suit, silky tie, and dark leather shoes.

"Please don't ruin my fun," I plead when his gaze drops to my hands as I shove the magazine into the gun. "I thought you had meetings all day."

He strips off his fancy jacket. Resting it on the back of a chair, he gets to work unbuttoning his cuffs next. My throat tightens at the sight of his muscled, tattooed arms when he rolls his sleeves up.

"Yeah, Cain," Rev says, fake pouting. "Thought you had meetings."

In a smooth move, he positions himself between me and Rev. "I'm learning to offload. Plenty of employees champing at the bit to prove themselves and earn that corner office."

With a hand on my lower back, Cain moves me up to the firing line. "Finger off the trigger, Ezra. Check that your safety is off. Good. Now take aim at your target."

I glance over at Rev who just gives me a wink and heads over to the table to prep his own guns.

Lifting the pistol, I gaze down the steel top and do my best to line up a good shot. Cain adjusts my arms, loosening up my elbows. He squares my shoulders and hips with the target. His hands linger every time he puts them on me.

Having him draped around me really fucking turns me on. Apparently, clutching a dangerous weapon does the same. Yeah, my heart is thudding fast, but not with fear.

Most of my life, I've been helpless. At the mercy of evil's hands, without rights and without means to defend myself.

But right now, I hold all the power.

"Go for it," Cain says, moving to my side.

The first shot I fire jolts my heart. My arms buzz from absorbing the impact of the explosion, but I don't break from my position. I'm not even sure what I'm waiting for. Maybe for someone to tell me that I did something right?

"Ezra, baby," Cain murmurs.

Something flutters around in my chest. I focus on my target, spotting the hole I made in the neck. An absolute rush comes over me. Like that destructive, negative energy churning inside of me was just blasted out of the gun in my hand.

Aiming again, I fire until I run out of bullets, only missing one shot to the head.

When I glance over at Rev, I beam at the surprise in his face. And when I look at Cain, there's only pride as he gives me a slow smile.

"Huh." Rev slams a loaded magazine into his gun and cocks it. "Honestly thought you'd be better suited for knives. I wanted to see you go off like a little ninja cat."

"I like sharp things, too," I say.

"Oh, kitten. You *are* trouble," Rev praises, waggling his eyebrows at Cain.

Cain sighs. "Let's stick with the basics first. He hasn't been with us that long."

"And he's already showing considerable promise. That bonus check can come anytime." Rev clips more loaded magazines onto his belt. "Guy was born for this."

Not true at all.

I was molded. Shaped by experiences I didn't choose. I was dealt a horrible hand in life, and now I'm going to make sure shitheads that hurt people are wiped from the earth.

"Now that you've got a feel for the gun, let's make some more corrections." Cain motions me back up to the firing line. "A hard thing to overcome is the urge to grip the shit out of the gun with your dominant hand and control the trigger."

Again, he moves into my space. I love that he towers over me. I fiddle with my lip ring, allowing him to touch me freely. He rests the handle of the gun between my thumb and index finger on my right hand and helps me wrap my left hand around my right fingers.

"Now, smoothly pull the trigger back until you hit resistance."

My hands shake as I do, my body bracing for the blast.

"Nothing's going off until you ease that finger back more, okay? Try again."

He slips my ear protection over my ears, then steps aside. When I pull the trigger this time, I see the difference proper form makes.

"Holy shit." I stare at the hole in the target's forehead. Who knew this could be such a thrill? I'm already obsessed. "Can I do this all the time?"

Cain chuckles. He leans in to press a kiss to the corner of my mouth. "My beautiful, destructive little tornado."

"God, you two are cute," Rev says, holding up a gun in each hand.

Flashing a grin, Cain nods me over to the table to reload as Rev shoots up his target. Then he sets me loose again after correcting my posture and grip.

I shoot for hours, not satisfied until I'm able to cluster my shots. My arms quiver from effort, and I take that as my sign to rest. I can't stop smiling like a fool.

"Hey, pretty boy. Want to watch me slaughter your man in a little friendly shooting competition?" Rev asks.

Sucking down a big gulp of my coffee, I hop up on the edge of the table. "Yes. Yes, I do."

Cain runs a hand through his hair, which seems to enjoy rebelling against his styling pomade. One lock of dark hair curls over his forehead. It's obscenely hot.

Rev spins one of his pistols around his hand. "Cain thinks he's a better shot, but he's dead wrong."

"Quit your shit talking and take your fucking shots," Cain retorts. He cracks his knuckles as he moves to the wall of more intimidating guns, removing what Rev told me was an AR-15 Platform—Cain's favorite gun.

The way Cain handles it, running his large hands over the black steel, shouldn't have me burning up on the inside, but I like that he takes time to appreciate details.

"Nope. No way," Rev calls out. "Handguns only."

A lethal edge transforms Cain's face. "Handguns. Then rifles. Fair fight."

Rev's smile slips, revealing the cold killer beneath. "Whatever, cowboy."

Lifting his right pistol, Rev lands a shot between the target's eyes. He does the same with his left pistol. Back and forth he alternates firing, hitting the same exact spot. My jaw drops in awe of his perfect aim with the seemingly lazy way he's shooting.

I watch Cain's confident movements as he steps up to the firing line in another bay. He repeats the pattern. Six shots with his right hand. Then he reloads and shoots the same gun with his left. His body is so fluid, his shots faster than I can even process.

Imagining Cain in action outside of an office setting, dressed in black tactical gear, has me practically drooling. I want to see that so bad.

Rev moves from target to target, and I snap my ear protection off to hear them bickering.

"How is it you fucked up your last mission so badly, but you have near-perfect aim? You lying to me about being in meetings all day?" Rev asks, anger laced in his words.

"What, you think I'm sneaking off and dropping criminals in secrecy?"

Rev shrugs. "Wouldn't put it past you. Ezra, come determine the winner, please."

I rush over to study both targets, amazed by the consistent, clean pattern on both pieces of paper. "I really can't tell. I think it's a tie."

Rev growls, pretending to melt into the floor. "This is fucking bullshit. Pistols are *my* thing."

"Weapons, in general, are both of our thing. Now pick up that rifle," Cain demands with an unsettling grin that makes a shiver run down my spine. I've never wanted the weight of his body on me more.

Rev does as he says, and I perch on the table again, securing my ear protection. The targets are moved back to the seventy-five feet marker. Rev takes his time, lining up his shot through the scope. He fires several times before moving aside for Cain to take position.

Cain unloads his magazine, and once again I'm ordered to the firing line to determine the winner. Before I can even push the words out, Rev mumbles, "Fucking ex-Special Forces bastard."

My brows lift as I look over at Cain, soaking in his lethal body. I knew he was in the military, but Special Forces? What had Cain been exposed to during his service? Probably doesn't make for easy small talk.

Rev drops his gun on the table and jabs a finger at my chest. "I expect to see you in the gym tomorrow during lunch."

Shrinking under his unhinged intensity, I nod. "Wouldn't miss it."

Rev strides out of the room, and Cain retrieves his suit jacket. "Not sure how late I'll be this evening. Order in food, if you want. My credit card's on the kitchen table."

He leaves me then, too. Ok, so he's still hot and cold. I really shouldn't have expected anything more.

Sighing, I check the wall clock. Three hours to kill and a seemingly endless supply of ammunition at my disposal. Maybe this night is salvageable.

CHAPTER TWENTY-FOUR

CAIN

The crack of a gun lurches me upright in bed. Instinct has me grabbing for my own weapon tucked in the drawer of my nightstand. My other hand reaches for Ezra and finds a cold, empty pillow.

No.

"Ezra?" I shout, ripping the sheets off the bed, willing my eyes to adjust to the darkness. Once they do, I spot him curled up near the end of the bed. Air whooshes from my lungs.

Ezra sits up, blinking and rubbing a hand through his mess of hair. "What's wrong?"

His hazel eyes meet mine, widening when they drop to the gun clutched in my hand.

Coated in a sheen of icy sweat, I'm still panting, though the wave of terror has receded.

"Fuck," I utter, ruffling my hair. "Just a dream."

His shocked eyes move from the gun back up to my face.

"Cain," he murmurs, his features scrunching up. "Are you... oh, no. No, no, no."

He crawls over to my side of the bed to straddle me. Stroking his fingers down my tattooed arms, he eases the gun out of my hand. Before he places it on my nightstand, he checks the safety.

All the while, I'm unable to move. The urge to tell him to go back to sleep sticks in my mouth. My tongue is swollen, my body limp like my bones have been excavated from muscle and flesh.

He tries to push me down flat on the bed, but I keep my back plastered to the headboard, not ready to slip into sleep knowing what my brain will make me see again, too many bodies for one man to have claimed without sacrificing his soul.

Ezra brushes locks of hair from my sticky forehead. He swipes at the dampness along my cheeks. Brows furrowing, I touch a hand to my cheek and find them wet with tears.

Ezra pets me for a while until my adrenaline drains.

"I thought that you... I thought I hurt..." I sigh, giving in to the smooth touch of his hands all over my skin. The comforting weight of him on top of me. "It doesn't matter. You're safe."

"I am," Ezra confirms. "Always safe with you."

I kiss his perfect mouth, wondering how he can walk through this world with such enviable lightness when he's experienced horrendous abuse.

I'm going to pick Gabriel apart like a vulture. And whoever is actually pulling the strings on this fucked up operation? Yeah, I'm going to spend some quality time introducing them to pain before I claim their soul, too. Add it to my fucking collection.

Sensing my rising anger, Ezra cups my face in his hands. He tips my head until our lips meet for a delicate kiss.

"You are so brave," I whisper, kissing him over and over again. "So incredibly strong."

Ezra's slow smile is everything. It moves the scar I cut into his face higher, and I brush my thumb over it. "I hate that I did that to you."

He wraps his hand around my wrist. "I don't. It's proof that this was real when you decide I'm not good enough for you and kick me out."

My face twists up, those fucking tears still leaking out of me. How long has it been since I've cried? Since Aiden's death? Did I even cry then, or was I still too angry over his betrayal?

"Baby, I need you to do something for me, okay?" I say.

He nods eagerly, running his soft hands over my brows and along my jawline. His touch is everywhere, like he can't get enough of me. Like he's trying to memorize the shape of me.

"Isaac wants to meet with you. Regularly. And I want that, too," I explain, praying he doesn't fight me on this.

Isaac told me he'd talked to Ezra about his position at Sinro, but he hadn't approached the topic of offering services just yet.

Ezra fiddles with his lip ring, his hands sliding down to trace circles over my bare chest. "You think he can straighten me out?"

I pinch his little piercing between my fingers, moving the ball back into his mouth. "He makes living a hell of a lot easier."

Ezra cocks his head to the side. "To repeat your earlier words at *my* demand, no promises. But I will try. He seems nice enough."

When he snuggles into my chest, I pull the sheet up over our entwined bodies. I keep one arm draped over his waist and the other buried in his hair.

I had no choice in the matter of getting tangled up in Ezra. His chaotic nature sucked me in, and I know I won't ever be able to escape him. I am changed at the very center of my being.

Altered.

And it fucking terrifies me. There's always that chance of losing him, just like I lost Aiden.

Which is why I'm going to do my best to make Ezra bulletproof. I'm going to turn him into a fucking threat, mentally and physically. No one, not even me, will be able to break him.

"Sleep," Ezra hums. "I can hear the gears whirring in your head. I've got you, okay?"

I hold back a chuckle. He *really* fucking doesn't. I'm the trained soldier, after all.

But I drift to sleep, anyway, letting Ezra believe he can protect me.

CHAPTER TWENTY-FIVE

CAIN

I used to hate the concept of dating.

Not that I ever did much of it, but Aiden was addicted to the attention we got when we went out together. Rare to see two men of our caliber being affectionate out in public.

But when I wake up wrapped in Ezra, I have the sudden urge to do this right with him. I want to make him fucking lethal, but I also want to pamper him with the affection he deserves.

Carefully, I slide out from under his arm and leg, tucking the sheet back over him, and brew a big pot of coffee. I rest the phone I bought him on the counter next to a plate of strawberry crepes, watermelon, bacon, and scrambled eggs. Then I sneak down to the lower levels to retrieve a heavy black box from the armory.

Rev catches me heading back to the elevator as he steps out of the gun range. His gaze drags over my lounge wear, a smile curling on his lips.

"Shut the fuck up," I mumble before he can mouth off.

Unfazed, Rev says, "You know I'm happy for you."

"Didn't ask." I cut for the stairs in hopes that he won't follow me.

Rev keeps stride with me. "That your M9 Beretta? Haven't seen you take that one out in years."

A muscle in my jaw ticks as I start the climb up the stairs, eager to get my blood flowing and muscles working. "You can't keep words inside your body, can you?"

Rev's a few stairs below me. "Hell no. You're giving it to Ezra, aren't you? I know you're secretly a romantic."

I roll my eyes. "Yeah, cause giving a guy a gun is romantic."

"We're mercenaries." Rev flashes a grin. "Guns are our love language."

I can't help a little snort at that.

"Hey, I actually wanted to ask you if I could run him through an exercise with my team today. He's so fucking stealthy, Cain. He's going to be a mad threat when he's all trained up."

It's exactly what I want, but reality has a prickle of worry creating an itch inside my chest. I peek down at Rev in the middle of the stairs. "Do you think we're making a mistake?"

"What? Pulling him into our world?" Rev actually takes a moment to think about it. "He was already up in this shit. I think we're doing the best thing we can for him. No one will ever mess with him again."

My chest tightens at the thought.

"Anyone tried, I'd fucking gut them," I mumble.

Rev chuckles. "Sounds like love to me."

I sigh, then start climbing the stairs once more. "Go ahead and introduce him to your team."

"Cain?" Rev calls out. "Don't let anything hold you back from letting him know how much you care, okay? You both deserve this."

"Again, didn't ask. I'm sending him your way in an hour. Make him fucking hurt."

Laughter echoes through the stairwell, and he sings his next words, "Love language."

Ezra's still asleep when I return to my apartment. From the edge of the bed, I admire him. I revel in the fact that he finds peace in my bed when it seems like he struggled to do that in the guestroom.

His features are soft. Feminine. Stunning. And his body is becoming strong, cut along his arms and his torso. I'll have to find a way to thank Rev for that without him gloating about it.

I drag the sheets down his body. Lazily, his head turns to me to give me a peek. He smiles in approval, stretching out his legs. Then he tries to burrow his head under the pillow.

"Oh no. You want to work for me, you need to get up early in the morning," I say, unable to hide a devilish grin.

He groans. "Isn't it like the weekend or something? Shit, I don't even know what day it is."

I grip his ankles and drag him down to the end of the bed. Flipping him over, I groan at the sight of the hard ridge straining against the fabric of his pants.

Unable to help myself, I run my fingers down his bare, smooth chest. I trace the ridges of his stomach and end at the V carved down his hips.

Ezra stares up at me with those lust-filled hazel eyes, his full lips parted.

"So pretty," I murmur, leaning down to drag my tongue up his naval. "You are such a distraction. Can I taste you, baby?"

His nod is so enthusiastic, a faint smile plays on my lips. Hooking fingers into the waistband of his sweats, I tug them down, enjoying the way his cock bounces free.

I drop to my knees and take him into my mouth. He bucks his hips forward, crying out when I suck him hard and draw him deep. Every time I pull up, I swirl my tongue over the head of his cock, addicted to the words he's babbling.

"Fuck, this can't be real. I'm dreaming. Too fucking good. Oh god, I want it so bad, Cain. Please don't stop."

I hum around him, and his whole body shivers in response. Sliding my hands around to sink fingers into his lush ass, I take him in long strokes.

His hands snap to my hair, gripping me as he thrusts up into my mouth. "Coming. Oh fuck, I'm gonna come."

He explodes on my tongue, his cock pulsing for what feels like an eternity. Greedily, I swallow down everything he has to give me.

When I pull away, I grin at the satisfaction on his face. He reaches for my pants, tented with my own aching erection, but I step back.

"I want to do it to you," he whines, sucking on that lip ring in a way that drives me crazy.

"No chance, baby. Your breakfast is getting cold, and I have a surprise for you."

My little tornado pops upright and bursts out of the bedroom. I catch him leaping up onto the counter to start digging into the food I prepared.

Rev's words replay in my head. *You both deserve this.*

I don't feel like I deserve anything. It's been years since I've let anyone into my life this far, and even when I had Aiden, I sucked at doing anything right. I was still the cold businessman when I walked through the apartment door at night, unable to detach my mind from work when Aiden just wanted to spill about his day.

I join Ezra in the kitchen and motion to the phone and the black case I placed on the counter.

"What's this?" he asks, eyes wide.

"Your new toys."

He sits there motionless for a while, and I worry that I took things too far too soon.

"Ezra."

He runs his fingers over the phone. Then he flips the locks on the gun case and opens it. His features light up with such joy, and my nerves settle. This was definitely the right decision.

While I still can't process the fact that I discovered his name on that drive, or comprehend how he survived on the streets, emotionally battered and caring for an elderly man with medical needs, I can only anticipate what he will become given the right guidance and training.

"No need to keep borrowing guns from the range now."

Ezra closes up the box and rests his cheek against it. "This is a real Cinderella story, isn't it?"

I smirk. "I'd like to think you're more of a morally gray hero."

After getting dressed, I rejoin Ezra in the kitchen. My brows shoot up at the black ring that somehow appeared on the counter next to his plate.

I'd forgotten I still had the wedding band I'd bought for Aiden. I honestly don't even know why I kept it, only that it seemed cruel to throw it away after removing every other piece of him from my life when he died.

"Sorry, I found it that first day," Ezra admits, unable to meet my eyes. "I'm done stealing. I promise."

My mouth dries as I pick up the ring and turn it in my hand. A long breath escapes me. "It's okay. That chapter of my life ended a long time ago."

I drop the ring in the trash and walk over to tip Ezra's chin up so I can kiss him. There's a spot of whipped cream at the corner of his mouth. I slide my tongue over it to lick it up.

"Is it inappropriate to ask if I can blow you now?" Ezra asks, eyes still heavy from sleep and his orgasm.

I chuckle. "Rev was right. You *are* a threat."

"Only when I'm left to my own devices. You're not leaving me alone today, are you?"

"Nope. You have special training with Rev, and then I'm taking you out tonight."

His brows quirk. "Out?"

"That's all I'm telling you, so don't even try batting those lashes at me."

Tearing my gaze away from his overwhelming fucking cuteness, I move to grab my phone off the counter. Something hits me hard in the back, and I can't help but laugh as his arm snakes around my throat to try to choke me out.

As gently as I can, I heave his body over my shoulder and drop him onto his back, cradling his head so it doesn't hit the floor.

He lets out a grunt, and I grin down at him. I spin him around until our bodies are lined up. A perfect fucking fit.

I force his legs up to his chest as I press my hard cock against his ass. "Maybe I should cancel our date, hmm?"

His eyes shoot wide, and he frantically shakes his head. "No, don't do that! I want it!"

Dropping down to press a kiss to the throbbing pulse point in his neck, I murmur, "Then be a good boy today."

CHAPTER TWENTY-SIX

EZRA

A good boy apparently runs through exercises with a team of mercenaries in the lower levels of Sinro Enterprises.

Rev introduces me to his team. Kate, a tall, dark-haired, intimidating woman, appears to be his right-hand. She takes up barking out orders when Rev spends time going over signals with me. She doesn't greet me like the others. I assume she thinks I'm deadweight.

But when Rev has me run through a training course on my own, set up to mimic infiltrating a house, I sneak in a window and take down all the targets without missing a shot. I do it in record time, spurred by the memory of my escape and what I witnessed on Cain's computer.

"Alright, where'd you find this guy?" Kate asks.

"You should recognize someone from your own stomping grounds, Kate," Rev replies, popping a wad of gum.

Her hawkish green eyes land on me, and I see a flicker of acknowledgement there. I give her a timid smile.

As a group, we run through another exercise to reach a victim locked up in a room at the center of a concrete maze. Half the team is designated to the rescue, and the other half are enemies.

It's different to rely on others. Difficult to determine when that figure popping around the corner is a teammate and not a threat. I've only ever operated alone.

But our rescue squad manages to make it to the victim, and I pick the lock on the door before Kate can even get her kit out.

I can't put into words the way this work makes me feel. I'm just satisfied to have purpose again. Jakey might not need me anymore, but there are other people out there that do.

Buzzing from the victory and coated in sweat, Rev checks his watch. "Mr. Vincent's waiting for you. Good job today, pretty boy."

"Thanks." I grin, then book it for the stairs, racing all the way up to the seventeenth floor.

Sure enough, Cain's sitting on a stool at the island, scrolling through his phone. He's got on a pair of black slacks that hug his massive thighs and a dark v-neck sweater under his peacoat.

Walking in to him waiting on me makes my heart throb in the best way possible. I can imagine a future like this. Nights coming home from work where we get to cook dinner and work out and shoot guns and fuck around with each other.

Cain looks me over and cocks a brow. "Go good, then?"

"So good." I nod. "Need a shower."

Darting for the bathroom, I scrub my body clean. I pull on the fanciest hunter green sweater Eduardo picked out for me and fitted black jeans with my combat boots.

Cain interlocks our hands and leads me out of the building to a flurry of snow tumbling from the sky. I drop my head back and let out a wild laugh as snowflakes kiss and melt on my skin. I know I have to be in a dream. Shit like this doesn't happen to me. I was never meant to have a happy ending.

Cain draws me against his chest. "What's going on in that head of yours?"

"I think... I'm happy."

He kisses my forehead. "Dates whenever you want them, okay?"

Taking my hand, he guides me down to the sidewalk. We walk the streets, admiring the lights and Christmas decor in the highrise window displays. I fill him in on my day with Rev, and he tells me about a new government contract to provide security for the mayor at a convention in a few weeks.

It's crazy to think about how many jobs he oversees. It makes me appreciate the time he carves out for me, knowing he's obsessive with his work.

We turn at the next intersection. Christmas music spills into the air from a giant skating rink. When Cain leads me to the skate rental booth, my brows raise.

"Are you serious?"

"If you want to do something else, we can," Cain says, frowning.

I rub a fist over my aching chest. "Ugh, I don't know if my heart can take this sweetness."

Relief floods Cain's face. "Oh, you're gonna take it, baby."

Skates tied to our feet, we wobble over to the edge of the rink. I grip the barrier wall with both hands, worried I'm going to make a fool of myself the second I step onto the ice.

Cain slides out with grace. He extends his hand to me. "Come on. I've got you."

His brown eyes hold me as I slip my hand into his warm one. He gives me a comforting squeeze.

Creeping onto the ice with his support, my feet somehow hold me upright on the thin metal blades. And after a slow circle around the rink, both of our athletic bodies find a good stride.

There's a deep-rooted pain spreading in my chest, but I don't think it's a bad one. I can't worry about what my future holds with this beautiful, dangerous man. Not when he's right beside me, clutching my hand like he doesn't ever want to let go. Sometimes he pulls me against him to twirl under the falling snow.

When the crowd thins out, we move over to a booth to buy hot chocolate loaded up with marshmallows. Cain sits sideways on the bench so he can keep his gaze on me.

"It's like you like me or something," I tease, heat flooding my cheeks.

Cain captures my jaw in his hand and turns my head to plant a kiss on my lips. "I love it when you're sassy. How did I do for our first date?"

Flustered, I blink back at him. "You did splendidly. Now can you please take me home so you can fuck me?"

The pad of his rough thumb moves over my bottom lip. "Such a pretty, filthy mouth. Actually, I wanted to ask you for a favor."

I straighten up. "Anything."

"I was hoping you'd come with me to visit my parents tonight."

"What!" The word comes out more of a squawk, and I smack a hand over my mouth, embarrassed by my outburst.

Cain averts his eyes. "You don't have to. No pressure."

"Um…" I give my lip ring a spin. "I've never done that before. I haven't even met my own parents."

His features twist with pain as he tugs my body closer on the bench. He kisses the top of my head. "My parents will love you, Ezra."

I squeeze my eyes shut. "What if I have a freak out moment?"

"They will understand. They've seen me at my worst, and it wasn't pretty."

I lift my head to look up at him, eyes narrowed like I can get a read on the darkest parts of his soul. "Angry?"

"Violent. And distant. I spent most of my twenties lost in my head."

I cup his face in my hands and kiss him. "Are they expecting me?"

"They're not even expecting me." Cain chuckles nervously and runs a hand through his dark locks. "We don't have to do this. Say the word and we go home instead."

His sudden discomfort has me popping up off the bench. I yank at his hand like I'm capable of moving his giant body. "Let's get this show on the road. I still want sex later."

"Christ, Ezra." Cain shakes his head with another laugh.

I'm not sure what I expected from Cain's parents, but running a commercial dairy farm outside the city wasn't in the realm of possibilities I'd conjured up.

Cain drives us down the mile-long gravel road, parking the Benz next to a sprawling craftsman home with a wrap-around porch. Isaac's sitting on the railing, chatting with a large man dressed in dark jeans and a red flannel shirt.

My stomach churns with nerves when their attention shifts to us as we climb out of the car.

"Ezra, you are a saint," Isaac says, giving us a wide smile. He's got on a slouchy hat that paints his dark locks to his forehead.

His physical similarities to Cain unnerved me the first time I met him, though he's a bit less put together, and he doesn't hold the same intimidating air as Cain. When Cain's present, everyone and everything revolves around him, caught in his gravity.

I fumble for a response, but I'm saved by Cain's father rushing off the porch. "Don't believe my eyes."

Cain meets him halfway with an extended hand, but his father clasps him into a tight hug, slapping at his back. "I've missed you, son. Your mother is going to be so happy. Lydia! Lydia, get out here right now!"

Indistinguishable yelling comes from behind the screened front door, revealing the cozy interior of the home. Pretty sure every fixture is on, spilling golden light out to push back the night.

I wait for the panic to hit me. I know I don't belong here. I belong on the other side of the river. I belong in ragged, stolen clothes. I belong in shelters and alleyways. My upbringing included four cement walls and a man who never shared his name, even after years of him owning me.

But there's no time to overthink and spiral out when Cain's father moves in front of me. He looks so much like Cain, too, that I can't help but relax. Or should I say, this is what Cain will look like in a couple of decades—tall, burly, salt-and-peppered, and handsome as all hell.

"Hello," I greet, accepting his handshake. "I'm Ezra."

Cain's father beams at me. "Nice to meet you, Ezra. I'm Will. Thank you for bringing my son home."

"Hey, I'm the one that planted the seed, okay?" Isaac complains.

The screen door bursts open, and a pretty woman with a plait of black hair leaps off the porch into Cain's awaiting arms with a heart-wrenching sob. "Don't you ever stay away from us that long again, you hear me? You know I can't handle the city. I'm sure that's why you holed up in the center of it," she scolds, tears streaming down her cheeks.

When Cain lowers her onto her heeled boots, she takes his face in her hands. "You look good, son. Real good."

"Yeah, I'm good. Ma, this is Ezra." He nods to me, and I'm swept up in a hug before anyone can warn her that I might lose my shit.

Only I don't. Because this touch is only meant to comfort. Her strong arms hold me together, and I can't help but wrap my own arms around her and nuzzle my head into her neck. She's the same size as me. I think the only one who missed out on the giant genes is Alaric, who seems to be missing from this reunion.

"This is nice," I murmur, and everyone chuckles.

"Lydia's a good hugger," Will says.

God, I really hope I don't find a way to fuck things up tonight. Part of me still wants to run away. Why would Cain bring me here with the threat of Gabriel's gunmen tailing me?

"You two hungry?" Will asks. "I made extra pork chops, and your ma made apple pie. She likes to test my willpower when I'm on a diet." He pats his flat stomach.

My mouth waters. "I'm starved."

Lydia's gaze cuts to Cain, and I see that same fire in her that dances at Cain's core. "Are you not feeding him properly?"

Cain sighs. "We were busy."

"Busy." Alaric snorts, appearing behind the screen door with a steaming mug in his hands. I catch the sharp look Cain directs at him.

Lydia wraps an arm around my shoulders, and I want to fucking cry. Shit, I *am* crying. Cain ruffles my hair as his mother clings to me.

"So sorry. Happy tears, I swear it," I mumble when Lydia takes my face in her hands like she did with her son. "This is all new to me."

"Oh, honey. Don't apologize. Come in and sit down at the table. Cain, are you two spending the night? Isaac and Alaric are."

Cain sighs and shoves his hands into his coat pockets. He tips his head up at the velvet night sky, and I follow his gaze, trying to puzzle out what's going on in that head of his.

"Didn't plan on it."

His response to his mother's simple request has me worried. Does Cain not visit home often? Did something happen between him and his parents? That seems unlikely from what I've observed so far.

I glance at Isaac and catch him frowning at his brother.

"We'd love to come back soon, if it's not too much trouble," I throw out, unable to stop myself.

Lydia rubs a hand up and down my arm. "Baby, we've got plenty of spare bedrooms here. You're welcome anytime."

Escorted inside, Cain's parents seat us at a worn table off the l-shaped kitchen and stuff us with enough food to make me question how long I'm going to have to work off all the calories.

After dinner, Isaac slaps a deck of cards on the table. "Alaric, get in here. You're playing hearts with us. No excuses."

Alaric groans but peels himself off the couch to join us.

"And Cain, put the phone away. Rev's more than capable of running that place for a few hours."

I giggle over Isaac's surprising bossiness. He seems to be the most vocal of the family.

Cain scowls but tosses his phone on the counter. "Fine. Don't know why you always insist on playing this game. You never win."

It's surprising how quick Isaac's attitude shifts when I end up winning most of the rounds.

"Hot wings for lunch?" I offer, hoping it'll be enough to earn Isaac's forgiveness for destroying him in cards.

He pouts. "Wings *and* beer."

I turn to Cain. "Can I have some money to buy Isaac lunch?"

Everyone but Cain bursts into laughter. Before he can open his mouth to complain, I lean over and peck a kiss to his lips. "Thanks."

Cain releases a low, frustrated chuckle as I hold up his wallet that I swiped from the pocket of his coat hanging on the back of his chair. "Little thief. I suppose we should talk about compensating you while you go through training. But I pay Isaac enough to buy his own damn food."

"Ezra, honey. Do you work for Sinro, too?" Lydia inquires.

Alaric and Isaac both snort.

"Cain, why don't you tell Mom how you held Ezra captive before you decided to bring him on as an unofficial, unpaid intern?" Isaac teases.

Both of Cain's parents look between me and Cain in surprise. I sink further into my chair. "I may have deserved it, sneaking into his company and all."

Alaric nods, sipping at the green martini Isaac made him. His face puckers. "Your attempt was quite entertaining to watch."

Cain's head snaps to Alaric. "So you *were* watching. I should fire you."

"No terminations at the dinner table, boys," Lydia commands. She turns her focus back on me. "Well, no matter how you met my Cain, I'm so pleased you're in his life."

I glance at Cain in time to see a twitch of a muscle in his jaw. I want to hound him for answers about why he seems distant from such a wonderful, loving family.

Soon, Alaric drifts off into the living room with Lydia to watch a Christmas movie, and Isaac goes to work making new cocktail creations that make me shudder. Cain ends up being ordered to the couch to sit on the other side of his mom. He motions me over, but I spot Will sitting in a rocking chair on the back porch alone and slip out to claim a chair beside him.

Will answers all of my questions about what the silos and barns hold, happy to detail out his operations on the farm. His laid back nature and skill with conversation remind me of Isaac.

"I don't think I've ever seen my son this content," Will says. The comment disturbs me because the word content doesn't really come to mind when I think of Cain. If this is him relaxed, I hate to think how unwell he was previously.

"I believe I have you to thank for that. So thank you, Ezra. From the bottom of my heart. I don't know how long you two have been together, but it's been a while since we've seen Cain. We worry about him."

"Because of how he was when he came home from serving?" I question, brows furrowing.

Will leans his head back against his chair as he rocks. "The country gained a hero when he enlisted, but we lost our son. He was such a sweet kid. Quiet and observant. I don't think he'll ever get back all the pieces he left out there in the world."

I'm speechless as that painful ache from earlier returns to my chest, and I come to believe it must be love. I'm in love with Cain. Shit. The very thought of him hurting has me wanting to scream into the chilled night sky.

"Sir, I should be thanking you for raising such a special man. He is so good to me."

Will sniffles. "That makes me happy to hear, Ezra."

We sit in comfortable silence until Cain comes out to check on us. Will rises from his chair and claps his son on the shoulder. "Headed to bed. Early morning. You guys are welcome to stay as long as you'd like."

"Appreciate it," Cain replies.

As soon as his father disappears inside the house, Cain strides over to plant his hands on my armrests and rocks me forward so he can kiss me long and hard. I'm left breathless, my eyelids fluttering. "They're smitten with you."

I snort. "I cried within minutes of meeting them."

"I ripped their front door off the hinges in a tantrum the last time I came home. They wouldn't let me leave until I had dessert."

"They're good people, Cain," I say softly.

He gives a little shake of his head. "I don't know what I did to deserve them."

I trace light fingers along his stubbled jaw. "Why do you stay away?"

Cain grimaces. "Because I bring dark clouds everywhere I go. Life after my service was tough. There's a serious lack of education on what to watch for when you come home. How hard those memories can slam into you. How the physiology of your brain has changed. How you might flip your fucking lid in the grocery store or over someone banging on your front door. I just wanted my parents to live in this bubble of happiness without me there to burst it. I assumed that meant I needed to remain out of the picture, at least until I leveled myself out after I lost Aiden. Ma just lectured me about all that, don't worry."

I grip the front of his sweater and tug him down so I can kiss him. "Thank you for sharing that, and thank you for bringing me."

"Always. You make me brave, Ezra," he murmurs, nipping at my jaw. The tip of his nose traces a line to the hollow behind my ear, causing me to shiver. "Now I think I'd like to take you home and sink my cock into your warm, tight body."

My heart skips and my breath catches. "Scandalous. I think I'd like that, too."

Scooping me up, Cain carries me through the house. He tosses out rushed goodbyes to his brothers, his mom already having snuck off to bed.

The drive into the city takes no time at all with his reckless speeding. I might be encouraging the danger with my hand stroking his hard cock through his pants. I even take him out and suck him into my mouth.

"Fuck. You're naughty." Cain sinks deeper into his seat. He groans in approval when I hum around him.

I keep him on edge until he parks the car. Then we burst into his apartment, mouths fixed together and bodies grinding in need of release. He hauls me over to the couch and drops me there. "Get naked, Ezra."

I fling off my sweater and struggle with the tight material of my pants as Cain disappears into the bathroom. He returns, stripped of his clothes. Struck by the beautiful shape of him, I almost miss the bottle he tosses on the couch when he sits down.

"Come here." His voice is a smooth, seductive rumble.

I waste no time climbing on his lap. The instant our cocks press together, my control snaps. I crash my mouth to his, and he devours me in return. My hands run over the rigid lines of his stomach. When I swipe fingers over his nipples, he growls and thrusts his hips up.

"God, you're so hard. Every bit of you," I whisper, wrapping my hand around his cock.

"And you are so sexy." Cain sinks his teeth into my bottom lip.

I hear the click of a bottle, and then his slicked up hand grips both of our cocks. His strokes are slow and deliberate, edging me toward catastrophic pleasure. I tilt my head back on a moan when his other hand glides down my ass to circle over my hole. He massages it, playfully dipping a finger in every now and then to set me off.

"Look at you, baby," Cain hums, running his warm, flat tongue up the column of my neck. "So fucking responsive."

"Fuck." I draw the word out.

"You good?" He trails teeth and lips and tongue over every inch of skin he can reach as he toys with my prostate and jerks us both off.

I dig my blunt nails into his shoulders and rock against him. "Yeah. Yes. Oh, fuck. Cain."

Cain presses a warm kiss behind my ear. "You wanna come all over my cock?"

My head jerks up and down. "Yeah, I want that."

"Go ahead, baby. Show me how you fall apart for me. My perfect little thief." His hand clenches us tighter. Between that and Cain beginning to unravel, panting and thrusting up against me, it's not long before I'm spilling on his cock and abs.

"Fuck, you are ruining me. You're so good for me." Cain claims my mouth again, right before his warm release shoots onto my stomach, dripping down to where our bodies are pressed together.

Panting, I rest my head on his collarbone. I keep my eyes squeezed shut, desperate to stay in the moment. I'm already so addicted to his touch, I don't think I could live without it. Without him.

Cain kisses my forehead. "Let's get you cleaned up."

He carries me into the shower. After we're both rinsed and dressed in loungewear, he lures me out of his bedroom by the hand.

"Go grab that throw blanket," he orders.

Brows furrowed, I do as he asks. When I return to the kitchen, Cain's waiting for me holding a bottle of wine and two fancy glasses.

I've never touched alcohol a day in my life. Never wanted to bring it around Jakey, what with his addictions and all.

Doesn't mean I'm not a little curious...

With the blanket draped over one of my shoulders, I let him guide me out of his apartment and onto the balcony. The nip of winter air has my teeth chattering instantly.

"Uh, Cain? I'm not really interested in becoming a human popsicle."

He smirks back at me. "Have a little faith in me."

Guided to a corner of the balcony, I spot an oversized outdoor couch covered in pillows and a large, concrete fire pit. String lights dangle from the building to the ledge over our heads. None of that was there the last time I came out to swim laps in the pool.

"You did this..." I start to say, trailing off as my chest swells with emotions.

"Sit, Ezra."

So I do, curling my entire body under the blanket on the couch. Cain sets the wine bottle and glasses on a small table before igniting the fire pit. Heat blazes over me, fighting back the cold, and I melt with a groan of pleasure.

Cain pours us both glasses of bubbling white wine, then settles in next to me. I throw out the blanket to cover us both, scooting against his body as I accept the glass with wide eyes.

"It's sparkling juice," Cain says.

"Oh."

"Sorry to disappoint. Alcohol's not something I ever want to dabble in again. I don't keep it on hand."

I shake my head frantically. "No, that's definitely best. I've never tried it, and maybe I never should."

Cain drapes his arm around me and pulls me closer. We sit in silence, gazing out at the city, warmed by the crackling fire.

I have never felt so relaxed or cared for in my entire life. Is this what normal humans experience? Is this what relationships are like? Because if so, I want this. Forever. So fucking bad it hurts.

I stroke my fingers over the pine trees inked into his arms. My lips curl up at the corner. "So much nature. And yet you live in the concrete jungle."

He turns his arm in the firelight, allowing me to trace the crows circling around sharp mountains reflected in a small lake.

"It was difficult when I first moved here. Crowds fucking sucked, but I needed time to adjust back into society without worried eyes on me all the time. Here in the city, I could hide. I could be anti-social. I could drown in work. No one looked at me twice if I was an off-putting asshole."

He sinks fingers into my hair, gently stroking over my scalp. "My parents have a big patch of pine trees on their property. My brothers and I used to build forts out of the fallen sticks. Our favorite game was to pretend to be heroes. Childhood at its finest, right? I thought maybe if I etched those memories into my skin, I wouldn't forget that carefree kid."

My breath catches in my lungs, and Cain sighs. "Turns out he's too far gone. Someone else took his place. Someone who scares me. He's bitter and angry. He makes it hard to enjoy all the good things in life."

His words pick at me, striking notes of overwhelming sadness. I may not know anger on the same level as him, but I *have* struggled to find the joy in life as a result of my own trauma. I've chased adrenaline to fill voids within myself, even though I know my thefts will never be enough to make me whole.

I hide part of my face in the blanket, hating Cain's suffering but also loving that he's giving me such delicate pieces of himself. He's got such a big heart. I don't think he even knows it.

My fingers curl around his inked arm and pull it tight to my chest. "Your tattoos are really pretty."

"Mmm." Cain musses my hair. "I suppose I like pretty things."

"Cain?" I murmur, pulse quickening.

"Yeah, baby?"

"You feel like home to me."

His reply is a long kiss to my temple before he rests his head against mine.

CHAPTER TWENTY-SEVEN

EZRA

Cain juggles me between his staff over the next two weeks.

I know he's trying to keep me distracted while he refocuses on hunting Gabriel. According to Rev, they have teams spread out day and night searching for him, but the shipyard raid must have spooked him. There's been no trace of the crime lord since.

I have my first session with Isaac. Instead of diving into shit that makes my stomach curdle, we go out for wings and beer, as agreed upon when I demolished him in cards. I don't know if he's being strategic and trying to create a base foundation of trust between us, or if he actually *wants* to be friends. Maybe he's just a foodie.

When I hesitated at the entrance of the building, stressed about putting Isaac in danger being seen with me in the city, he just laughed me off.

"I'm a competitive shooter, Ezra. When I'm not in the office or competing, I snipe shit stains from rooftops for shits and giggles."

Definitely related to Cain.

While I'm starkly aware of Cain's absences in the mornings, Rev pushes me to the limit in the gym every afternoon. In total, I've gained four solid pounds of muscle—and a couple pounds of fat—since Sinro locked me in that meeting room. It's a noticeable difference on my lean frame.

But it also means I have more energy. With Cain working late nights, I end up channeling that destruction into target practice at the gun range until I'm ready to pass out or I run out of ammunition. By some magic, ammunition boxes are replenished the next day, as if bullets grow on trees around here.

I also get a full day of rest to spend with Jakey. I nap on the carpeted floor of his little home under the watchful eye of Salem, smirking as the two of them shout at a football game on the TV.

Salem joins us for dinner. She gracefully dodges my questions about her jobs, but I'm still hopeful that one day I can assist her.

Unwilling to return to an empty apartment when Salem finally drops me back off at Sinro Enterprises, I hit the elevator button for the thirteenth floor.

The office is silent, with the exception of Cain's keyboard clacking away. I peek my head into his doorway. When he finally notices me, his eyes drag up and down my body in appreciation.

"Ezra," he says in the low, sensual tone he saves for me.

"Hi," I whisper back.

Cain lifts his chin to motion me over, and I move around his desk to nestle on his lap. He doesn't try to hide his computer screen from me, just studies me as I take in details of a missing child report.

This time I'm prepared, though. The chaotic energy that lives in my veins has been drained by all of my recent activities.

"I want to do more. Please." Taking his stubbled cheeks in my hands, I place kisses all over him. His dark brows. His strong cheeks. His beautiful lips. "I'm tired of shooting paper targets. I've been doing so good."

"You little minx," he hums. "No need for persuasion tactics."

He skims a hand up my spine, clasping it around my neck to pull me into a kiss. It leaves me in a daze, and I blink back at him.

"What?" he asks.

"I don't know. You're just... way more affectionate than I expected."

"Do you want me to stop?"

I shake my head furiously. "Never. I like it."

Frowning, Cain strokes his fingers along my thigh. "I won't stop you from doing what you believe you need to do. Rev wants to take you out on an operation. Would you want that?"

I flip my lip ring back and forth. "Yeah, I'd like that a lot."

"Good. Ezra," he says hesitantly. "I want to be serious with you. I want us. I just... fuck, I suck at relationships."

My heart swells in my chest. I pivot to face him fully, pecking a kiss to his lips. "It's okay. I've never been in one."

Cain winces, his head shaking. "I'm going to let you down. I'm terrible with communication. I'm dominating in bed. I have horrible OCD and will flip my fucking lid over messes and pretty much anything that doesn't go according to plan."

My laugh is wild. "Cain, I'm a fucking train wreck."

He takes my jaw in his hand and kisses me. "No. You are precious, Ezra. You are perfect. Promise me you'll call me out whenever I'm lacking. You tell me your needs, and they will all be met, okay?"

Jesus, he's burrowed his way so far into the center of my rapidly beating heart.

I tug on his earlobes. "Promise. I won't let you get away with anything. I'll be demanding and needy."

He plants a kiss on my neck. "Beautiful boy. What do you need from me right now?"

"Just all of you," I whisper.

Cain is the exception to the laws of my universe. He must sense that. He must know how I look at him. How the air electrifies when we're close to each other. How something inside of him calls to me.

He lifts me up and sets me on my feet. I already miss his body heat, but as soon as he logs off his work computer, he's on me, slotting his mouth against mine and pushing me backward out of his office.

He shoves me against the elevator wall. His hands slide up my shirt, flicking over my nipples. My gasp allows him access to delve his tongue into my mouth.

Addicted to his taste, I climb up his body and lock my hands around the back of his neck. I suck on this tongue while I grind my hips against his erection.

"*Fuck*. Ezra." His hands slide beneath the waistband of my pants to squeeze my bare ass.

The elevator doors open, and Cain carries me into his apartment, never breaking our consuming kiss. We don't even make it past the kitchen. Pretty sure Cain's trying to fuck me on every surface of his apartment, and I'm okay with that.

He lays me out on the island, dragging my shirt over my head and tossing it aside. His mouth and tongue are everywhere, tracing my stomach, running over my sensitive nipples. He sucks and bites at me as I moan and arch my back, already so fucking achy.

Gripping his shirt, I use it to pull myself upright and rip his buttons, sending them pinging around the apartment. His OCD ass will be searching for them for weeks.

Cain takes my mouth aggressively, rolling one of my nipples between his fingers. "You think that's funny?"

I rake my hands through his hair, unable to help myself from touching him back. "Don't wear shirts anymore. You don't need them."

He chuckles and flicks open my jeans. "Yes, I'll conduct all business naked from now on."

When his hand wraps around my hard dick, my spine loses support. I curl forward, my forehead coming to rest against his smooth chest. "Good. You. Naked. It's... it's good."

Cain grips my jaw in his other hand and seals his mouth to mine. There's nothing hesitant about the way he's kissing or touching me. No testing boundaries. No giving space for feelings or doubts.

Cain kisses me like he wants me just as much as I need him, and I'm toast.

He hooks his hands in my pants and tugs at them. "Fucking skinny jeans."

Whipping out a serrated knife, he slices down the fabric before I can protest, cutting through my boxers, too.

"God, just look at you." He drags his fiery gaze down my body. "I want to fuck you so hard you can't sit for a week."

"Yes, please." I suck on my lip ring.

A yelp bursts from my mouth as he hauls me off the counter and flips me so my chest and stomach are pasted to the cold countertop.

"Ah, shit!" I hiss, but soon forget my discomfort when Cain spreads my cheeks and flattens his tongue to my hole. "Oh, fuck."

He licks his way down to my balls, tracing a maddening pattern. And when he sucks on my rim, I know my dick is leaking pre-cum all over the side of his counter.

"Cain," I whine.

He growls. "Not yet, baby. I'm not done playing with you."

Teeth sink into one of my cheeks. I cry out, hips tilting forward, desperate for friction.

"No coming," Cain orders. "I *will* spank you if you do."

He pushes his tongue inside of me, and I lose my mind, my hands snapping out to grip the edges of the counter. I rock back against him.

He continues torturing me, moving his skillful tongue in and out of my hole, soaking my rim with spit.

When I'm a shuddering mess, his hands draw me back from the counter enough so he can jerk me off while his tongue continues to trace my rim.

"Jesus Christ on a fucking bike. Fuck me already."

Cain replaces his tongue with a finger, sinking it deep inside me. "You good, baby?"

I moan. "No, I'm in agony."

His hand clamps down on my cock, holding me in place. "I don't think you are. You're not screaming yet."

There's pressure as he begins to push another finger inside of me. I groan as he eases it out and spits down my crease before sinking it further this time.

"You say the word and I stop."

"Don't stop," I pant, eyes shut and body trembling.

Cain works a third finger in and strokes that magical spot that has me moaning on every slide of his hand along my cock.

"Oh my god, that's good."

His fingers leave my body, and I groan in protest.

"Keep gripping the counter, Ezra," Cain orders.

I hear feet padding across the floor, and my heart races in anticipation.

I squirm impatiently until he returns to push lubed fingers inside of me a few slow times before he breaches me with his cock. As if that isn't enough to drive me crazy, he reaches around to stroke my erection again. When I get too shaky, teetering on the edge of detonating, he stops moving and squeezes me at the base of my cock.

"Jesus Christ," I mumble, white-knuckling the counter.

"I know, baby. I want to stay buried in you forever."

He thrusts deep, and my weak legs tremor beneath me. There's too much sensation. Cain is everywhere. His tongue and teeth dragging over my skin. One hand jerking me. The other holding my hip so I don't bang into the edge of the counter as he begins to fuck into me with purpose.

"Oh fuck. Fuck. Shit. Cain."

"No coming until I say so." He growls, slamming his hips to my ass, shooting sparks of pleasure through me.

His pace is brutal, fast and hard just like I need. But I'm far too close. I don't want this to be over. I don't want us to be over. Not when I've just started breaking through his steel walls.

"I can't," I force out between moans. "You're too good. So good."

Cain drags me up off the counter, wrapping his arm around me to pull me tight against his chest. He's got me restrained and mewling uncontrollably as he fucks up into me.

"You can. You take me so well, baby," he praises. "So hot and tight and perfect for me."

"Oh no. I'm gonna come." I tip my head back on his shoulder, bracing for the orgasm that's already curling my toes and causing a full-body shudder.

Cain stops moving. His hand tightens around the base of my dick. "Don't you fucking do it, Ezra. I didn't give you permission."

"Cain," I whine, trying to wriggle in his hold. "Please."

He pulls out of me.

"Oh, come on!"

Spinning me around, he heaves me up over his shoulder. He smacks my ass, and I reach down to squeeze his cheeks, earning a snarl that causes me to giggle.

"Only fair," I mumble.

He throws me down onto his bed. Shit, I think he might be broken. He's staring down at me with madness blazing in his dark eyes, his shirt ripped open, pants undone to show off his proud cock.

He strips off his clothes and descends on me, claiming my mouth as he plunges his cock inside of me without warning. I whimper against his lips. My cock weeps on my stomach as I try to hold back the building pressure in my spine.

Cain grips my hair, tilting my head so he can drag his hot mouth down my neck.

"Oh, fuck. I'm so sorry," I whisper, right before I erupt, shooting cum between us, my ass clamping down on his cock. The orgasm hits me hard enough to darken my vision for a few seconds of bliss.

"Ezra." Cain groans, and then his hips are jerking erratically as he hits his climax, his warmth spilling inside of me.

We don't make it out of bed to clean up. Just collapse in a sweaty, messy heap and pass the fuck out.

CHAPTER TWENTY-EIGHT

EZRA

I wake up to the apartment door clicking shut.

Mornings without Cain suck, but I can't mope around. I slip on a t-shirt and ripped black jeans before stepping out into the kitchen to find a mug of hot coffee and a plate of french toast on the counter.

My heart swoops in my chest. He fucking spoils me.

After devouring the meal, I head for the gun range. There's nothing quite like unloading explosives at paper targets shaped like aliens with dumb faces. I imagine they're Gabriel or his masked cronies or predators, like the man who bought me and locked me away for his own personal, sadistic enjoyment.

Emptying a magazine, I flick it to the side and shove another full magazine in at lightning speed, feeling a rush of adrenaline. This is where I belong. Finger on a trigger, gun aimed at sin. It makes me feel alive to think that maybe all the shit I'd gone through was necessary to get me to this exact point in my life.

Maybe I should start unpacking some of these thoughts on Isaac, because I'm not sure they are healthy.

When I turn to retrieve more ammunition, I discover I have an audience. Rev's leaned up against the wall by the door. He's dressed in black cargo pants and a black jacket with a bulletproof vest. His face is void of emotion.

"Um, hi," I say. "What am I doing wrong?"

Rev looks me over with indifference. "Nothing, Ezra. Absolutely nothing. We've got a job tonight."

"We?" My brows lift, and a thrill shoots through my veins. "You serious?"

"You already shoot like you've been doing this for years. You can wriggle your way out of holds in the ring. You can pick locks. You don't fear pain. And, I know you'll be highly motivated to fuck Gabriel up when the time comes to take him down."

My heart leaps. "When do we leave?"

"Right now. Bring your gun, lover boy."

Excitement buzzes under my skin as we ride the elevator down to the lower levels. Rev scans his hand on a pad outside a heavy metal door revealing what looks like a locker room, only for murderers. Dozens of mercenaries glance my way. I recognize some from training with Rev.

Rev waves me over to the row of metal cubbies along the wall. "This gear should fit you. Suit up. I'll fill you in on the operation shortly."

I reach for the vest and grunt at the surprising weight of it.

"Tomorrow, we start exercising with gear on," Rev says with a frown.

"You got it," I reply with a nod.

"Pretty Ezra." Rev pinches my cheek. "Cain tried convincing me that you're too much of a brat to fit in on my team, but you take orders exceptionally well."

"I act up for Cain in hopes that it will result in sexual punishment."

Rev tips his head back and lets out a hearty laugh, striding away to collect his own gear.

Nerves kicking in under the scrutiny of trained killers, my obsessive time in the gym and gun range suddenly doesn't feel like enough. Just how big is this operation? Are we taking Gabriel out tonight?

A guy I've heard called Forest leans over and pats a gloved hand on my shoulder. "First one is always an emotional rollercoaster. I threw up all over my uniform, but you'll do just fine."

A hesitant smile eases onto my face. "Oh, yeah. Thanks. Um, how do I strap this on?"

I hold up a gun holster, and Forest chuckles. Before he can take more than a step toward me, a towering figure slips between us. Cain leans down to capture my mouth. The kiss is a bit indecent for an audience, but I can't help melting into him, my fingers hooked in his bulletproof vest.

When we break apart, Forest is shaking his head, grinning. "Fucking knew it."

Cain helps me into my gear. I should probably be embarrassed. I'm surrounded by professionals. But his possessiveness only makes my body heat in the best way possible.

His mouth brushes the shell of my ear as he murmurs, "You look sexy as hell, baby. When we get back home, you better run upstairs and get prepped for me."

My jaw drops. Cain steps away, leaving my cock stiff and achy. This little problem only gets worse when he takes over leading the show.

"Any issues tonight, and you retreat to call in reinforcements. As much as I want to tell you all to shoot away, we need to track these fuckers back to their ant hole," Cain instructs. "Gabriel's definitely not in charge, so stay sharp."

I don't have time to question what the plans are as teams file out a back door into the underground parking garage.

"You're with me, pretty boy," Rev says, hitting the unlock button on a key fob for a black SUV with tinted windows. We climb in, and I check the mirrors for Cain, spotting him loading in a navy SUV with Forest.

Forest blows us a kiss. I hang my body out the window to blow one back at him, earning a glare from Cain. That's what he gets for pawning me off on someone else.

Cain pulls his vehicle up next to us and points a finger at Rev. "You don't leave his fucking side tonight."

Rev salutes. "I'll be all over him like a bear on a honey hive."

I clutch the oh shit handle as Rev whips the car out of the parking spot and guns it toward the exit ramp.

"Why are so many teams going out?" I ask.

"Alaric found consistencies among the addresses on the drive," Rev says, racing through a red light at deadly speeds.

"Consistencies? Jesus, are we in a hurry?"

He glances over at me, brows furrowed. "No. Why? My driving too much for you?"

"It's... aggressive," I offer.

"Yes. Consistencies. Several kids were tagged at the same couple of addresses. Foster homes. Shelters. Churches. Youth activity buildings."

Blood drains from my body. All places that were supposed to be refuges for people like me. I shift in the seat, eager for movement to keep the panic from creeping in.

My hands curl into fists. "I was taken from a foster home."

"Yeah. Your address was one flagged."

Stomach churning, I sink into the seat, trying not to let the weight of his words crush me. I stare out at the streets, not really present in my own body.

Rev's eyes flick to me. I can't help but feel like this is a test. A mercenary doesn't lose his shit out on a job. Emotions cannot rule me, especially when lives are at stake.

"That's not... where we're going tonight, is it?" I ask, not sure how to process that possibility. I hadn't thought I'd ever see that foster parent again. I spent years hating her for giving me over to a man who had abused me. I blamed her. How could she not have seen the evil in his eyes? How come no one from child protective services ever came to check up on me?

Because these people target nobodies like me.

I'd spent so much of my existence plotting revenge against both of them. But when I escaped, I wanted nothing more than to shed every piece of that life. I fled, only taking with me the trauma I couldn't seem to shake.

"No. Chances are we won't see any action tonight. Teams will be on rotation at the flagged addresses until this entire ring is shut down."

"Who's going to my address, Rev?"

He hesitates, swinging the car down a quiet, littered street with decaying brick buildings. "Cain."

I flip my lip ring back and forth with my tongue. Is that why Cain assigned me to Rev? Because he wanted to murder the woman responsible for almost destroying me? Does she have other kids in her home listed on that fucking drive?

Yeah, I'm not sure I would have been able to stop myself from storming inside that house and pumping her full of bullets. And if she *did* have foster kids, that's the last thing they needed to witness.

Rev parallel parks the SUV along a street of rough shops four blocks away from our destination. He reaches over and zips the keys in one of my vest pockets. "No pressure, Ezra. You can drive right back to Sinro if you need to. Isaac will buy you pizza and force you to watch reality TV with him."

"I'm not leaving. I want to do this."

He flashes a wicked grin. "Now that I've relayed Cain's words, I'll give you mine."

My head jerks to him in surprise, catching him pouring a box of nerds candy into his mouth. "If someone shoots, you fucking kill them, okay?"

Back in West Bank, I'm in my element. I trail Rev around buildings and through dark alleyways, hyperfocused on our task, despite my sugar buzz from the pop rocks Rev forced upon me.

Our address is a graffitied shelter on the corner of a run-down intersection. Thankfully, it's not one I've stayed at before or I might have come unglued. I'm still battling to keep myself in check after learning about the foster home situation.

Pressed up against an abandoned building, unease spider walks down my spine when I spot an unmarked black van parked at the end of the street that doesn't belong to Sinro.

"Rev," I say under my breath.

He reaches for his gun. "Good instincts. I feel it, too. You should head back to the car."

I shake my head. "No way. I stay with you."

The crack of a gun splits the night. A bullet crumbles the brick right over Rev's head. He whirls around and fires a shot to the corner of a roof overlooking us, dropping a body to the street with a sickening crunch. "Guess you're getting baptized by gunfire."

Heart hammering against my ribcage, I whip out my gun and sweep my eyes over the streets.

Another bullet whizzes by, and Rev orders me behind the cover of a dumpster in the alley. Peeking around it, I catch a silhouette in the second-story window of the building across from us. I aim my gun at the lower level window and pull the trigger when the shadow appears. It drops out of sight, and my heart dips in my chest as I stare at the broken glass, ears ringing from the blast of my gun.

Rev takes my chin in a gloved hand. He turns my head to meet his icy eyes. "You with me? First one can fuck you up."

A slow grin eases onto my face. "Yeah, I'm good."

Two guys down.

"Do you think all the addresses were a setup?" I ask, pressing my back against the dumpster. I keep my eyes moving over the streets.

"Not sure. Can you call in for back-up?"

I fumble for the comm piece in a vest pocket. Jamming it in my ear, I hit the call button.

"Alaric. We've got company. Not sure how many gunmen."

"You and three of the other teams," Alaric replies. "I'll send reinforcements."

Dread sluices through my body as Alaric hangs up. Was Cain safe? I had to trust that he would make it home. I couldn't let my brain spiral me into a panic right now.

Out of the corner of my eye, I spot a figure darting across the street behind us.

"Got another one," I mutter.

"Go fetch," Rev says, and I take off, loaded gun in hand.

Adrenaline streams through me, propelling me forward. I can run miles without tiring. This guy is as good as dead.

I know Cain's going to be pissed about this entire situation, but I've never felt so alive. Never felt so in control of my thoughts and emotions.

Never felt so powerful.

I don't know what that says about me that I get off on chasing down bad guys, but I want to keep fucking doing it.

I raise my gun to fire. The shot misses. Aiming while running is more difficult than I expected, but I've trained far too hard to let someone who traffics kids get away.

A thought strikes me, and I lower my gun. Eventually rats have to go back to their nests, right? Hopefully Rev doesn't get mad at me for going a bit off the books here.

I pull back, slinking in and out of alleyways, letting the guy think he's gotten away. I stalk him all the way to a building pulsing with industrial music and strobe lights in East Bank.

Shedding my tactical gear behind a pallet of empty cardboard boxes, I slip into a group of young, scantily clad partiers as they enter the club.

Heavy bass assaults my eardrums. Multi-colored lasers flash across the dim interior, the beams reflecting off thick clouds of smoke.

Shit. It's gonna be hard to spot the guy in here. I slip onto a stool at the bar, checking that my gun is still tucked into my waistband, and order a drink with a fake ID I swiped as a teen.

After Alaric's admission about catching me on security cameras when I thought I'd snuck into Sinro, I don't feel so confident about my ability to track this guy. I should probably call Rev or Alaric.

But then I spot him darting up the metal staircase in the back, leading to an overhanging balcony for VIPs.

My heart stutters. From my spot, I can make out Gabriel lounged on a red sectional between two women and three other dangerous looking men dressed in black. My guy leans down to speak in Gabriel's ear.

I stiffen as a pair of hands slide around my waist. A body leans against my back. "You want to have some fun tonight?"

Turning, I take in the pink streaks through the woman's light hair and the fake lashes that weigh her eyelids down, giving her a sleepy look. Glitter sparkles on her high cheekbones.

I force a smile at her while I ease her arms off my body. "Sorry, but I'm pretty gay and very taken."

She steps back. "Bummer. Have a good night, cutie."

Failing to swallow the lump in my throat, I glance back up at the balcony. Another man has joined the couch overlords. Dressed in a black button-up and slacks, he clashes with the others. His light brown hair is short, and a pair of wire-framed glasses perch on his nose.

I know this man.

Blood drains from my body, leaving me a cold husk. I'm thankful for the seat under my ass, or I might have collapsed to the floor, which would only draw unwanted attention.

The man that held me prisoner leans over to chat with Gabriel, a drink in his hand.

God, is it possible to pass out and throw up at the same time? Panic slithers through my body, mixed with disgust and fear and white-hot rage.

He should be dead. I thought the wound to his neck was enough to end him. I wish I could see the scar where I stabbed him to confirm that this isn't just a figment of my twisted imagination.

Suddenly, the gun tucked into my waistband does nothing to make me feel strong. I can't fucking do this. Who can be a successful mercenary when they react like this?

I slide off the chair, nearly losing my balance when my feet hit the ground.

"Hun, you gonna finish that?" the bartender shouts.

I glance back at her, which is a huge mistake. Awareness of eyes on me ices my bones. My gaze darts up to the balcony.

My abuser is staring back at me. I'm eight years old again. Filled with hope that I found a forever home, only to have that hope crushed. Instead, I find myself shivering in a dark basement, starved of human interaction and brainwashed to submit to his whims.

Bile singes my throat. I clench my teeth together to keep from getting sick. Even from a distance, I feel him too close to me. His evil has a fucking presence. A shadow-like form that wraps invisible hands around my throat to suffocate me.

His slow, wicked grin is my undoing.

I bolt for the door, panic coiling around my chest, strangling the air from my lungs.

I can't do this. I can't. I can't *breathe*.

I stumble out of the club and make it half a mile down the street before I slip behind a restaurant and plant my ass on the wet street. My head hangs between my knees as I start slamming my spine against the brick wall behind me, breaking open my skin.

Over and over and over again.

CHAPTER TWENTY-NINE

CAIN

E zra's a mess when his call comes through.

There's only cries and indistinguishable ramblings on the other end, and it drives my heart into a quick rhythm.

Alaric had informed me that the shelter Rev and Ezra arrived at was under Gabriel's watch. Three other locations were, as well.

I would have preferred the firefight to the scene I'd busted into at Ezra's previous foster home. Six children, malnourished and clad in soiled clothes.

Salem got them all out before I lost control and splattered the kitchen in the woman's blood.

I hate that my teams are spread too thin tonight. I'm overwhelmed by the urge to be in several places at once.

But Ezra comes first. Always.

"Baby, what is it? What's going on?" I demand, bolting for the SUV parked outside the foster home. I rip open the door and slide in, smashing down on the gas before I even have his location pulled up on my phone. Forest can hitch a ride with Salem.

"It's so fucked." Ezra sobs. "So fucking fucked."

I slam the gas pedal to the floor, swerving through cars and red lights. "Just hold on, okay? I'm on my way. I'm coming for you."

When I check his pin on my map, it shows me fifteen minutes away. It might as well be hours. This city's too fucking big, and Ezra's too far away for my comfort.

"Are you hurt?" I ask.

His little hiccups have my stomach lurching this way and that. Rev should have alerted me if something had gone south. What the fuck had happened?

All that matters right now is that Ezra's still with me. Despite how much his call is shredding my insides, at least I know he's alive. I can get to him. I can fix this.

"I'm sorry, Cain," Ezra whispers. "I'm so pathetic. He...he's going to hurt me again. He's never going to let me go."

Rage spills through me, and I white-knuckle the steering wheel. I growl. "Who's going to hurt you, Ezra? Gabriel? I'll flay him alive."

No one is safe from me if I find a single mark on Ezra's body. Hell, I might burn the entire city down tonight. It's filled with scum, anyway.

His pin directs me toward an alley next to an upscale restaurant. What the fuck would he be doing here? My heart pounds in my throat as I ditch my vehicle in the middle of traffic and rush toward him.

Gun poised, I charge into the alley. Only when I'm certain it's clear, do I let my gaze drop to Ezra. He's curled into a ball in a dirty puddle, rocking back and forth with that toxic fucking energy that sets me on edge. His fingers spasm on top of his knees, and his hair has been tugged out into a wild mess like he's been trying to rip it from his scalp.

Pretty sure my heart hits the bottom of my stomach. I can't seem to push it back into place as I rush over to scoop up his cold, wet, shivering body.

"I'm here, baby. I won't let you go," I murmur, resting my forehead on his for a few painful breaths.

Questions burn on my tongue, but I put them in check. I need Ezra safe first. With him in tow, I dart back to the SUV, but Ezra clings to me when I try to place him in the passenger seat.

I curse at our situation. As if to underline this shitty night, a bullet whizzes past my head. Cradling Ezra in one arm, I turn and fire a shot through a muscled guy's head, dropping him on the street.

People begin screaming as I try to buckle Ezra in the passenger seat again, but he refuses to unhook his fingers from my vest. So I jog around the front of the vehicle, move the driver's seat back, and climb in with him tucked on my lap. One-handed, I speed to Sinro Enterprises.

Ezra's silent the entire ride. As much as I want to haul him into Isaac's office right away when we get back to Sinro, I have to respect that Ezra will talk when he's ready. He just needs a minute to process whatever happened and find a center within himself. Until then, I'll bend over backwards to take care of him.

I send a voice message to Alaric with details on where I found Ezra. He texts back that he'll have Rev and his team sweep the area.

Carrying Ezra into my apartment, I plop us down on the couch in the dark. Wrapping both of us up in the throw blanket, I hold his shaking body. I stroke my fingers through his hair and rub slow circles along his lower back until I'm convinced he fell asleep.

The fact that he can find such peace with me is truly a blessing. One I don't feel like I deserve. Not when my kill count is too high for me to remember names, only faces, and they haunt me behind closed eyes.

I focus on Ezra's breaths until I feel like they are stable enough for me to extract an arm and check in with Rev. All he texts back is that Ezra took off after one of Gabriel's guys. The urge to grill Rev is strong, but I leave him to hunt, hoping he slaughters the piece of shit responsible for Ezra's pain.

When Ezra finally stirs, I loosen my hold on him so he can sit up. "Can you tell me what happened?"

His voice is weak when he replies, "Gabriel's working with him."

I brush my fingers along his lower back beneath his damp shirt. "Who, baby?"

He shakes his head. "I don't know his name. He never told me. I thought I killed him. He's supposed to be dead, Cain."

Fresh tears spring to his eyes, and my chest presses in on my lungs.

"Okay," I say, struggling to wrangle my emotions. Right now, I just need to listen, no matter how much my body wants to take action and solve world problems. "You've met this guy before?"

Ezra pushes his face into my chest and unleashes a frustrated growl that has my stomach tying in intricate little knots I don't think I'll ever be able to untangle.

"Hey." I drag my hands through his wet locks, gripping the ends tightly so he's forced to hold my gaze. "No matter what you tell me, nothing changes between us, okay?"

He stares into my eyes like he needs to see evidence that my words are truthful.

"You have become vital in my life. Nothing changes, Ezra."

His throat bobs, and his bottom lip trembles. "I wasn't supposed to get out. He wasn't ever going to let me go."

My jaw clenches hard enough to ache down through my neck, but I wait for him to continue. "He... I... I was his pet, Cain. He kept me locked up in his basement. If I was good... if I didn't fight back, he... he let me wander in that space. But if I wasn't good, if my panic took over, sometimes he'd chain me up."

"Jesus fucking Christ." My hands slid down to his hip bones, fingertips pressing in tight to hold him upright. Anger rears up inside of me, aching to rip something apart.

Ezra shudders before he forces a deep breath. I fight the urge to crush him against me, knowing he needs to get all of this out.

"Sometimes he'd take my clothes. Make me... eat without my hands. Sometimes, he convinced me that I deserved to be there." He squeezes his eyes shut. "Sometimes the memories get a bit weird and I question what was real. It was so *wrong*, Cain. I know that now. So very evil."

"Did he..." I can't finish the question. I don't really want to know the answer. But Ezra shouldn't have to carry the burden of his horrors alone.

Ezra's silence is enough of an admission. He starts to pick at his chipped fingernails. I capture his hands in mine to stop him.

"He came down to fix a broken fixture. He dropped the screwdriver and I just... lurched for it. I stabbed it into his neck. Stole the key for my restraints and never looked back. I should have checked that he was dead."

Ezra shifts positions, hauling one leg over my lap so he's straddling me. He rests his forehead on my collarbone, and I stroke a hand along the back of his neck.

"Don't make me talk about it anymore," he whispers.

"Ezra," I say, my voice thick with emotion. "I would never make you do anything you didn't want to do."

"Okay." After a pause, he adds, "I should have shot them all."

The mercenary in me wants to agree. To drill him for information on this man so we can track him down, and I can rip him into pieces. There's a solid chance he's the one who hired Gabriel.

He's a fucking dead man walking.

Too many unfinished tasks swirl in my head. Discussions I need to have with my teams. With Alaric and Rev and Isaac. But I shove all of that aside for now.

Swallowing, I rest my chin on top of his head. "What do you need from me, beautiful boy?"

"To not feel so pathetic. I fucked up. Everyone's going to be disappointed in me. They were right there in front of me, and I couldn't keep my head on straight."

"Fucking hell. You can't say shit like that, okay?" I snap back.

Ezra pulls away to meet my eyes, fear swirling in their mesmerizing depths. "I... I'm sorry."

I groan at my loss of temper and press a kiss to his forehead. "No, it's just... that kind of talk is like a razor blade to my fucking heart. No one is disappointed in you. Did Forest tell you he puked on his first mission?"

Brows furrowing, he gives a weak nod.

"He probably didn't tell you that he pissed himself, too. And Rev shot one of his superiors in the ass cheek on his first operation. We're all human, despite the fact that we try not to act like it, because humanity is messy. You experienced completely valid emotions tonight."

"Okay." Ezra deflates against me. "I think I'm hungry. Too much sugar. Rev fed me candy."

Sighing, I pick him up and carry him to the kitchen island. I set him down in his favorite spot while I retrieve ingredients to make him homemade alfredo.

After dinner, I run a shower for him and help strip him down, my gaze never leaving his, always assessing his reactions. I hate the dark circles under his eyes. The heaviness to his shoulders. I know that defeat. I've gone to war against it countless times. The fucking effort it took to get out of bed some days, with the weight of what I'd witnessed, what I'd done, pressing me down into the mattress...

It's nothing in comparison to what Ezra must have suffered. Treated worse than an animal. Degraded and tortured and forced to submit to a monster of a human being.

When I angle his body toward the shower door, I growl at the sight of the broken skin along his spine. Three quarter-sized wounds along his vertebrae have crusted over with blood.

Invisible hands throttle my insides. I have to step back from him to suck in a big gulp of air so I don't punch a fist through something.

Once I'm level enough, I strip down, too. I help him into the shower, washing every part of him carefully as he just stands there with his head bowed and eyes closed.

We're so close, and yet I get the sense that he's drifted somewhere far away. Somewhere I fear I can never reach.

Still, I press my body against his back and wrap him up in my arms. For once, I appreciate that I'm so large. I've always believed I was built for pain, but right now, I can almost blanket Ezra in comfort. It's one small thing I *can* do for him.

Ezra hums as he leans back against me. My slick hands run up and down his chest and abs, eager to soothe.

His hums quickly turn into little moans. He leans forward to rest his head against the wall. One of his hands finds my wrist and lowers my hand down to his stiffening cock.

"Please," he whispers. "I need it. Wring me out so I can sleep tonight."

My own dick jerks in response as I grip his shaft tightly, like I know he wants. I slide my hand up and down his length, twisting at the top. I drop my other hand to his balls, alternating between tugging and massaging, letting his perfect noises guide me.

"Beautiful Ezra." I plant kisses on the back of his neck. His hand clutches me tighter as I work him over. Soon, he's barely able to hold himself up, and I turn him around, easing him gently against the tiles as I drop to my knees.

Ezra hisses through his teeth as I suck him into my mouth. I take my time, running my tongue over every glorious, solid inch of him, trading off between sucking him hard and deep-throating him as the hot water sprays down on us.

When his toes curl and his fingers tangle in my hair, I pop off for a second. "Let go, baby. Fuck my mouth. Punish me."

So he does. He digs his fingers tighter into my hair and slams his hips forward, forcing his dick deep into my throat. I know I'll be feeling it after, but I moan and grip his ass to encourage him.

Ezra pumps recklessly until he's spurting down my throat, pulsing through an orgasm that has him sliding down the tiles onto the floor. When he's eye-level with me, I kiss him hard.

"You're mine. No one is ever going to fucking touch you again."

"Yours." Ezra nods, cradling my face in his hand. "But you belong to me, too."

I wake up before dawn to Ezra sucking my cock.

The sheets are crumpled at the bottom of the bed, and the glow of the city illuminates him nestled between my legs. Both of us went to bed naked, too tired to even bother with clothes.

Still drowsy from sleep and now dissolving into pleasure, it takes a few slick movements of his mouth along my shaft before I summon up the decency to try to ease him away.

Ezra slaps my hand and makes an angry sound on my cock that has my eyes rolling back into my head.

"Fuck. Okay. Do as you please."

It's like I dreamed him up. I think I've waited my whole life to find him. My perfect, sweet Ezra. He's so eager to please me, bobbing up and down in a maddening rhythm as his hands grip my thighs. I can't help but rock my hips into him.

"Such a good little thief." I slide my fingers into his wavy hair, gripping it at the roots. He moans on my cock, and I growl in return.

I lift my head up enough to watch him fuck me with his mouth. I can't tear my gaze away. His hazel eyes are so vibrant green when they flick up to look at me through dark, full lashes.

He's the sexiest person in existence.

"You take me so good. Love your pretty lips wrapped around my cock, baby."

His lashes flutter, and his body melts a bit.

I don't last long. Groaning, I unload a hot stream of cum into his mouth. When he pops up, my seed still coating his tongue and his beautiful cock hard for me, I have the sudden desire to give him more than I've ever given anyone.

"Come up here," I order, tugging him into a deep kiss. His lips are salty from swallowing my release. He grinds his erection against my thigh, eagerly chasing his own pleasure now.

"Don't worry. We're going to take care of that," I murmur. "Get the lube."

Ezra lurches up, now straddling my thighs. His wide eyes drop to my softening cock. I bite back a laugh.

"Do as I say, Ezra."

He leans over to grab the bottle from my nightstand, and I take the opportunity to squeeze his full ass.

"Slick your cock up, baby," I command, spreading my legs wider.

His brows knead together as he stares down at me, but when I add fire to my gaze, he coats himself in lube.

I take the bottle and squirt some onto my fingers before dropping them to circle my hole.

Ezra's eyes shoot wide open. "Woah. I thought...you only topped."

I can't hide a sinister grin. "You never asked."

"Oh, fuck." A bead of pre-cum appears in his slit as he squeezes his dick. "I've never..."

He's flustered now, and it ignites my temper. I quickly squash it so I don't ruin this moment. "You will be the first I've ever let into my body."

"Oh, no. I'm going to splooge too soon," he whines, biting down on his lip. "I'm about to let you down so hardcore."

Never thought I'd chuckle while shoving two fingers inside my ass. I'm getting hard again just from the idea of him breaching me.

I don't bother with a third finger when I'm too fucking amped up for Ezra to lose himself to me. I grab his hips and draw him closer to my ass, right where I crave him.

"I'm yours, baby," I say.

Ezra leans down to kiss me as he pushes the head of his cock up to that first ring of muscle inside me. I fight the urge to tense up. The burn and resistance is worse than I'd expected. Not that he's small—I just underestimated those muscles in my body.

Maybe I should have played with toys or worked in a plug to start. Honestly, I wasn't sure I would go through with this.

"Are you okay?" He's nearly breathless already, and that just turns me right the fuck on. My hard cock throbs against his stomach.

"Good." I nod, rising up to nip at his jawline. "You're doing perfect."

I've never been a vulnerable person. I rarely give up control. But things are different with Ezra. He is the most precious thing to me. And I want to show him that. I want to give him everything.

Ezra bottoms out inside of me, and I'm surprised that the burn is completely gone. Instead, I feel full. That pressure is making my dick leak. It's fucking phenomenal.

"Is this what you feel when I'm inside you?" I ask.

"God, it's so fucking good, right?" Ezra replies. "Am I okay to move?"

I slap his ass, then grip both smooth cheeks in my hands. "Get to it."

Ezra rolls his hips, hesitant at first. But when he summons the first moan from my lips, he finds a confident, smooth pace.

"Fuck. Fuck. Fucking shit, Cain. I can't last." He pants, squeezing his eyes shut. "I'm so sorry. You need to stop being so hot. Oh, God. You feel criminal."

With my hands still clenching his ass, I force him to keep fucking me, angling him just right to hit my prostate. Pleasure sparks where he pounds against me, building and building.

"Then we'll... just have... to do this again," I grit out right before I come hard enough to roll my eyes back in my head.

"Oh, shit. I can feel that." Ezra moans and slams into me one last time, spilling his warm release. When he slides out, panting and spent, he plops down beside me in dramatic fashion, and I chuckle.

"Shower. Coffee. Work."

"Sex. Sex. Sex," he replies, and when I turn my head to look at him, his goofy little grin releases the invisible binds that tied themselves around my chest when I found him in that fucking alley.

I can finally breathe again.

With a laugh, I shake my head. "Insatiable. I'm glad you're feeling better."

He nods, draping his body over me. The fact that he's become so comfortable touching me like this, letting me touch him, has my heart soaring.

Someday, Ezra will realize his worth and find somebody better. More stable. More human. Just *more*.

Until then, I'll do everything in my power to make him happy.

"What can I say? You really do it for me," he says, rubbing his cheek over my bare chest.

I run fingers up and down his spine. "Yeah. You're it for me."

CHAPTER THIRTY

EZRA

To say I've become hyper-focused on the idea of murdering one man would be an understatement. I don't think I'll be able to sleep a full night again until my abuser is buried six feet under.

Sex with Cain has been a solid distraction, but he's not always able to fuck this destructive energy out of me.

The gun range isn't doing the trick, even after upgrading to rifles, and Rev can't seem to work me hard enough in the gym. No matter how long I run or how many reps I knock out with weights, my mind is still haunted.

So it's no surprise I end up outside Isaac's office two days earlier than our scheduled appointment, leaned up against the wall as I wait for him to return from lunch.

He freezes when he sees me, a paper bag of greasy food clutched in one hand and a giant milkshake in the other. His eyes dip to my fingers, twitching restlessly against my thighs.

"Hi, Ezra. What can I do for you?"

"I think I have panic attacks," I blurt out. "Possibly anxiety, too."

Isaac's dark brows touch the ends of his hair curling out from under a slouchy hat. He recovers with an encouraging smile. "Why don't you come in, and we can talk about it. Here, you look like you need this more than me."

He hands over the chocolate milkshake, and I can't *not* consume it. Only after my belly is sluggish from the ice cream treat, do I get up from the chair in his office and begin to pace.

"I don't want this to be about me," I start off. "I want to do this job. I want to help hunt down bad people. But my head doesn't want to cooperate, and I need it to cooperate because this is about other people who need help, not about what happened to me fucking centuries ago."

Isaac doesn't seem phased by my sudden aggression, almost like he could see down into the core of my pain the first time he met me.

We spend three hours talking, and after I've unloaded most of my fucked up past—I can't give him all of it—I find that the disgusting feelings in my chest ease up just enough to take the edge off. I think it's just Isaac's ability to take everything I say in stride. He might be a wizard.

"I can come back tomorrow, right?" I ask, hesitating in the doorway.

"Of course you can. And just know, it doesn't always have to be to talk about things. I want to be friends with you, Ezra. Our lunches have been immensely enjoyable."

His words strike me in the chest, deflating my lungs. I force a shy smile, and then I'm on to my next mission. I'd made so many plans last night while lying awake in bed and counting Cain's breaths.

The lower levels are empty, with the exception of Alaric. He's browsing through files on his computer at alarming speeds, a fresh cup of black coffee perched atop old pizza boxes on his desk.

"Hey," I greet softly.

He startles, spinning around in his chair. "Shit, what? Oh. Hi, Ezra. What are you doing down here?"

My fingers run over the scars on my arms. "I was hoping you could research someone for me."

"Um. Yeah, sure thing." He rubs his hand up and down his cheek. "You, uh… wanna pull up a chair?"

After disclosing everything I can remember about my tormenter to Alaric, I still can't seem to find my way back to a normal rhythm. Or what I've come to know as normal in my time at Sinro.

How long have I been here now? Over a month, for sure, but I've lost track of the days.

I end up in the steaming pool on the balcony of the seventeenth floor, swimming laps until my muscles feel loose and my fingers prune up.

Heaving my body out of the saltwater, I splay out on the patio and let the droplets of water rolling off my goose-bumped skin turn cold in the bitter winter air.

Sometimes my brain likes to play games with me. Like, how long would it take me to freeze to death? Would I die upon impact if I jumped from this height? How quick would I bleed out if I just took that cut deeper into my skin?

I swallow and clench my eyes closed, forcing those thoughts back under lock inside my chest. They share a space with things I've convinced myself didn't happen. If I tell Isaac that my innocence was taken from me, then that makes it a reality, right?

What the fuck is wrong with me today?

The elevator dings, and my heartbeat quickens in anticipation of seeing Cain. When he appears in my vision, dropping his briefcase in a wooden lounge chair, I lick the icy saltwater off my bottom lip and watch him as he loosens his tie.

He drops down onto his hands and knees until his face is hovering just over mine, upside down. As I stare up at him, wide-eyed and wounds exposed, I think I glimpse heaven in his loving gaze.

The searing need he creates within me is venomous, spreading through my veins and seeping into cracks to fill me up. I never imagined it would be possible to feel this way about anyone.

But here I am, aching for him. Probably on an unhealthy level.

"Hey," he murmurs before sealing his lips to my pouty bottom one.

I part my mouth for him, letting him sweep his tongue inside. He kisses me slowly, ravishing both of my lips. Sucking and licking at me. Our tongues meet and roll and twist together in the most decadent way.

When he draws back, he keeps his eyes locked on mine.

"Hey," I whisper.

"I have meetings over the security detail for the mayor tomorrow. I think you should go spend the day with Jakey."

I fight back a wave of tears, realizing I'd been so wrapped up in Sinro and my own demons that I'd forgotten about visiting Jakey. My world used to revolve around him, and now I feel guilty that it has expanded so much that he's become less prominent in my life.

How horrible am I?

"Okay."

Cain's brows knead together. "Salem won't be there."

My heartbeat falters, and my hands snap out to grip his forearms. "What the fuck. Is Jakey okay? Someone should be with him."

"Ezra." Cain's tone comes out a little sharp. I clamp down on my anxiety, not wanting to push his buttons. Not when I feel so fragile today. So close to shattering into a thousand sharp, ugly pieces.

"Jakey means everything to you, and you matter the most to me. Kate's there with him. We needed Salem's expertise in the field the other night."

Pulse still racing, I wince. "There were kids."

He sweeps his thumbs over my temples, easing back damp locks of hair. "We got them out safely."

I hate the emotions rising up in my chest. They make my throat swell and my skin itch. "Rev said you went to my old foster home."

Cain hesitates, breaking eye contact. "Yeah."

"Did you... kill her?"

His features twist up. "How do you want me to answer that question?"

I lift a hand to stroke fingers over the furrow in his brow. "With honesty."

Dark brown eyes fall back to mine. "I put six bullets in her head."

I nod. "Good."

Cain lets out a heavy sigh and drops his forehead onto my bare shoulder. "I'm tired. Should we order fast food tonight?"

The porch crew at Madera Estates is on patrol when Forest drops me off at the doors in his mustang the next day.

One of the elderly women cat calls, "Oh, another one of them handsome, dangerous looking men visiting today."

"Good morning," I reply, though my brain snags on her comment. Who are the other dangerous men visiting residents? Kate is supposed to be here on watch. Did Cain send more than one person? I wouldn't put it past him. He's definitely the overprotective type, but I like it. I think I need it. No matter how hardcore I pretend to be, I'm weak on the inside.

"Why don't you come sit and chat with us?" another resident asks.

I force a polite smile. "Oh, um... maybe after I check on my Jakey."

I can't squash the bubble of worry in my gut. Hurrying past the empty office, I'm eager to lay eyes on my friend. Why did I stay away so long? Why am I so fucking selfish?

I knock on his door at the end of the hall, but there's no answer. When I peek over at the glass exit doors to my right, I notice the security pad is green instead of red. Splotches of blood decorate the sidewalk outside, disappearing around the corner.

I grab the handle to Jakey's home and shove the door open. Dread takes me under, flipping the world around me when I find the interior dark. I stumble back and drop into a crouch in the middle of the hall as my lungs stretch and contract in desperate need of air.

Jakey normally has his lamp on and his TV blasting sports or music. He prefers the background noise.

God, if he's not inside... or if he is, but he's hurt...

I need to call for help. I need my gun. Why didn't I bring my fucking gun?

I hold back the scream of rage building inside my lungs. I want to blame Cain for stealing Salem away from Jakey, but would she have been able to handle Gabriel's men on her own?

Get it together, Ezra. Jakey needs you.

This is no different from a job. I've run through dozens of exercises just like this. I need to check that Jakey's okay. Maybe he just forgot to lock his door and fell asleep or something.

I just need to breathe and move my body.

Easing into the dark room, I don't call out for Jakey. I don't find anything close by to use as a weapon either. Good thing I'm decent with my fists.

Rev's training has me dipping into the first doorway in Jakey's home to clear it. But what I find has bile surging up my throat. I barely make it to the toilet before I get violently sick.

Someone dumped Kate's lifeless body in the bathtub. She'd been taken to with a knife, I think. I don't have the strength to check. Blood paints the walls in a scene that will forever be burned into my brain. Hand prints and streaks where fingers clawed at the tiles.

Fuck. Fuck. Fuck.

This isn't good.

A cold sweat overcomes me as I move into the living room on high alert. Immediately, I'm jumped by a large figure dressed in all black. He wraps an arm around my neck and snaps a rag to my mouth that smells like acetone.

I slam my elbow into his stomach, breaking his hold. Unleashing my rage, I flip his hefty body over my shoulder and onto the floor.

I don't hesitate. I'm on top of him in seconds, slamming fists into his face until his nose crunches and blood splatters over the carpet and my throbbing knuckles.

Reaching for his gun, I rip it free and shove the barrel against his skull.

"Where's Jakey?" I demand, madness creeping into my tone.

The guy moans and writhes beneath me, but I keep him pinned between my thighs. I smack him hard with the gun. "The old man! Where is he?"

"Crazy senile motherfucker?" He turns his head with a groan and spits blood. "Nearly bit off my thumb. I'm not fucking chasing him down."

My head jerks toward the windows along the back wall overlooking the green space. Jakey escaped. He's out there somewhere, probably lost and freaking the fuck out.

Focusing back on my target, I cock the gun. My hand shakes as I stare down into his wide eyes. He wouldn't be the first person I've killed, but somehow doing it up close always hits a little different.

I reach into my pocket to grab my phone, prepared to call Rev, but something strikes me hard in the back of the head. The room fades to black as I slump forward.

CHAPTER THIRTY-ONE

EZRA

I regain consciousness in a dim space, vision still spinning from get-ting fucking hit in the head. *Again.* Which just further convinces me that Gabriel's shitheads are behind this attack.

Odd that they would strip me down to just my black pants, though. It makes me squirm in the chair I'm resting in, and I quickly discover the rope securing my wrists and ankles. My heart lurches down into my stomach, and a bubble of sickness expands in my gut.

I'm so tired of being kidnapped.

My head drops back as my breathing grows frantic, my lungs strug-gling to find air.

It's okay, Ezra. We can handle this. Isaac taught me new coping skills. This is just another test.

I focus on assessing my surroundings instead of feeding the panic unfurling inside of me. The weird shaped room holds a musty odor. Probably the ancient red carpet. The eggshell walls are barren except for a crooked wooden cross. A lone stain-glass window cracked to let in a gust of cold air that raises the hairs along my skin.

A fucking church?

My stomach worms itself into tight knots. Rev mentioned that there were church groups aligned with the trafficking operation.

Immediately, I wish I could erase the thought from my brain. Instead, I fight against my restraints harder, ripping my skin on the coarse rope binding me in place. Warm blood drips down my fingertips.

Would Cain even think to search for me in a church? How many of them are there in the city? Hundreds?

Fucking fine. If this is my end, so be it. I just wish someone knew to look for Jakey. God, this sucks in every way possible.

A woman with curly, ink black hair and near-black eyes to match enters the room from a set of heavy wood doors. She's wearing a cross necklace and earrings, as if advertising her faith eliminates the fact that she's got me bound like a pig in a holy house.

She touches the end of a knife under my chin, and I stop fighting to free myself. No point going out that way. I *do* have some pride.

The woman cocks her head. "You smell like sin, though I suppose you *are* pretty enough to keep. Father Mason will be pleased to have you back."

I don't need to ask who she means. Panic expands in my chest, putting pressure on my heart and lungs until they feel like they're going to explode. Flashes of that cold, dark basement infect my brain. The weight of heavy chains on my bare skin. The drip of a leak somewhere in the foundation, often the only sound to accompany me in purgatory while I questioned if I was slowly going insane.

Father Mason.

After years under his control, I finally have a name, and it makes it so much worse.

The woman runs the tip of her blade down my sternum, drawing a line of warm blood and a slow note of pain. "Ah, there's the fear."

Doors creak open once more, and I sense his presence before he even steps into view. He was never an intimidating man in appearance. It was his voice and his touch that slithered inside of me. The patience he had for breaking me down.

"Oh, Leo," he hums, features alight with pure joy. Every step he takes toward me is another nail driven into my throbbing heart. The terror he summons in me is unnatural. It cleans me out with razor claws.

Father Mason stands before me and drinks me in behind his glasses. "How I've missed you. What a game of hide-and-seek you play. Fate has brought us back together, and I'm so grateful. I never found the right replacement for you."

I thrash against my restraints. "Don't fucking touch me."

I hate this weakness bleeding inside of me. I hate that I can't help but give away how much this man still affects me. Cain and Rev tried to make me strong, but I think I might be a hopeless case. I'm nothing more than a frightened child in the presence of demons.

And this demon isn't going to make the same mistake of letting me get away.

Soft, glacial fingers dip into my hair, and I can't help but shudder. His fingers trail down my cheek to play with my lip ring. "This is new."

When I jerk my head away from him, he lets his hand drop to my bare chest. I swear my bones dissolve. I slump in the chair, desperate to put as much space between us as possible.

"I don't like that you're bigger than me now," Mason says with a tilt of his head. "I'll have to keep you restrained all the time. Learned that lesson the hard way, didn't I?"

My eyes drift to the scar on his neck. Had I just been a little stronger back then, had I struck a little deeper, I wouldn't be in this position.

He leans in, bringing his mouth close to my ear. "But the rest of you... yeah, the rest is the same, isn't it, Leo?"

My insides curdle. God, please just take me. Maybe I could piss Mason off enough to kill me. Would Cain continue to protect Jakey even when I'm dead? Would he burn this entire fucked up trafficking ring down to avenge me?

I can be a martyr if it means other children will be spared of these horrors. Gladly, I'd die for them.

Swallowing, I ask, "Why are you working for Gabriel?"

"Working for him?" Mason's laugh is low. "Oh no, Leo. You've got that backwards. I hired Gabriel to help me with my business. I needed extra hands to keep up with demand."

Dread coasts through my body. "You're in charge."

"I'm in charge." He sweeps fingers over my pebbled nipple, and I let out a pathetic whimper. "You would have fetched a steep price, too, had I not been so captivated by you."

I rage against my bindings once more, even though I know it's fucking useless.

"Love is a powerful motivator. It can make you do foolish, out of character things. Like storm right into a trap. At least, that's what your hot-headed CEO is going to do."

No. No. No.

Tears leak from my eyes as I snap them shut, splattering onto my jeans. I pray for this to be a nightmare. A test.

"Sinro will no longer play vigilantes in this city. Then we'll go back to the way things were. You and me, Leo. Forever."

I start to sob as he slides a piece of silk fabric over my eyes.

CHAPTER THIRTY-TWO

CAIN

Alaric calls in the middle of a meeting. I hit decline and carry on with my virtual presentation, but the peace doesn't last more than two minutes before Rev's bursting into my office. His frenzied expression is one I've never seen him wear before.

"Apologies," I say to my clients on the video call. "I'm going to have Rorik step in to finish the security run-through. He's quite capable. He'll be leading the team assigned to you. Thanks, Rorik. Thanks, everyone." I click out of the meeting and turn my full attention on Rev. "What the fuck is going on?"

"It's Ezra."

I push up to my feet, dread spilling into my gut. "Where is he?"

"We don't know. Forest called. Kate's been found dead. Jakey's missing. And no one knows where Ezra is."

Immediately, I reach for my cell and speed dial Ezra. The call goes straight to voicemail. I open up the app to track him. Ezra's phone pings

outside of the city, and my heart stops beating for a few seconds. I grip
my phone tighter. "Why the fuck..."

I shoot the location off to Alaric. Two minutes later, his text comes
through. *It's an abandoned estate about seventeen miles north off the
highway. I'll send over details.*

I smash my phone down on the desk, not giving a shit about the
audible crack of the glass screen. Rev doesn't try to console me. He'd
suck at it, anyway.

"I need everyone on this, Rev. I need him back."

"Already on it. Teams are prepping now."

Sometimes I wonder if I have any business running this company
when Rev is always a step ahead of me.

Ten minutes later, all available teams are loaded up in armored vehicles, scanning over maps Alaric feeds to our phones. I clutch the gun I
gifted Ezra in my hands, my anger threatening to boil over at the fact that
he doesn't have it with him while I try not to let my brain conjure up
horrible outcomes.

But when it comes to Ezra, I've never been in control of anything.

"He's gonna be alright. We've run hundreds of successful extrac-
tions," Rev assures me.

I tuck Ezra's gun away before I sink a bullet in Rev. His ability to
remain calm in stressful situations grates on my nerves. I have to remind
myself that he was built differently, and that comes with its own chal-
lenges.

I drag a hand through my hair. "I'm more worried about the condition
he'll be in when we get him out."

Why do I already feel like I've fucking lost him?

Parked a half mile from the targeted estate, my teams spill into the
woods.

I rush the grand doors at the back of the home. Forest covers me as I pick the lock. We sweep in, clicking on flashlights to illuminate the dusty, abandoned interior.

The silence eats away at my nerves. I run statistics in my head. It hasn't even been twelve hours. I saw Ezra this morning before work. It's not like he's been missing for days.

He's okay. I'll make sure he's okay. We just need to get him out.

We scour the first floor, winding through pitch-black, boarded up rooms and hallways littered with old furnishings. The light on my gun catches several pairs of footsteps in the dust coating the floor like a light snowfall.

I wave Forest closer, motioning to a staircase that leads down into what looks like a cellar. It makes my chest tighten as I recall Ezra's admission about being held in a basement.

My blood boils as we hurry down the stairs, guns raised. The shoe prints lead us to a stack of wooden crates in a damp, windowless room that feels more like a crypt.

I glimpse a lit-up phone on the corner of one of the crates. When I step closer, I see that it's Ezra's phone, and it's connected to a FaceTime call.

My entire world comes crashing down around me.

Faintly, my brain registers the scent of sulfur and the ticking of a timer, but I'm glued to the visual of Ezra, *my Ezra*, on the phone—half-naked, blind-folded, and tied to a chair in the middle of a plain white room. Dried blood covers his chest.

I'm going to murder a lot of people tonight.

My focus hones in on a cross hanging behind his head. A church? But which one? There are hundreds of fucking churches in this godforsaken city.

Forest nudges my arm, bringing me back to reality. I wave him up the stairs with my gun and tap my comm piece. "Place is rigged to blow. Everyone out now."

I snatch Ezra's phone, pocketing it, then bolt up the stairs. Hearing Rev's curses echoing from the second floor as he yells orders to his team, I linger on the back porch.

The word fuck replays like a mantra in my head. I was so quick to dispatch these teams, we barely had time to run through plans. If someone gets hurt, this is on me. All because I got too emotionally attached to someone. Again.

"Move your ass, Rev," I roar.

Seconds tick by, and my pulse thuds harder beneath my too hot skin.

Rev slides into view and we bolt for the tree line. He lags behind me on shorter legs, so I grab him by the arm, yanking him faster.

The instant the detonation goes off, I throw my body over Rev's. Heat sears my back. I grunt as something hits my thigh, bringing with it a pain I haven't felt since I'd been shot.

"Cain!" Rev eases me off his body, shielding me from the raining debris. Black plumes of smoke and hungry flames climb the gray sky behind him.

"Fuck, don't look at your leg."

"Call Alaric," I force the words out, handing him Ezra's phone. "We need him to find Ezra. Church. He's in a church."

Rev ignores my demand, working to rip his belt off and strap it around my burning thigh. When he pulls it tight, I lean up enough to glimpse the chunk of wood sticking four inches out of my leg. Judging by the volume of blood escaping me, I'd say quite a bit of the wood is hidden inside my body.

I hiss. "That's not great."

"No shit. We'll storm the fuck out of those churches, but first we need to get you to the doc. I don't think it hit a major artery, but there's a ton of blood, so I guess we'll find out in a few minutes."

Rev and his morbid fucking humor.

"I'm not dying from a fucking splinter."

Rev hauls me into one of our armored vehicles. Salem climbs in with us and positions my head on her lap. She keeps a warm hand resting on my cheek.

Warring against dizziness, I mumble, "Alaric. Call him. Now."

I watch Rev dig out his phone with bloody hands. Only when he relays details to my brother, do I let a heavy darkness claim me.

I'm laid out in a hospital bed when I pry my eyes open, my thigh wrapped up tight and itching something fierce, and my head bogged down from too many fucking drugs. The room spins in my vision, and my limbs won't respond as fast as I need them to.

I squeeze my eyes shut in frustration. All I see is my beautiful Ezra, bound and blood-stained, his chest heaving with panic.

He's suffering, and I'm not there for him. I can't hold him through this meltdown because I didn't slow down to think about the situation for a single goddamn minute.

I'm so fucking gone for this man, and I'll stop at nothing to get him back. I hope he knows that. Hope it gives him something to cling to.

The more I think about it, the more fury tumbles through me unrestrained. I think about that fucking drive. The picture of him as a child, posed on that couch. The emptiness in his eyes. I see him in my kitchen, a knife pressed to his forearm and that wild, broken desperation in his eyes.

It fucking kills me. Opens up gaping wounds inside of me until I'm sure I'll die from this invisible pain.

I can't live without him. I can't live with the idea of him broken, either.

Growling at my pathetic state, I jerk up from the bed. I rip the IV from my arm, tape and all. Then I leap from the bed, hissing when my injured leg crumples, unable to support my weight.

"Fuck!" I yell, clutching the railing of the bed to keep from hitting the ground. I shove the bed across the room and stumble back against the windows.

Regaining my balance, I lurch forward and wrap my hands around the monitor that was assessing my vitals. I hurl that across the room. The commotion gains the attention of the nurses. They rush in, quickly followed by Rev dressed in his tactical gear.

He gives me a look of warning. "Hey there, big guy."

I turn the full heat of my gaze on him, knowing the nurses are no match for me in this state. They can try to sedate me. I've fought through every imaginable hellish scenario. I will win this fight. I will get to Ezra.

"Where is he, Rev?" I push out. My insides are an inferno, melting away the remaining slivers of my humanity.

Rev sighs and shakes his head. "We're still searching."

I snarl at him, fists clenched. "You need to fucking do better! He deserves better!"

"I know, Cain. We'll find him."

"Yeah? In fucking pieces?" I roar. My leg crumples beneath me, and I barely catch myself on the windowsill. I'm shaking all over. "I can't lose him, Rev."

Rev doesn't reply. I think he might be at a loss for words.

One of the nurses leans close to him to say softly, "We need him off that leg."

"Yeah, okay. I got him." Rev takes a few steps toward me. "You going to cooperate, Cain?"

I curl my hands into fists, and Rev's eyes flick down to catalog the movement. Stumbling forward, I swing a clumsy arm at him. Rev dodges. His fist strikes me in the jaw, and I go down hard.

I'm not sure how long I'm out. Only when I wake up this time, I'm clear-headed and my thigh hurts something fierce. At least it's not fucking numb anymore.

Without hesitation, I slide from the hospital bed, rip out another IV, and tear the stupid hospital gown from my body.

A shout comes from behind me. "Woah. Jesus."

I turn to find Rev sitting in a chair by the open door, still dressed in his gear, and an arm thrown up over his eyes. "Put that weapon away. Clothes are on the table, hotshot."

I reach for the pile of belongings Rev must have retrieved for me. Wincing, I drag on a pair of boxers and basketball shorts. Then I tug on an oversized black hoodie.

Rev catches my arm when I hurry toward the door, limping heavily. "What the hell do you think you're doing?"

"Finding Ezra." I growl, yanking free of his hold.

Rev's eyes dip to my leg. "Yeah, but you're fucked like that."

I shove at his chest, slamming his head back against the wall. "And Ezra's fucked if we don't help him! Don't you fucking get that, or is that too much for your fucked up head to understand?"

Rev pulls out Ezra's forgotten gun, and for a second, I wonder if I've finally pushed him to the edge. Instead, he slaps the gun down in my palm. "You were supposed to sleep through the operation. Alaric just found the church. He pieced together information Ezra had previously given him on his abuser. He's some priest at St. Peter's Catholic Church. Salem, Rorik, and their teams, plus a few others, are headed there now."

"Fuck. Why is there always a religious figure involved in these rings?" I grit out, tucking the gun into the front pocket of my hoodie. And this sick fuck in particular seemed to be in charge.

He needs to die. As much as I want to be the one to rip him to shreds, his soul belongs to Ezra.

Rev helps me hobble out of the hospital room. Greg, our go-to ER doc, yells at me to lie back down. Rev just waves at him. "All good here, Greg. You know where to send the bill. We'll see ourselves out."

"See you back here when he rips those stitches," Greg replies with a shake of his head.

Rev loads me in the passenger seat of his silver truck. He retrieves my AR-15 from a utility box fixed to the bed of the truck and drops a comm piece in my palm.

"Yeah, I'm always prepared for worst-case scenarios," Rev says when I give him a surprised look. He whips his truck onto the street. "Why does this feel like it's about to be completely unhinged?"

"Because we usually have a solid plan in place when we do this kind of shit, and right now, we don't."

In no time at all, Rev swings his truck into a parking spot across from the church. It dominates an entire block, its stone towers and sharp spires aspiring to penetrate the heavy clouds.

Definitely well-funded.

"We need to reach out to our government contact," I say. "Something tells me we're just scratching the surface of a much bigger organization."

"Agreed." Rev nods, tucking his dual pistols into their holsters. "Can we kill some people first, though?"

"Oh, we're going to kill a whole bunch of people first."

The arched doors at the front of the church crack open, and two rough looking men in leather jackets step out to light up cigarettes, their breaths visible in the chilled air.

I grit my teeth. Is the entire church on this priest's fucked up payroll?

Hopping out of the truck with a grunt of pain, I glimpse shadowy figures darting around the side of the church. Salem, in all of her vampiric glory, leading her silent team to the back doors.

Rifle cradled in my hands, I limp toward the church, prepared to raise fucking hell on holy ground.

Two rounds of a sniper rifle crack, dropping the men at the front before I can fire off shots. I search for the gunman and spot Isaac on the roof of a grocery store about a hundred yards away. He gives me a salute. At that moment, I feel a surge of pride.

Yeah, I love my brothers. Might need to get better at showing it.

My teams flood the building from alleyways and neighboring buildings. It's a beautiful fucking sight. Had I not been so worked up over Ezra's kidnapping, I might have basked in the moment. This rush of adrenaline used to keep my heart beating.

Spurred on by the need to get my arms around Ezra, I limp up the church steps. Rorik appears at my side to sling my arm over his shoulders.

"Boss, you need to stop pushing your limits and start paying attention to your health."

"We'll all take some time off when this is over," I lie. "Company party or something."

Rorik snorts and helps prop me against a column in the entryway of the church as bullets erupt from all directions. Where you'd expect people engrossed in worship, there are only criminals wielding guns.

"Even the fucking nuns?" Forest exclaims.

Sure enough, I watch one of them withdraw an assault rifle from her robes and fire over the pews.

"Merry Christmas to you, too," Rorik mumbles, peeking around a wall to drop the nun with a perfect shot to the temple.

"Filthy animals," Forest adds, and Rorik flashes him a wide grin.

I pick off a guy creeping toward the pew Forest's ducked behind.

While reloading, Rorik asks, "Ever heard of the movie Nude Nuns with Big Guns?"

Rev snorts, popping out of the coat closet on my other side to shoot down two gunmen from the balconies. "You making shit up again?"

"Nah, it's a real movie," Rorik says.

"Focus," I command, shoving another magazine of bullets into my rifle. This is why I leave victim extraction to Salem and her team. She doesn't make light of the situation. These guys are all numb to death.

I press the comm piece in my ear. "Salem. Update."

"We're in the basement. Halfway through extraction." She lets out a heavy breath. Salem was usually so put-together, so good at hiding everything but her warmth and kindness. "There are a lot of kids down here. So sorry, Cain. No eyes on Ezra."

Beneath my growing storm of fury, a sense of failure burrows deep. My business exists to stop shit like this from happening, and yet it has been happening on such a large scale in my own city.

Of course, that sick fuck wouldn't have kept Ezra with the others. Ezra is probably special to him. Just the thought has me coming unglued.

My eyes scan the balconies, homing in on hallways leading deeper into the church. Gritting my teeth, I push through the pain in my thigh and rush the interior staircases, blasting my way through nuns and criminals.

"Stitches!" I hear Rev shout at me.

Fuck that. I'm too enslaved by my rage to care.

CHAPTER THIRTY-THREE

EZRA

"Do you believe in God, Leo?" Mason asks, easing my head back with his hand tangled in my hair.

I should scream and spit and lash out at him, but I can't seem to find the will to do anything except fall apart. Robbed of my sight by the blindfold, all of my muscles are tensed up in anticipation of what he's going to do next.

"I... I don't know," I admit.

"An agnostic, then. That's okay. I never shared religion with you. Your lack of faith is as much my fault as it is yours. I'll do better with you this time."

Mason slides his fingers down to my jaw. My throat bobs, every part of me chilled and itching like I'm covered in insects. Nerves fire messages of warning that make me squirm and whimper.

I can't do this again. I don't want to do this.

My brain tells me even if I get out of this situation, I may never get myself back to a good place. Why does he get to be in charge of plugging and unplugging pathways in my brain?

"Kill me. Please just kill me," I plead, tears leaking from beneath the soaked blindfold.

Mason withdraws his hand.

"I'm offended, Leo. Were our times together so bad? You never opposed. You were so malleable, weren't you?"

I can't find any fire within me to counter that I was a fucking child. He was an adult. One who should have cared for me properly. I shouldn't have had to tell him I didn't want his touch. That my body didn't belong to him.

Cold fingers drift down my arms, tracing over scars.

"No track marks. I suppose that's a blessing. Though we'll still need to cleanse you before I take you home. Who knows what you've picked up in our time apart."

I let out a horrible sob, my mind giving into hopelessness as his hand brushes over my abs. It dips lower, a knuckle sneaking under the waistband of my pants.

"No one has touched you here, I pray," Mason murmurs.

I shudder, bile rising in my throat. Even if I could manage a response, the glorious sound of gunfire pops off from somewhere in the church. Mason's uttered curses are my salvation. My heart skips in my chest, and I push myself upright in the chair.

Cain's here.

The doors creak open, and the room is filled with the echoes of shouting and guns exploding, a symphony to my ears.

I'm left alone and blind to fight with my restraints, unsure of how much time I have to try to get free before Mason returns. I struggle against the rope hard enough to draw fresh blood from my raw wrists and ankles.

My body locks up when the doors creak open once more.

"Ezra."

Another sob escapes me at the sound of Cain's voice. "You came."

Quick swipes of a knife free my hands and feet. I push the blindfold off my head and launch myself into Cain's awaiting arms. He catches me with a grunt, dropping to his knees. I bury my head into his neck. "You came. You're here."

"Baby." Cain eases me back, and I glimpse pain etched into his face.

My mind sharpens instantly. "What's wrong?"

I search his body for signs of injury, dread pooling in my stomach when I glimpse the blood soaking through the back of his pants. "Cain, you're hurt. Why are you hurt?"

"Priest fuckhead tried to blow us up." He cradles my face in his hands. "Ezra, I love you. My adrenaline's waning, and there's a strong possibility I'm gonna pass out soon."

"What?" I gasp, my heart leaping. "Wait. Did you say... God, Cain. I love you, too. Don't you fucking confess to me like you're about to die. I love you so much. We need to get you to a hospital."

He holds my gaze with his steady brown eyes. "Not until you put a bullet in that fucker's head."

I shake my head, body sagging a bit in his hold. "I...I don't think I can do it."

"Look at me," he orders, and my eyes snap back to him. "I need you angry, baby. You *will* put this fear to rest. You will not be afraid of him. He doesn't get to keep his hooks in you. Do you understand?"

I sniffle, nodding. "I kill him, and then we go straight to the hospital, right?"

"Right." He hands me my gun and picks up his rifle from the floor.

"I'm not leaving you alone like this," I say in a firm tone.

When he struggles to stand, I tuck my gun in my waistband and wrap my hands around his torso, hauling him through the doors.

"Where's Rev?" I ask.

Cain doesn't respond, and it makes my heart skip with worry. Fuck. I think it may be up to me to get us out of here. I'm shirtless, caked in blood, and edging up to major freak out territory. My heart is thundering in my chest. I can feel my pulse throbbing under my skin.

But I won't fail Cain.

Sucking in deep breaths, I steal the comm piece from Cain's ear. "Rev?"

"Hey, Ezra," Rev replies. "Good to hear your voice. I'm assuming Cain's in rough shape?"

Guns pop off from his end of the line.

"Definitely an understatement."

"Can you get him close to the balcony? I'll be up there in a minute."

I heave Cain upright, grateful for all my commitment in the gym. "I'll get him there."

Pulling out my gun, I let pent-up energy flow through me. I kick open the heavy doors to the hall. This is just like target practice. Only these targets fire back. And I'm hauling a behemoth of a man in one arm.

I move through the hall as fast as I can usher Cain. One of Gabriel's guys steps up, and I blast a shot into his skull. It's amazing how quick I've become numb to the idea of killing, but my body recognizes this as a life or death situation.

I drop two more gunmen around a corner and spot Rev at the top of a staircase by the balcony doors. His gaze sweeps over me, brows raised at my half-naked, bloody state.

He helps me rest Cain in a balcony pew as shots continue to fire below us.

"Are those... nuns?" I pause, cocking a brow.

"Wildly inappropriate, right?" Rev says.

I glance down at Cain, frowning at the sheen of sweat covering his pale face.

"Go," Cain orders. "I'm good here with my rifle for a minute."

Muscles tensed, I linger until Cain hefts his rifle up onto the ledge and takes aim at our enemies. I lean down to give him a quick kiss.

"Please don't let him die," I say to Rev.

"No worries. Go fuck shit up, grasshopper."

Out in the hall, I cut toward the back of the church first. My heart strikes against my ribs like it wants to leap out of my chest.

I just want this over with. I don't ever want to be in Mason's presence again.

But Cain's right. I need to kill him for real this time. I need to watch the life leave his eyes.

I catch Mason slipping down another hallway. Raising my gun, I sink a bullet into him. He yelps, but I don't hear the satisfying thud of his body hitting the floor.

Something barrels into my side from an opened door in the hall. I don't even check who it is. I just let my chaotic emotions drive my fist into the guy's face. He stumbles back, and I strike out with my gun, hitting him in the temple. Then I step back and fire a bullet into his head.

I start after Mason again, following a trail of blood under a locked door. Searching the hall for something to pick the lock, I come up short. So I slam a boot against the old wood. I keep kicking, driving my fury into breaking down the door. I'm like a bloodhound on the hunt. I can practically smell Mason's fear.

The old lock gives, clattering to the floor as the door swings wide. Mason's pacing inside, one hand clutching his side where I clipped him and the other shaking as it yanks at window latches in desperation.

"No running from this." I lift my gun, aimed at his head.

"Leo," he says cautiously, backing up a step. He fails to mask the terror on his face. "It doesn't have to be like this. You don't have to be a killer."

"Too late for that," I say, dropping my aim to fire a shot into Mason's foot. He howls and stumbles back into the corner of the room.

I don't have much time to spare with Cain's injuries, but I give in a bit to the viscous, white-hot rage overcoming me. "In what universe do you think I would show you mercy for the hell you put me through? Why shouldn't I kill you?"

"Leo," he pleads between sobs, blood oozing from between his fingers clenched around his shoe.

I cock my gun, and he flinches. "That's not my fucking name."

I'm trembling again as I lick away the salty tears running over my lips. "I wish there were other victims here to punish you like you deserve. Wish I had the strength to lock you up and torture you for *four fucking years*." I scream the last words at him. "Deprived of food and water and clean clothes and warmth and human fucking decency."

Mason shakes his head frantically. "It was never my intent to hurt you. I was always gentle, wasn't I?"

"Gentle?" I push the word through my clenched teeth, my features twisted in disgust.

"I told you I love—"

I pull the trigger, splattering his brain across the stained glass windows. No more of this. I'm so fucking done.

My heart chugs with heavy beats as I stare down at his body for a while. I fire another round into his skull for good measure. Watch him bleed out on the floor, eyes wide and glasses askew.

This time I know he's dead. His evil will never see another day.

So why don't I feel better? Less disgusting on the inside? Is it because I'm still riddled with fear over Jakey and Cain?

I crouch over his corpse, my eyes burning with tears, and my hands shaking too hard to properly operate my gun if someone else comes barging in here.

I touch my fingers to my abuser's neck. I know he's dead, but I still need to check. I let out a weak cry when nothing thuds beneath his skin.

God, I hate these feelings bubbling up inside of me, threatening to overcome me. I *hate* them. Had Cain not been injured, I would fall apart in this room. But the worry over his safety has me shoving my emotions down, down, down. I know they're going to crush me later.

I let myself sink into that place where I existed during my abuse, locking everything away until I operate on auto-pilot. It's like a different Ezra takes over. One not affected by emotions. He exists, but just barely. He's alive, but he's not human.

I rush for the balcony. Thankfully, the gunfire has ceased. Rev is heaving Cain up by the arm as he flags in and out of consciousness. The pool of blood left behind on the pew has my heart lurching in my chest, threatening to unleash what I just caged up.

"Jesus, Cain," I mumble, reaching out to wrap my arms around his other side.

We carry him down the stairs and load him in Rev's truck. Then Rev hands me the keys and my phone.

"My leadership skills are needed here. We still haven't found Gabriel. Have Alaric send you the address for our doc. He's already expecting Cain."

I stare down at the keys with wide eyes. "Rev, I don't know how to drive."

But he's already darting across the street. He shoots me with finger guns. "Gas on the right. Brake on the left. You'll figure it out."

CHAPTER THIRTY-FOUR

EZRA

We made it to the ER but not without difficulties. I ran two red lights, nearly took out a street sign, and parked the truck on the sidewalk. Somehow, Cain remained calm throughout the chaos, which only proved to me that he wasn't well. No one fully conscious would let my lack of driving skills slide without aggressive commentary.

The doctor informed me Cain had indeed ripped his stitches. They fixed him up and wheeled his sleeping body into a room where they'd posted me up.

No one blinked twice at my half-naked, cut-up state. I suppose if the staff tends to Sinro's employees, they've seen far worse.

Isaac stopped by to drop off spare clothes and check in with me. I mumbled replies to his generic questions, assuring him that I was fine to watch over Cain for the evening.

In reality, I don't think I've ever been so far from okay. The fall from adrenaline has me sinking deep into a pit. If I could untangle my emotions, maybe I could figure out what the fuck I was actually feeling because it's too much all at once.

I spend the evening pacing the hospital and checking my phone for updates from Rev on the search for Jakey. By the time sunlight pours through the windows, creating what look like dreamsicles on the tiled floor—sleep deprivation at its finest—I'm running on empty. I'd nearly worn through the skin on my fingers, rubbing them over the gold coin I hadn't realized I'd stolen from Mason's pocket.

Something to remind me that he's really gone.

Cain is dismissed shortly after a terrible hospital breakfast. I listen to the doctor's strict orders on auto-pilot. Then I'm loading Cain into Rev's truck in the connected parking garage, perspiration beading on my skin from the effort of supporting his massive body.

"I may have been out of it last night, but I could have sworn you parked *on* the sidewalk," Cain says as I buckle him.

"I moved the car. Possibly twenty times last night," I admit. "City parking is stupid."

"Ezra."

I ignore his weighted gaze, seeking to pry under my weak armor. "I'm fine. It's fine. Everything's fine."

Of course it's not, but we make it back to Sinro without another word. Isaac meets us at the garage elevator. He helps me drag Cain into his bed and forces pain meds into his mouth. I watch Cain settle in, aware of Isaac sneaking concerned glances at me. I'm so over it.

"Ezra, you should rest," Isaac says. He's perched on the edge of the bed by Cain's feet.

"Not while Jakey's still out there."

"How about you wash up, then? I'll make sure Cain stays in bed."

I shake my head. Isaac doesn't understand. Honestly, I just want him gone. I don't want to talk. I don't want to relive anything right now. I don't know what I need, but I know it's nothing anyone could offer me. Feeling a prick of guilt, I lie and claim I'm hungry.

"Food. Okay." Isaac nods. "That's a good idea. I can grab something across the street."

Isaac rushes out of the apartment like if he's not quick, I might do something drastic. And that might be the plan. I hear the door click and rise from the edge of the bed, my heart sprinting in my chest.

Cain latches a hand on the hem of my shirt.

I sigh, my shoulders dropping in defeat. "Thought you'd fallen asleep."

One blink, I'm standing, and the next, he's got me laid out in the bed beside him. Part of my brain screams to fight against him, but it's no use. Even injured, Cain would kick my ass.

I can't seem to find a scrap of energy to get myself on my feet again, so I rest my head on his pillow, close enough to feel his breath against my skin.

"Sleep, Ezra," Cain orders, slinging an arm over my waist. He nuzzles into my neck and presses warm, slow kisses there.

I open my mouth to argue, but his large hand cups my jaw, guiding it to meet him in a lingering kiss.

"Jakey will be okay. I need you to be okay, too."

I can't help but uncoil under the warmth of his body and the gentle stroke of his fingers along my spine. This, right here, is what I need. Cain wrapped around me, keeping me firmly planted in reality.

Eyelids drifting closed against my wishes, I sink deeper into the bed. "Someone needs to hunt down Gabriel."

"We'll find him. Sleep, or I'll be tempted to get up and work."

I grab his shirt in both of my hands as if I could threaten him. "Don't you fucking dare."

"Mmm. Then you better stay put to hold me down."

I wake with a jolt, my heart thundering in my chest.

Lurching up in bed, I struggle to make out my surroundings. The room is dark, and that sets my panic loose with claws out. I scramble from the bed, convinced I'm right where Mason wants me. He's locked me up in that basement. I never escaped.

This must be purgatory.

My pulse doesn't calm, even after I pace the entire apartment. I can't wake up Cain. He needs to heal.

But I don't know what to do. Isaac's probably asleep, too.

I end up in the bathtub. I'm not sure when I got the knife, but the process of removing all eight of my safety pin earrings brought me some relief in anticipation of the pain I'm about to bring myself.

Sometimes the process leading up to my self-mutilation is enough to calm me. Sometimes I truly need the pain. Maybe enough pain to make it all stop this time.

I killed that man, but he remains, like a stain in my head.

Tears burn in my eyes. I shouldn't be doing this. Cain is going to hate me. Isaac's going to realize I'm unfixable. Rev isn't going to want somebody this broken on his team.

Tilting my head up to keep the tears from spilling, I don't register the door clicking open until a giant figure looms in my peripheral.

Cain doesn't say anything, but I feel his rage simmering through the dark room. He walks over to the tub. Then he heaves his bad leg over the edge with a grunt, coming to a seated position in the tub with me, crowding my space.

I should scold him to go back to bed. He's going to injure himself again.

Instead, I let him pull my body against him. Let him hold me as I fall apart. I sob so hard I'm half-convinced my chest is going to burst open. I sob until both of our shirts are soaked with my tears. I feel physically sick from the effort of shedding all of this pain churning inside of me like hurricane winds.

"I need help, Cain," I cry out. "I've never wanted anything more than you and this job in my entire life, but I can't do this. Look at me. I should be taking care of you right now. I'm a fucking mess. I told you I was. I don't deserve you. Kick me out, please. I'm worthless. I belong on the streets."

Cain growls, wrapping his hands around my hips and tugging me closer. "You belong in my arms. You belong with me. Hell, I think some part of me knew it the moment I laid eyes on you."

He strokes hands over my hair and presses kisses to my forehead. Then he tips my chin up so I'm looking directly into his eyes. "Listen to me. You are worthy of every ounce of love others want to give you. Do you understand? You deserve love. So let me give it to you until you're healed enough to believe it, too, okay?"

All I can do is nod and bury my face in his chest.

"We'll figure this out, baby. We'll talk to Isaac."

It sounds more like he's convincing himself at this point, and that tears me up more.

"You really love me," I murmur, sniffling.

"I really fucking do."

"Will you hold me until morning?"

A heavy breath comes out of him as he wraps his arms around me. "Always."

The ringing of a cell phone snaps me awake. Morning light streams through the bathroom door. I'm laid out on Cain as he sleeps, his head cocked at what appears to be a painful angle.

Shit. He's going to have knots in his muscles. I'll have to massage them out when I get him back into bed.

I scramble for my phone on the nightstand, rushing into the kitchen to answer Rev's call so I don't wake up Cain. There's a note from Isaac on the counter about food in the fridge.

"Did you find Jakey?" I ask.

"Can't say anyone really found him. He walked through the front doors of Madera Estates this morning like he'd gone out for a grocery run."

I push out a breath of relief. "Is he injured?"

"Well..." Rev chuckles. "He's missing an ear, but he refused medical attention until someone served him breakfast."

I can't help but unleash a breathy laugh, too. It's not an ideal outcome, but at least Jakey's alive and back to stirring up trouble.

"Sometimes I forget that he survived on the streets long before I showed up." Honestly, he was the only reason I'd made it this far in life. "Thanks for checking on him, Rev. Thank you for being so—"

"We talked about the kind word," Rev warns. "Bossman still high as a kite?"

I peek into the bathroom, taking in the strong shape of Cain laid out in the tub. "He's sleeping."

"Why don't you check in with Isaac and then go visit your old man? I promise I'll call when we make headway on Gabriel. Fucker has your name written all over him. Oh, and you owe me for the damage you caused to my precious truck. Better kiss up to your sugar daddy."

He ends the call with a laugh before I can shift the blame on him. I warned him that I couldn't drive.

Standing in the kitchen for a few breaths, Rev's words sink in. Hot tears burn my eyes. Anytime Jakey got lost, he would always end up outside the scrapyard where we first met. Almost like that was his reset spot. His checkpoint. His beginning. It was definitely mine.

The fact that his spot has moved reassures me that Cain made the right choice in moving him to Madera. No matter how much I worry about Jakey, I could never uproot him from a place that feels like home to him.

But it also makes my chest ache. Jakey doesn't really need me anymore. I have to accept that reality. I have to deal with my fucked up mental health, too.

I call Isaac first, not wanting to cause any panic from my sudden absence. "Hey, Cain's asleep in the tub. Might need help getting out."

"Like... with water?" Isaac's voice hitches up.

I give a sad chuckle. "No. We never filled it. We may have slept in there last night."

"Ezra." He blows out a breath. "Are you okay?"

I drag a hand through my wild hair. "No, I'm not, but I think I need to visit a friend before I word vomit in your office."

"Take your gun. Come right back to us. I'll handle Cain, but you know if he wakes up and you're not here, he's going to be a handful."

Hanging up, I tuck my gun into my holster and slide on my jacket. Then I grab Cain's keys to the Benz.

My lack of driving skills earn me countless blaring horns and middle fingers, but I make it to Madera Estates in one piece.

I find Jakey sitting in his recliner, knitting away. His ear is covered in gauze, taped to his shaved scalp. His eyes meet mine, and a goofy smile spreads on his face. "My Ezra. Knew you'd show up soon."

"Fuck around, Jakey." I curse, striding over to examine his wound. "Does it hurt?"

"Would hurt less if I took those pain pills, but I won't touch 'em." Jakey shakes his head. "I'll be alright. Now you wanna tell me why you look so sad?"

I drop down on my knees to rest my cheek on his thigh and wrap my arms around his waist. "I was scared you were done for. I'm still scared."

He pats my head. "I'm just fine. Can handle my own."

"You lost an ear. All because I got us both tangled up in a mess with criminals."

"Bah. If it wasn't gonna be criminals after you, it was gonna be my past catching up to me in some way."

My tears soak his pants, but he doesn't complain. Just keeps brushing shaky fingers over my hair like he used to do when the shelters were full and we had to sleep on the streets.

"I know you aren't mine by blood, but that never did matter to me, you know that?" Jakey says. "My boy went to heaven, and I got to pull you out of hell."

My body quakes as I cry, and I let out every horrible, gutting emotion pent-up in my core. I'd never fully disclosed to Jakey what had happened to me, but I guess he sensed it was something inhumane.

"You were the only person who ever made me feel safe," I admit.

"And you filled a hole in my heart, sweet boy."

I turn and rub my tear-streaked face on his pants. "You can't just say shit like that, Jakey."

"I'm gonna say a few more things, so listen up. I won't be around much longer, Ezra."

"Don't talk like that. You're going to live forever."

He pats me again. "I don't want you to keep hanging on to me. You've got your whole life ahead of you. And you've got a nice man who loves you and wants to take care of you."

I'm rendered speechless. I'm drowning in a sadness that permeates my very bones. Can you grieve the loss of a relationship as you knew it? Because this feels a whole lot like parts of me are dying and falling off.

"I'll be just fine here. This is what we always dreamed of, right? We made it to East Bank. So it's time to let go of the past and move forward. Can you do that for me, Ezra?"

I sob uncontrollably for a couple of minutes, clinging to his pants. After I compose myself, I nod. "I'll try. But I'm still going to come visit you."

"I'd like that. Bring that lovely angel with you when you do."

"Who, Salem?" I can't help but laugh. I wipe my eyes on my sleeves and give Jakey one last squeeze. "I don't think I could keep her away from you, handsome."

CHAPTER THIRTY-FIVE

CAIN

Nothing pisses me off more than not being able to work. Actually, I think threats to Ezra take the cake for the quickest way to push me into a rage now.

I spend far too long sleeping because someone, either Ezra or Rev, keeps slipping me something to knock my ass out. So when I do finally wake up, I'm in a ripe fucking mood, made worse by the fact that my phone is missing and the sky is pitch-black outside the windows of my apartment.

"Ezra," I shout, pushing up onto my feet. Blinding pain shoots through my body, but I do my best to ignore it as I limp into the kitchen.

The scene I walk in on dissolves my worry instantly. Ezra's darting between a pot of water bubbling over on the stove and a smoking pan he tossed into the sink, caked in burnt tomato sauce. The kitchen island is covered in enough groceries and trash to make one of my eyes twitch.

"Fucking hell." Ezra tips his head back, shoulders slumping. "Why is this so hard? Cooking will be the death of me."

A full laugh rises in my chest. I can't help but drink him in, pathetic state and all, dressed in my t-shirt and sweats, and feel my heart fucking swell with love.

I have never experienced an all-consuming need like this in my life. That desire hasn't weakened even a fraction in the time we've spent together. It feels like Ezra has been in my life forever.

Shuffling across the kitchen, I reel him into my arms, pulling his back against my chest.

"I just wanted to cook you something for once. Rev told me how to make spaghetti, but it's way more difficult than he made it sound." He deflates, tossing the spoon in his hand onto the counter. "You should be laying down."

I curl my body around him, resting my head in the crook of his neck. I breathe his scent into my lungs and brush my lips back and forth over his smooth skin. "I just want to hold you."

"Well, then the kitchen's probably going to burn down and you're going to rip your stitches for the second time."

I chuckle. Reaching out a hand, I turn off all the burners on the stove and lean us back against the counter for support. I trail kisses across every inch of his exposed skin. Behind his ears. Along his cheekbones. All the while, I slide a hand under his shirt to run over his toned stomach, tracing each delicious ab muscle.

"Who took my phone, Ezra?"

"I'm not telling." He gasps when I pinch his nipple. "Fuck. Rev did. This isn't fair."

"And who drugged me, little thief?" Nice and slow, I circle my fingers over his other nipple, enjoying the way he arches back against me. My cock hardens against his ass.

"No one drugged—"

I sink my teeth into the muscles between his neck and shoulder, earning a moan from him that has me grinding against his ass.

"Shit," Ezra says breathlessly. "The doctor said—"

My hand slides down, dipping beneath the waistband of his sweatpants to brush over his half-hard cock.

Ezra breaks away and whirls on me, cheeks flushed and chest heaving with labored breaths.

"Oh, I'm in a much better mood now," I smirk, loving the effect I have on him.

"Go back to bed, Cain." Ezra tries to look commanding, but all he's doing is turning me on more.

"I'll go if you come with me."

He throws out his arms in frustration. "What do I do with this mess?"

"Leave it."

"But I destroyed your kitchen."

"*Our* kitchen," I correct. "You can make it up to me."

Stalking forward, I lift him into my arms and haul him to bed, ignoring his sass about my injury. I drop him down on the sheets, struggling to hide my wince as I climb over his body.

I grunt as Ezra flips me over with surprising strength, positioning himself on my hips to keep me immobile. "Sorry if I hurt you," he says, his brows furrowed and nose wrinkled. "But no more getting up."

My hands drift to his thighs, giving them a squeeze. "You're the boss."

"No, *you're* the boss."

"And you're in charge of me. So that makes you in charge of everyone, Ezra. How does it feel to run a multi-billion dollar company?"

He shakes his head, a little smile raising the corners of his perfectly shaped mouth. "It's too much power. Good thing I have you to do all the work for me."

I chuckle. "Good thing I have Rev to pick up the slack. Want to order pizza?"

"I want to eat spaghetti." He pouts. "But obviously, that's not happening. So yeah, I'll call in the order."

We end up devouring two large meat lovers pizzas in bed while Ezra fills me in on his visit to Jakey and his new treatment plan with Isaac, and I give detail to how a piece of wood got lodged in the back of my thigh.

Only when we're snuggled in bed, staring into each other's eyes, do I glimpse the sadness he's fighting to hide.

"What do you need, Ezra?" I tighten my arms around him, snuggling our bodies closer.

His pulse throbs under my touch. "You. Always you."

I capture his full lips in a long, slow kiss. And when I sense him retreating into his head, I pull back to give him space.

"We don't have to do anything tonight. Nothing changes. Nothing you do could ever make me love you less."

He blinks back at me. "You said love again."

"I did." I raise up enough to peck a kiss to his cheekbone. "I love you. No fucking question about it."

Tears leak from his wide doe eyes, and I work to swipe them away as they tumble free. "Ezra, baby."

He flattens me out on the bed. I can't help but release a low laugh, my dick twitching at the way he's handling me tonight. "I think you need to lay off the gym time with Rev. Not sure I can give up being the dominant one."

He cracks a grin, his beautiful hazel eyes glittering down at me. He whispers his next words against my mouth. "I love you, too."

CHAPTER THIRTY-SIX

EZRA

While Cain heals, I split my time between therapy and helping Rev and his teams comb the city for Gabriel. We barely cover any ground. Sinro Enterprises still has endless jobs to oversee, and Rev spends hours holed up in meetings with government officials after disclosing information about the trafficking ring in the city.

Eager for our lunch break in the gym, I perch on the edge of Rev's desk and run my fingers over the gold coin I swiped from Mason's corpse.

"Where'd you get the old train token?" Rev inquires, swiveling in his desk chair.

"Huh? Oh, um... it fell out of that priest's pocket when I shot him."

It had become somewhat of a fidget toy for me in replacement of my safety pins. I transferred it into my pocket every morning.

He leans forward in his chair. "Can I see it real quick?"

I drop it into his outstretched hand.

"Seems like a weird trinket for a holy man to carry around. Avid train enthusiast?" He flips it over his fingers smoothly. "Or could it be the perfect hiding place for the leftovers of a criminal organization?"

My heart skips a beat as I slide off the desk, already buzzing with adrenaline as Rev calls up Alaric for information on closed train stations in the city.

"Two locations that could be your jackpot," Alaric replies. "One of them in particular used to serve as extra parking for a Catholic church next door. It was supposed to be demolished due to safety issues a decade ago."

"Fucking bingo. Got you, you piece of shit," Rev says. "Not you, Alaric. Your research is always appreciated. Thank you so much."

"Sure it is," Alaric mutters. "Don't let the building collapse on you."

Before I can fully process what's happening, four teams of mercenaries gear up and load into SUVs with heavy ammunition, Cain included, because he threw a temper tantrum about being left behind.

Parked a few streets over from the ancient church, my eyes drift to Cain resting against the back of a black SUV, his injured leg propped up on the tail, and his new M110 semi-automatic sniper rifle cradled in his hands.

He looks like a fucking dream. His dark locks are tousled so perfectly. His black zip-up jacket is pulled snug over his cut biceps, and his black cargo pants taper into his military boots.

It's so wild to think he would ever take an interest in me, but he's made sure to let me know every morning and night how much he cares for me. However long he wants me in his life, I'm going to do my best to love him.

I catch the little hitch in his mouth when he moves his leg wrong. I hate that he's here when he's not even remotely close to one hundred percent. Rev offered to tie him down in the interrogation room back at Sinro, but that would mean we'd actually have to get the jump on him. A messy fight would put him at risk of re-injuring himself. Again.

Instead, we settled on him coming, but only on the agreement that he perched up with the snipers.

I wipe the drool off my chin, and focus my attention on Rev as he splits us into groups. Isaac helps Cain post up across the street on a warehouse rooftop, and Rorik's got both sides of the train tracks covered with his team.

Rev motions our group forward. He tails me to the back doors of the abandoned building, where I swiftly pick the lock. We sweep inside, silent as death.

The earthy scent of moss hits me, patches of it growing over the crumbling interior walls. Voices below have our teams spreading out to surround the building along the upper level. When I peek my head over the railing of the platform, I spot a collection of large, tattooed men sitting around collapsible poker tables near the railways, Gabriel included.

Rev gives the signal and gunfire pops off like a fucking firework festival. Gabriel and his men reach for weapons, overturning tables in their scramble to take cover.

I pull the trigger on my rifle as one of the men rushes the platform stairs. He crumples to the ground, and my heart pounds faster in my chest from the adrenaline.

We have the element of surprise, flushing Gabriel's gunmen out into the trainyard and right into the scopes of Rorik's team. Snipers crack in the distance, a sound that brings me comfort.

No one is escaping today.

I spot Gabriel back-pedaling toward the dark interior of the station and chase after him. He blasts a couple of shots at me. I dart around a support column for cover, pushing out a slow breath as the tiles shatter and dust clouds the air.

My pulse is throbbing, and a grin curls on my lips. Everything inside of me screams to claim the kill. I am the hunter now.

I spin around the column, gun raised, but Gabriel's gone. Rushing inside the station, I soon find myself staring into a pitch-black hole leading down into the earth, Gabriel's footsteps echoing below.

The room begins to dissolve around me as my heart races. My messed up brain feeds me visions of my concrete prison. Visions of a man I know for a fact is dead.

There's a twisted part of me that believes he got back up after I left that church. I thought I'd killed him once before. Maybe evil never truly dies.

Shit. I don't want to go back into the dark. Am I really going to have a fucking panic attack right here?

Squatting down, I nestle my gun between my thighs and stomach as I go to war against my body's overreaction to a stupid set of stairs.

"Baby, you there?" Cain's voice comes over the comm piece in my ear. Other employees can hear us, but no one is going to harass the boss for supporting me during an operation. Pretty sure most of them know Cain's got a soft spot for me. He doesn't hesitate to claim me in public.

"I'm here. Gabriel's in the basement."

There's a long pause, and all I can hear for several moments is my heart thudding too loud in my ears.

"You got eyes on him?" Rev asks.

"No," I whisper, burning with shame. "But he's not far ahead of me."

He's not far ahead, but I don't think I can do this.

"Ezra. No one will say a word if you're at your limit. You've done enough," Cain replies.

I shake my head. "I need to see him dead."

"I'm right here with you. The moment you want out, we'll all be racing to get to you, okay?"

A voice that sounds like Forest comes on the comm. "I'm very fast, Ezra. I'll be there before you can blink."

"We've got your back," a rougher voice sounds, most likely Rorik.

"I'll throw myself off this seven story building to get to you," Isaac adds.

"I would walk five hundred miles—"

A half a dozen other voices start yelling in my ear, and I can't help but release an exasperated laugh.

When they finally quiet down, Cain says, "Just keep taking deep breaths, baby. You've trained so hard for this. We all have faith in you."

With Cain as my guide, I suck in a big gulp of earthy air. Over and over and over again, I breathe. Soon my heart settles back into a rhythm that doesn't feel like it's going to explode my chest. My vision sharpens, and my boot finds the first stair, prompted by Cain's patient instructions.

Three more stairs, and the desire to put Gabriel and his crimes to rest becomes stronger than my fears. I've come so far in such little time, it only encourages me to push myself harder.

And if I *do* have a full-on meltdown, which is the main reason Cain threw a fit about coming with us, I have a whole team of support to pick me up and carry me home.

I don't let myself overthink the remaining descent into the basement. I move fast, focusing on the heavy steel in my hands and the supportive buzz of familiar voices in my ear.

A shot fires at me when I reach the bottom. I spin back behind a stone wall, hissing at the pain in my bicep.

"You good?" Cain demands.

There's a burning sensation in my arm, and when I glance down, I see a streak of blood where a bullet grazed me. If Cain knew I'd been shot, he'd pull me out.

"Yeah, I'm good."

I charge around the wall and fire off shots as I rush into what looks like old service tunnels for the station.

A yellow overhead light flickers ahead, giving me a view of Gabriel when he darts beneath it. The sheer panic contorting his features makes me want to laugh.

"What the fuck do you want from me?" His ragged voice reverberates through the tunnels. "You want money? I can give you money. You want drugs? I'll hook you up for life."

I fight back the urge to shout out the word "justice". Seems a little early to make light of the situation and pretend I'm Batman. If I want to be a professional, I have to act like it.

And I have to do my fucking job.

Like the boogeyman, I stalk Gabriel into a small electrical room. He raises his gun at me, but I shoot it out of his hand before he can fire, blasting off two of his fingers. His screams are music to my ears.

"What I want is you dead," I say, sinking a bullet through his eye.

His head snaps back, but just like with Mason, I shoot again. I keep shooting until I unload my magazine. It's a waste of bullets, but I'm convinced he can feel the pain of each shot I bury into his skull.

Isaac and I talked about this moment. What to expect when this all came to an end. When my abuser and the crime lord responsible for capturing and distributing children were dead.

We'd done our best to prepare for my panic attacks. For my fear and sadness and emptiness. But all I feel right now is rage. It's not enough. Bullets aren't enough. One body isn't enough. Mason's corpse isn't enough. Not when so many fucking kids suffered.

That destructive part of me rears its ugly head, demanding I burn it all down.

"Ezra, are you there?" Cain's voice comes over the comm.

I press the button on my earpiece. "Gabriel's dead."

"You're a superstar," Rev cuts in. "You need Cain to limp in there and rescue you?"

My smile is weak. "No, but would you be opposed to me setting the place on fire?"

Laughter erupts on the comm system from multiple people.

"Get your ass out here, and we'll get you all the gasoline you want."

Heart still pounding, I sling my rifle over my shoulder and rush out of the basement like demons are clawing at my heels.

Rev meets me at the back doors with two cans of gasoline. Two more are already lined up against the building.

"Was this the plan all along?" I ask, cocking a brow.

"Nah, but it's all good. Government approved of us wiping out Gabriel's operation. And the city's scheduled to demolish the building. Two birds with one stone."

"But gasoline?"

Rev shrugs. "I don't think Cain will let me have the corner office if I let you play with C4."

I can't help but crack a toothy grin.

Assured that the building is cleared, I prowl through it, dumping gasoline over the bodies and decaying, hand-carved wooden furniture.

I shouldn't be so thrilled about lighting the place on fire. It must have been beautiful back in its glory days.

But the city plans to level it, anyway, and I can't help the part of me that wants to cause mayhem. Maybe that will never be fully healed. At least with Sinro, I'm allowed to wreak some havoc.

Positioned outside the train station, mercenary teams at my back, I ignite a match and drop it on the trail of gasoline. Flames consume my vision, climbing the smoggy sky. Others scoot back from the heatwaves, but I stay firmly rooted to the spot, needing to feel the burn on my skin.

Strong arms wrap around my waist, and a chin rests on top of my head.

"You okay, beautiful boy?" Cain asks softly.

My gaze never leaves the fire as I watch my past burn to ashes.

"I have no right to ask anything of you. Not when you've given me so much. But I'm really hoping you can find patience for me. I'm going to be okay, Cain. I want to be okay. I just don't know how long it's going to take. And that scares the shit out of me."

Cain spins me around. He tips my head up, and I glimpse flames crackling in his rich brown eyes. "Ezra. Baby. Etch this into your brain. I will wait eternity for you. And I will do it standing by your side. It took me years to get to where I'm at now mentally, and I'm still not convinced I'm worthy of you. So don't ever think that I won't be patient. Not for a single minute."

His words burrow deep into my chest, both painful and relieving at the same time. All I can manage in response is a nod before I stretch up on my toes to kiss him.

CHAPTER THIRTY-SEVEN

EZRA

I sleep like the living dead, all thanks to Cain fucking me in every way imaginable last night. His determination to wring me of toxic emotions and pent-up energy, while striving to not aggravate either of our wounds, was enviable. Gold medal level, really.

Maybe a little of it was punishment for refusing to go to the ER for stitches. I settled on Isaac's steady hand to fix me up instead.

Eyes still closed, I let my hand drift to Cain's side of the bed. I lurch upright when I discover his spot empty. I groan at the pain in my muscles, not just from our sex marathon, but yesterday's operation, too.

I drag my ass into the closet to get dressed, chuckling at the new clothes shoved onto my side of the rack. He literally cannot stop pampering me.

Out of defiance, I steal one of his gray t-shirts and pair it with skinny black joggers and my combat boots.

I expect to find Cain in the kitchen, sipping a cup of coffee, but there's only a travel mug of coffee next to a handwritten note to check in at the office.

Face scrunched in confusion, I grab the warm travel mug and load into the elevator. It's probably not professional to show up to the office in loungewear, but Cain's already disclosed to everyone about our relationship. And since I was never officially hired on at Sinro Enterprises, no one can complain that I get special treatment.

Not that they would when Cain's best friend heads up HR.

The doors ding open on the thirteenth floor. Gwen glances up at me from her desk. She gives me a big smile and two thumbs up.

"Hi, Gwen. How are you this morning?"

"So lovely, dear. You look... well-slept." She giggles. "Cain's waiting in the meeting room for you."

I sneak by her desk, prepared to throw myself at Cain. But when I stride into the meeting room, a crowd of employees greet me. Salem waves from her spot next to the counter, littered with boxes of pastries and juice. Rev spins in a chair, beaming at me. Rorik mumbles something while his mouth is stuffed with donuts, and Forest looks at him with disgust. Isaac and Alaric are locked in a battle over the last sprinkled holiday donut in the box.

And Cain heads up the show, positioned at the table in his pristine suit, dark hair styled and deep brown eyes burning into my soul.

I notice several things laid out on the meeting table. A bulletproof vest, military boots, a fancy black bag from a suit shop, an open case with shiny new guns, and an ID badge on a lanyard.

"What's this about?" I ask, looking everyone over.

"It's your first official day at Sinro Enterprises," Rev explains.

My gaze darts back to Cain, seeking answers in his hard expression. Underneath that glacial coldness is more kindness and love than I could have ever imagined.

"First official day?" My brows furrow.

"Paychecks and benefits and everything," Rev says. "You're already in the system."

"Unless you'd rather not take the job." Cain cuts Rev a stern look, giving me the choice to back out. Always giving me choices. Something no one else has ever done.

I can't help the overflow of tears. They spill down my cheeks, and I swipe at them as they tickle my jaw.

"Aw, Ezra. I told them springing this on you might be overwhelming," Salem says, coming over to pull me into a gentle side hug.

"No, it's good. I'm just so fucking happy."

Before I know what's happening, Cain has me in his arms. He claims me with a deep kiss that makes Rev bleh in feigned disgust.

"Bossman never stood a chance with this one," Rev mutters.

"Called it first," Alaric replies.

Cain breaks our kiss to search my face. "No pressure, baby."

I let out an airy laugh. "I got to set a building on fire yesterday. So that's a big hell yes I'll take the job. Did you buy all of these guns for me?"

Cain presses a warm kiss to my neck. "Everything is for you, beautiful boy. My heart included."

EPILOGUE

CAIN

TWO YEARS LATER

"Twenty bucks he takes you down in five minutes," Rev shouts over the hip hop music pulsing from the sound system in the gym.

I crack my neck and toss my Chief Operating Officer a glare. Rev's gone so far as to hang banners and streamers for the 2nd annual company team building event he started up. Ever since I gave him a new title and a corner office, he decided he had all the power at Sinro Enterprises.

I was fine to let him believe it—I've had my hands full with Ezra in the best way possible—until Rev pitched the idea of letting the staff beat the shit out of each other.

Took weeks for both him and Ezra to convince me that it would be a good idea, and honestly, it's done wonders to bring everyone together. Nothing like a little pain to bond one another.

One hundred and fifty employees are crammed in the gym this afternoon, fists pumping and spirits high. Some watch through the windows from the patio. And those uninterested in the boxing matches lurk around the pool or the community living room, drinks and appetizers in hand.

"Five minutes?" I raise my brows, letting my gaze stray over to the fiery, blonde-haired beauty in the other corner of the ring.

Ezra doesn't look so confident this year. Might be the plug I sank into his ass this morning. But there will be no repeat of him making a fool out of me. My little thief has mastered takedowns. He's become a better marksman than me, too.

Regardless of the outcome today, I still win out because I get to take him back to our bed and ravish him.

My heart thuds chaotically fast as I look him over. Yeah, anyone could see that he's my fucking weakness, but I don't care.

Ezra clasps hands with Forest and Rorik in the crowd, then he turns his head my way.

I smirk back at him, loving the rosy flush of his cheeks. Bet that plug feels real nice.

Sliding fingers under the hem of my shirt, I peel it off. Rev whistles, and employees break out into excited hollers. It has the intended effect, locking Ezra up with wide eyes.

Only, Ezra strips off his shirt, too. I'm in awe of the defined strength he's gained over the last two years under his perfect, golden skin. He's put in so much work—in the gym, in the gun range, and with Isaac.

I can't say he's a completely changed person. I think he'll always be a bit quirky and hyperactive. A bit broken, too, but I absolutely adore every piece of him. Even his horrendous cooking failures. His ability to destroy appliances is astounding. His lack of memory when it comes to finding his car keys and wallet frustrates me, but he makes up for it in sexual prowess.

Christ, don't get me started on his skill at coaxing me to visit my parents for every holiday. I'm fucking whipped for this man.

Ezra gives me a tight-lipped smile, and I know he's doing his best to keep from jumping my bones. Our match has gained too much attention among the employees to call it quits. Bets have been placed. I can't lose again.

I stride into the middle of the ring, adding a bit more swagger to my movements.

"Trying to intimidate me?" Ezra cocks a brow as he squares up with me. He bats those dark lashes, and I fight the urge to take him right here. His sexy whimpers from this morning as I spread him out on my desk and sucked his cock while stretching him for his gift still play in my ears.

This tangle won't end in the ring. I look forward to spending time in bed with him. Only Rev knows that I took a week off work to dedicate to Ezra.

Gazing down at his beautiful face, I can't help but stroke my fingers along his jaw. I give his chin a little pinch. "Baby, we both know you're not scared of me. I'm just trying to put on a good show for our fans."

"Alright. Alright. Enough of that shit. We're here to see some blood," Rev shouts out.

Smirking, I raise my fists. Ezra mimics my moves, beginning his quick, predatory circle around me.

It must come as a shock to our enemies how fucking deadly he is. He's so stunning, I know I'd end up with a bullet in my chest in seconds if I were up against him.

Ezra strikes first. His knuckles graze the sweet spot on my jaw, and my heart stutters in my chest. Fuck. How embarrassing would that be to get dropped so soon?

I slam a fist into his stomach, hissing at the contact against his solid abs. He barely slides backward, already hooking a right fist up to my jaw.

Dodging his punch, I pull him into my arms and lower my mouth to his ear. "No holding back this year, huh? My slutty little thief in a hurry to get fucked?"

Ezra hooks an arm around the back of my neck. Planting his foot on my thigh, he swings his body around me to strike at the back of my knees with both of his feet. I drop to the mat.

He kisses my cheek. "You play dirty, baby. I've been fighting a boner from hell all day."

Reaching back, I lock an arm around his waist and flip him over my shoulder. His back hits the mat hard enough to draw gasps from the crowd.

Ezra rolls back before I can get him in a hold. Still on my knees, I let out a delighted laugh.

As I'm rising to my feet, he charges me and kicks out a leg to sweep my feet, but I jump back in time. I don't miss the little shift in his features as the plug hits him just right. He's slow to get up, and I leap at my opportunity, knocking him onto his back once more. This time I get his arms pinned above his head, my hips pressing him down hard.

Rev starts his countdown. Ezra squirms beneath me until I drop my mouth to his ear and whisper, "Marry me."

His body goes slack, and his eyelids flutter. "What?"

I grin down at him. "You heard me."

Rev continues his countdown in the background, but the cheering from my employees fades away as I stare down at the man I want more than anything else in this world. The little thief that broke into my building and stole my heart.

Tears glisten in Ezra's eyes. "You're such a fucking cheater."

"I am," I agree. "Can you blame me? I sit behind a desk all day while you train."

Rev shouts out my name as the winner, and there's mixed reactions among the employees. I know most of them bet on Ezra as the champion, which is why I planned out this strategy to assure my victory.

"Are you serious? You want me?"

"Forever, Ezra."

He breaks my hold without effort, surging up to wrap his arms around me and plant a kiss on my mouth. "Then I'm yours. Forever."

AFTERWARD

A nd here comes a super sappy note...

This book wouldn't be in existence if not for two very important people in my life. As someone who severely lacks self-esteem, I've had so many moments of doubt on this journey as an author. The more stories I write, the more that doubt seems to fester. Which is obviously not a fun thing. But it *has* motivated me to get serious about my mental health, something I like to promote in my books.

Honestly, if not for the support of my husband and my best friend/alpha/beta/proofreader/everything, I would have definitely given up by now. They've withstood my wallowing, meltdowns, and depression and somehow still want some sort of relationship with me. Mad respect for their patience. And mad respect for their ability to be firm with me and enforce boundaries when I'm clearly not capable of taking care of myself or recognizing my limitations. True MVPs.

I have to send love to my editor, Sarah, too. Thank you for being so professional, reliable, and flexible with me. Thank you for the entertaining conversations and for talking me off ledges with my stories when I'm spiraling out.

Of course I have to thank my betas: Stacey, Rebecca, Wendy, Nattie, KJ Harrowick, Jenise, Cheyenne, Kersten, and Theresa. What a list of wonderful people! Thank you for the early encouragement, notes, and support. I cannot put into words how much I appreciate you.

Also, I just wanted to thank everyone for reading my work and sharing the love when my stories hit right. I've found such a great community among readers. It's everything an author dreams of.

Anywho, Rev's story is up next!

Sign up for my newsletter for updates on future projects:

Newsletter Sign-up

Other Books by Abigail Glenn

DRAG ME DOWN
Emotional MM Rockstar Romance

FORGED IN CHAOS
High Fantasy Romance

Printed in Great Britain
by Amazon

40306235R00185